MIDWAY

a tiny powder keg in the Pacific, an island so crowded with munitions and fuel it was a bomber's dream. To explode it and knock America out of World War II was Yamamoto's fantasy.

THE JAPANESE

Admiral Yamamoto—world's top-rated naval genius, commander of the Japanese fleet.

Captain Kuroshima—the young "God of Operations"; surprise was the key to his battle plan.

Commander Watanabe—a bad-tempered junior officer who understood what was wrong.

THE AMERICANS

Admiral Chester W. Nimitz—the shrewd Texan in charge: CINCPAC.

Admiral William F. Halsey—his motto: "Hit hard, and fast, and often."

Captain Matt Garth—he hated human frailty.

Lieutenant Tom Garth—he loved Haruko, a Japanese-American.

General James H. Doolittle—his daring raid on Tokyo infuriated the Japanese—and started it all.

THE MIRISCH CORPORATION PRESENTS

CHARLTON HESTON
HENRY FONDA

MIDWAY

Guest Stars
JAMES COBURN
GLENN FORD
HAL HOLBROOK
TOSHIRO MIFUNE
ROBERT MITCHUM
CLIFF ROBERTSON
ROBERT WAGNER

Co-starring
Robert Webber
Ed Nelson
James Shigeta
Christina Kokubo
and
Edward Albert

Written by DONALD S. SANFORD
Music by JOHN WILLIAMS
Directed by JACK SMIGHT
Produced by WALTER MIRISCH

A WALTER MIRISCH PRODUCTION

A Universal Picture

Technicolor®   Panavision®

MIDWAY

A Novel by
Donald S. Sanford

MIDWAY
A Bantam Book / June 1976

*Bantam Books wishes to thank the Caidin-Wolff Archives
for the use of U.S. Navy photographs.*

ISBN 0–553–02824–3

Published simultaneously in the United States and Canada

*Bantam Books are published by Bantam Books, Inc. Its trade-
mark, consisting of the words "Bantam Books" and the por-
trayal of a bantam, is registered in the United States Patent
Office and in other countries. Marca Registrada. Bantam
Books, Inc., 666 Fifth Avenue, New York, New York 10019.*

To the Reader

Both the American and the Japanese strategy in the conduct of World War Two had become deeply rooted in the belief that the aircraft carrier was to be the decisive naval weapon.

The development of the carrier as the keystone to naval strategy had not come to its fruition overnight; it had taken a long, long time.

Even in 1903, when the Wright brothers had first flown their powered kite, a fragile affair of wood and cotton fabric, there were dreamers at work. The American aviator Eugene Ely and Captain Irving Chambers of the U.S.N. were trying to persuade the Navy Department to allocate funds—and take the considerable risk—of experimenting with the frighteningly radical idea of using the cleared deck of a large vessel as a landing field.

And eight years earlier, the French aviator Clement Ader (who had antedated the Wright brothers' achievement by thirteen years with a fifty-meter flight of his steam-powered craft the *Eole*) had published a book on military aviation in which he wrote:

. . . an aircraft *carrier* will become indispensable. Such ships will be very differently constructed from anything in existence today. To start with, the deck will have been cleared of any obstacles; it will be a flat area, as wide as possible, not conforming to the lines of the hull, and will resemble a landing strip. The speed of this ship will have to be at least as great as that of cruisers, or even greater. Servicing the aircraft will have to be done below the deck, and access to this lower deck will be by means of an elevator long enough and wide enough to take an aircraft with its wings folded . . .

In the year 1910, a light aircraft actually took off from a ship in Hampton Roads, off the coast of Norfolk, Virginia.

It was to be a hair-raising exploit.

The ship was the U.S. light cruiser *Birmingham*, on which a superimposed platform had been built, eighty-three feet long and twenty-two feet wide, sloping down toward the bow at a carefully-calculated angle of five degrees, and the man in charge of the experiment was the persistent Captain Chambers.

Chambers had approached Wilbur Wright, then at the height of his fame, with an invitation to use this steel platform as a flying-field. Wright had taken one look at it and flatly refused to have anything at all to do with such a perilous venture. Chambers then approached another aviation pioneer, Glenn Curtis, who in turn got in touch with that same Eugene Ely who had been agitating for just such an experiment as this.

Ely promptly agreed to try it.

His little Curtis biplane, powered by a single 50-horsepower engine, was hoisted on board the *Birmingham* on the morning of November 10, 1910, and Ely went aboard to await a break in the overcast that would permit him to see what he was doing.

It came at three o'clock in the afternoon.

Chambers began to take his ship out of the Roads, and even before it had gathered speed—it was sailing at only ten knots—Ely climbed into his open cockpit, gunned the motor, and sent it speeding down the inclined deck, a mere fifty-seven feet of "runway."

The plane practically fell off the edge of the platform. It dipped so alarmingly that the propeller blades actually hit the water and were splintered by the force of the impact. Nonetheless, Ely somehow contrived to keep stability, swing the craft up into the air again, and make a safe landing ashore.

Within two months, Ely had devised a way in which a plane could also be *landed* aboard a ship at sea. He slung three arrester hooks on ropes from the tricycle undercarriage of his plane, and arranged for twelve cables to be strung across the deck, one foot high, some of which, he hoped, might catch in his hooks and pull him to a halt. If not, there was to be a canvas screen at the end of the improvised runway into which—again, he hoped—he could crash without too much damage.

Weighted ropes for arresters, and a makeshift screen to crash into; it was a primitive combination of such alarming potential that any but the toughest-minded aviator would have been horrified at the thought of it.

Not Gene Ely . . .

The ship this time was the armored cruiser *Pennsylvania*, and the landing platform had been enlarged to a length of 102 feet and a width of thirty-two feet. And although at the time of Ely's attempt, the cruiser was lying with a ten-knot wind behind her (thus increasing his landing speed from thirty to forty miles an hour) he succeeded in bringing the plane in to a landing. Its hooks caught in the last of the cables stretched out to stop him after a touch-down run of eighty feet.

Forty-five minutes later, to the cheers of the enormous crowd which had gathered to watch him, this indomitable pioneer turned his plane around and took off again.

Sadly, but perhaps predictably, Eugene Ely was killed in a flying accident very soon thereafter.

Further experiments continued on both sides of the Atlantic.

By 1914, when World War One started in Europe, the French were using the near-obsolete cruiser *Foudre* as a carrier on which a crude hangar housed the planes. In Great Britain, primitive box-kite aeroplanes were being adapted to use at sea, with air bags for floats, to be carried on board naval vessels. More serious interest was aroused when the first aircraft to launch a torpedo, weighing 800 pounds, was based on a light cruiser. It was a seaplane which was lowered into the water by a crane and later recovered in the same manner.

The first offensive ever mounted by carrier-transported seaplanes was a British strike against the German bases at Cuxhaven and Wilhelmshaven in December of 1914. But the seaplane system was slow, cumbersome, and relatively ineffective, and naval thinking started to swing back to Ely's idea of a wheeled aircraft landing on and taking off from the deck.

A Bristol Scout biplane, a lightweight fighter plane, was sent up from the deck of a small packet-ship named the *Vindex* to attempt to shoot down a German zeppelin which was impudently hovering over British waters, keeping naval shipping under surveillance. The experiment was a complete failure; the plane never reached its target.

Limited success in this type of endeavor was not achieved for another nine months, when another zeppelin was attacked by a carrier-launched fighter plane that flew above it and dropped incendiary darts. Even though the attack did not down the zeppelin, it was at least a demonstration of latent possibilities.

By now, passenger steamers were being taken over by the British Admiralty and converted to carriers. And the corner was turned, the proof provided, on August 4, 1917, when a Sopwith Pup—the most popular Allied aircraft of World War One—was launched from the deck of H.M.S. *Yarmouth* to attack an L22 zeppelin that had been spying out the fleet's movements in the early stages of the great Battle of Jutland.

The pilot, Lieutenant B. A. Smart, clawed his way up to an incredible—for those days—seven thousand feet, swooped down on the huge, gas-filled monster, and opened up on it with incendiary bullets from his machine gun.

The spectacle was tremendous as the zeppelin went down in flames; and now the lesson was fully learned: The aircraft carrier could be a weapon of formidable importance, freeing the plane from its confining dependence on land bases. Now the plane could be carried to where it was needed, launched, and safely recovered. The weaning stages were almost over.

In America, these activities were being closely watched by a limited number of enthusiasts who were convinced they were witnessing the birth pains of the weapon of the future, but it was not until 1919 that the collier *Jupiter* was converted into the first flush-deck carrier of the United States Navy.

One of those enthusiasts, General Billy Mitchell, demonstrated the superiority of aircraft over the battleship by pounding the surrendered German dreadnought *Ostfriesland,* to destruction in an effort to convince the military establishment of the importance of aviation.

In the early 1930s, the 14,500-ton carrier *Ranger* was built, followed in 1934 by the 20,000-ton *Enterprise* and ... the *Yorktown.*

Across the other side of the world, the Japanese, like the French, had been primarily interested in the use of seaplanes—mostly Sopwiths and Shorts obtained from Britain—but the British success with flight decks, and the American experimentation with arrester gear —which essentially constituted the crux of the whole matter—had inspired them to a keen interest in the carrier's future.

They succeeded in flying the popular Sopwith Pup off ramps built onto their battleship *Yamashiro* in 1920, and by 1921 they had engaged a semiofficial mission from Britain, under the command of Colonel Sempill, to advise them on the application of aircraft to naval warfare.

They launched their first carrier, the *Hosho,* in November 1921, and became the proud possessors of the world's first, specially-built, fully-operating aircraft carrier.

Though only 7,470 tons in displacement, the *Hosho*'s flight deck was 500 feet in length—a far cry from Eugene Ely's eighty-three feet—and her speed was twenty-five knots. She carried twenty-eight aircraft, with all maintenance facilities on board, including repair shops. A small island on the starboard side housed the bridge and the signal mast, as well as three funnels which could be swung horizontally over the side to give a clear flight deck from end to end.

An unusual aspect of her construction was the inclusion of a complicated series of lights and mirrors on board deck to assist the pilots in landing, a system improved on by the British and later perfected by the United States.

The Five-Power Treaty, limiting naval armaments,

permitted a total of 135,000 tons for the USA and Great Britain, 60,000 for France and Italy, and 81,000 for Japan. The Treaty expired in 1936 and the Japanese moved full speed ahead with carrier construction, building the *Shokaku* and the *Zuikaku*, each with a displacement of 25,675 tons, a speed of thirty-four knots, and a complement of seventy-two aircraft.

The Americans were slow to take advantage of the lifting of the treaty's restrictions, and it was not until September 1939 that construction on the carrier *Hornet* was begun. And at the time of Pearl Harbor, the Japanese carriers outnumbered those of the American's Pacific fleet by eight to three.

The Battle of Midway was to be the first all-out combat between two fleets which depended on carrier-based aircraft as their primary offensive weapon, and where victory or defeat would be calculated on the fate of the carriers and their planes.

For the Battle of Midway, and the diversionary attack in the Aleutian Islands, the Japanese were to employ, counting all carriers, battleships, cruisers, destroyers, submarines, and supply ships, 200 vessels, 700 aircraft and 100,000 officers and men.

The American total, of all ships, was to be fifty.

The outcome was to be the turning point in the war for the Pacific.

Prologue

The miniscule islands, of no historical significance whatsoever, lay thirteen hundred miles to the northwest of Honolulu, and just east of the international date line, an arbitrary line approximating the 180° meridian but deviating in part to bring the Aleutian Islands and Alaska into the same dating as the United States, and to avoid any land masses that might be considered "of consequence."

They were discovered a little more than a century ago by a Captain N. C. Brookes of the United States, and were first called Brookes Islands. Made up of two small sandspits, known as Sand and Eastern Islands, they were windswept, constantly lashed by storm and surf, and completely uninviting—particularly since the whole was encircled by a five-foot-high coral reef which presented a treacherous hazard to navigation. Their total land area was approximately two square miles—one-fifteenth the size of Manhattan Island—and their indigenous population was only four hundred and fifteen souls.

The United States made formal claim to the islands in 1867. Then, in 1903, Theodore Roosevelt designated them a naval reservation, and by that simple process pushed the United States frontier almost three thousand miles to the west. In the same year, they became a connecting station for the telegraph cable that was being laid from Hawaii to the Philippines.

Inexorably, and almost unnoticed, the islands were at last assuming a significance that had always been denied them.

Nonetheless, for thirty-five years or so, these pinpricks in the enormity of the Pacific Ocean's sixty-three

million square miles were scarcely even named in the
American press, nor brought in any other way into the
consciousness of the American public. Few people had
ever heard of them; few could guess where they might
be. Fewer still even cared.

But on December 7, 1941, simultaneously with their
attack on Pearl Harbor, the Japanese fleet shelled the
islands, and were driven off after inflicting severe losses. In the general shock of Pearl, this lesser incident so
far from home went almost overlooked by the American public. Pearl Harbor was the prime target, and it
was at Pearl that the crushing blow—to both American
naval power and American pride—was most acutely
felt. No one cared much about the shelling of a tiny
sandspit in the mid-Pacific.

It was "Remember Pearl Harbor" that became the
rallying cry, the slogan that unified the country just as
"Remember the Maine" had aroused the righteous
wrath of another, older generation. The totally unexpected calamity which the great naval base at Pearl
Harbor had suffered was paramount in the minds of the
American public and press. In the aftermath of that
shock, almost no one gave thought to that other battle,
to those other islands now known as Midway.

It was not until six months later that this far outpost
of the American frontier was brought to the forefront
of historical and military observance with the greatest trial of naval strength since Jutland.

But Midway was more than an isolated battle.

It was the turning point in a war that, up to this time,
had consisted of a long series of humiliating defeats for
the Americans and their allies, disasters from which, it
seemed, they might never recover.

The Japanese numerical superiority in this battle
was overwhelming. Against an American force of three
heavy carriers, eight cruisers, eighteen destroyers, and
nineteen submarines, the Imperial Japanese Navy
launched their attack with four heavy carriers (this single advantage in heavy carriers was considered enough
in itself to swing the battle into Japanese favor), three
light carriers, two seaplane carriers, no less than eleven
battleships, fifteen cruisers, forty-four destroyers, fifteen

submarines, and numerous smaller craft. The odds were alarming.

More frightening still was the *long-range potential* of a Japanese victory.

For the war in the Pacific, in which the main contestants were the United States and Japan, was still only part of a world-wide conflict, with the Allies on one side and the Axis on the other. The future course of this larger conflict, a conflict which had already engulfed half the civilized world in its flames, would have been irrevocably changed, had the strange combination of foresight and lack of it, meticulous planning and carelessness, of overconfidence and overcaution, and finally sheer luck, swung the tide around in the direction of a Japanese victory.

Had the Japanese triumphed, Hawaii would undoubtedly have fallen next; and with the long and almost indefensible Pacific coastline of continental America left wide open to Japanese assault, there would have been little interest in the USA for a protracted war in Europe. The threat at home would have been too great to allow of anything but the immediate concentration of all of America's resources for the defense of its own mainland. Consequently, there would have been a drastic lessening of American power in other parts of the world where that contribution to the Allies' chances of success was of overwhelming importance.

It was not only Europe that would have suffered. Japanese plans for the invasion of Fiji, Samoa, and Australia could not have been halted. More importantly perhaps, with the American armies concentrated for the defense of their homeland, there would have been no Normandy landings, no checking of the sweep that Germany was making in its highly successful *drang nach Osten*. Britain had borne the burden of the war in Europe alone for two years—the only one of the European Allies to hold out against the massive German war machine—and was not capable of mounting an invasion of Europe alone. And if, as was always possible, the awakening might of Russia had led to the defeat of the Germans, then the Iron Curtain, today, would be draped across the whole of Europe.

An American defeat at Midway would have had a shattering and incalculable effect not only on the morale and the safety of the American homeland; it would have changed the course of history itself, and redrawn the map of the world.

But the Americans did, indeed, remember Pearl Harbor.

They struck back with courage, with tenacity, and with brilliance. Under the overall command of a blue-eyed, sharp-witted Texan named Chester W. Nimitz, they sank all four of the Japanese heavy carriers, and in doing so, knocked out almost all of the best-trained and most combat-experienced Japanese naval pilots. They brought some semblance of parity back to the Pacific, and from this point on the war could be fought on more acceptable terms.

If any single battle might be called the turning point of World War Two, then this was it.

The fact that it was fought at all was not entirely due to Japanese determination. From the moment the Midway operation was conceived, there was strong, almost fierce, opposition to it by the majority of the naval General Staff in Tokyo. That opposition was swept away on the morning of April 18, 1942, by General James Doolittle's daring air raid on the Japanese homeland.

The raid had been mounted more as a demonstration of bravado than anything else. Compared with the devastation that had recently been inflicted on a somnolent Pearl Harbor, its consequences vis-à-vis the military strength of the enemy were certain to be minimal, its effect on the balance of power almost nonexistent.

For the events of December 7, 1942, had not only gutted American naval strength, but American morale as well; they had not only increased the relative strength of the Imperial Japanese Navy—already far superior to the U.S.—but had given the Japanese an overweening sense of invincibility. After so many long years of repression by the terms of the Five-Power Treaty of 1922, Japanese morale crested to the point of euphoria.

It was all a question of how the people *felt*. On the

one hand, humiliated and distressed; and on the other, jubilant and enormously assured.

The raid was a calculated attempt to blunt the edge of that self-confidence, and soothe America's humiliation with the balm of offensive action. It would show the Japanese that they, too, were vulnerable and that America was not content to lick its wounds at the opposite extreme of the huge Pacific Ocean, awaiting helplessly the next blow to its pride and to its military capability.

The pilots had trained under conditions of security so tight that they themselves did not know just where their target would be. From the Carolines in the south to the western Aleutians in the north, the western half of the Pacific was Japanese territory now. There was just no feasible objective that could be attacked by the land-based bombers in which they were training—practicing ultrashort takeoffs, precision bombing, and low-altitude navigation.

Some of them thought that Australia, the nearest landmass in the path of Japanese expansion, was to be their future base. Others thought they were ticketed for the airfields on Wake or Guadalcanal or Port Moresby. Almost nobody thought of Japan itself as a target, for how could *any* plane—even the legendary B-25, around which a mystique of its own was already developing—hope to cover the three thousand miles and more of Japanese-controlled waters and return to base?

Throughout the training period, great stress was laid on economy of fuel, on close-formation flying, and on skimming over the treetops at minimum throttle. The crews worked, and sometimes slept, in steel helmets, and each man was armed with a Colt .45 automatic pistol. And they were all volunteers for a mission that was described to them only as "dangerous, important, and interesting." They trained at Columbia, South Carolina, and at Elgin Field near Pensacola.

It was there that they first met the famous stunt flyer and barnstormer James Doolittle, the man who, in 1931, had set a new record by flying from Los Angeles to New York in eleven hours and sixteen minutes. He was cheerful, friendly, dedicated to the mysterious mission—and totally uncommunicative about it. He told them only to work, work, work, to get to know every foible, every idiosyncracy of these marvelous new planes, treating each one as an individual mechanism with a mind of its own.

To further the mystification of the young pilots, the navy suddenly took a hand in their training. A Lieutenant Miller came over from Pensacola to instruct them in short, quick take-offs. By learning to drop their landing flaps and push their engines to full power, they gradually reduced the runway distances to a minimum they never dreamed possible.

When the top-secret Norden bomb sights were removed from the craft and replaced by what became known as "dime-store sights" because, as Doolittle explained blandly, it was inevitable that some of the planes would fall into enemy hands, the crews became more mystified, some to the point of alarm.

They took their planes from Fort Myers, Florida, across the Gulf of Mexico at water level, then back to Elgin—the first of many long-distance flights to test their fuel consumption. On landing, the tanks were drained, the fuel measured down to the last drop, and it became apparent to the crews that every ounce was to be vitally important in the task for which they were being so meticulously groomed. They flew to San Antonio, and then on to March Field, with only a single refueling stop at Phoenix, Arizona. Doolittle was waiting for them there, and their planes were refitted with the new three-bladed props. Also, all their radio equipment was removed.

At San Francisco, where they were ordered to report, they flew over the Golden Gate Bridge (one of them flew *under* it), and saw the carrier *Hornet* lying sedately below them. There were three of the land-based B-25's already on her flight deck, hoisted over her side on winches. Now, at least, the secret of the quick take-offs was out. Obviously, they were going to fly their planes off the deck of a carrier. They had visions of their fuel-laden aircraft toppling off this ultrashort runway and sinking into the sea. But they could still only hazard a guess at what their destination, their target, might be. Not even the navy knew.

But then a few mornings later, on board the great carrier, it was finally made official.

Doolittle called them together in the mess hall and greeted them: "Well, men, for the benefit of those of you who haven't already guessed, we've been assigned a very juicy target—Japan." He paused, half-smiling at the astonishment on their youthful faces. Then he went on: "We're going to bomb Yokohama, Osaka, Kobe, Nagoya, and Tokyo. The navy will take us as close as they can. Then we'll take off from the deck of this carrier, drop our calling cards on Tojo and land . . ."

His voice trailed off. He sighed, scratched the lobe of his ear, and finally said, "Well, landing is going to be a bit rough. This carrier can't wait for us to return from our mission. The minute we clear her decks, she'll have to run like hell to get out of the range of the enemy's long-range, land-based bombers. So, we're gonna have a crack at reaching the Chinese mainland."

There was a murmur of disbelief from the gathered crews. He waited for silence, then continued: "We'll attempt to reach those parts of China where the Japanese aren't. Obviously, it will have to be somewhere along the coastline, because none of you are going to have more than a few drops of fuel left by the time you get there. If you get there at all." He paused again to study their reactions and decided they were going to be all right. They were grim, tense. He was glad. It meant there'd be no horseplay, no carelessness on this mission.

Doolittle went on: "The Chinese are cooperating fully with us. They've prepared a number of landing strips. Some of them are just bean fields but they'll serve your purpose. You'll set down at the first flat piece of land that comes under your bellies. Understand?"

They nodded silently and he continued: "There'll be plenty of gasoline waiting for you. It's all been taken care of. When you're gassed up you'll fly on to Chungking. And when you get there, I'm going to throw the biggest, wildest goddamn party in history. For the survivors, that is. If any."

It was on the morning of April 18 that the first warning of Doolittle's raid reached Japan. The fishing boat *Nitto Maru,* at her station on the picket line of sentry vessels seven hundred and twenty miles east of Tokyo, radioed that she had spotted a fleet of large, unidentified ships on the horizon, steaming at high speed toward the Japanese coast.

The Japanese could not believe that any American vessels could penetrate so deeply into waters over which they held undisputed control. Yet there was very little consternation in the Imperial High Command. Seven hundred miles of water made for a very comfortable barrier against assault. There was time to plan, to debate, to make preparations against whatever the arrogant American might have up his sleeve.

But the *Nitto Maru* was seen by the *Hornet*'s destroyer escorts, and recognized at once for what it was— a sentry vessel, stationed to keep the homeland alerted of any possible danger. It was obvious that the hoped-for element of surprise had been lost. In the *Hornet*'s wardroom, a hasty conference was called at which the attack plan was reviewed.

That plan had called for Doolittle's flyers to take off in the afternoon, when the *Hornet* was five hundred miles off the Japanese coast, so that the planes, close to their maximum safe range from Japan, could reach their target under cover of darkness. But now that they had been detected, it was decided that an immediate take-off was necessary, even though this alteration would stretch the great range originally decided upon by almost 40 percent. Moreover, an immediate launching would change the time of the strike from the hours of darkness to full daylight, with all the attendant dangers of a daylight assault. Nonetheless, the choice was made.

It was now that the tactic of using the longer-ranged, land-based B-25 was to pay off. For the Japanese were well aware that carrier planes, in order to reach their target and return to safe landings aboard their ships, would have to be brought considerably closer to the mainland. They reasoned, therefore, that the earliest possible takeoff time would be the early hours of the following morning. This meant that they had ample time in which to prepare a shattering reception for the invaders.

They dispatched four battleships of the 2nd Fleet with orders to intercept the American carriers and engage them. They scrambled thirty-two bombers, escorted by twelve Zero fighters, to search eastward in the Pacific for the impertinent enemy.

But they found nothing. And having failed to make contact, they assumed that the Americans, aware that the *Nitto Maru* had spotted them, had abandoned the mission. Under normal circumstances it would have been a perfectly plausible assumption.

They were wrong. By the time the Japanese High Command received word from its sentry ship, at 06:30 hours, Colonel Doolittle's planes were already taking off from the deck of the *Hornet*.

And thus, as at Pearl Harbor only four months before, the defenders were caught unprepared.

What Doolittle and his men could not have known, or conceived in their wildest conjectures, was that their daring but puny raid would silence all opposition in the Japanese Naval General Staff to a plan which, until then, had almost no chance of ever being implemented, an elaborate blueprint for the capture of two tiny specks in the mid-Pacific.

This is the story of that battle, the Battle of Midway, and of the men who fought it.

1

For the younger officers of the Japanese forces, there had never been any doubt about the eventual outcome of this war. For them, it had always been a question of *when,* rather than *if.*

The rapid succession of their sweeping victories, and the relative ease with which they had overcome all attempts to halt them, had led to a heady air of euphoria, a sense of invincibility which inspired them and augmented their courage.

That courage had never been lacking, nor had their devotion to their sense of conquest. To the eager young soldiers, airmen, and sailors, the fruition of a destiny that had long been denied them seemed inevitable. Their dreams of glory, of a greater Japan that would rule half the world, nullified any doubts they might have had if they had stopped to contemplate the sheer size of America and its awesome industrial potential.

It was only among a few of their elders who had traveled abroad that doubts arose. For them, the peril that was inherent in that enemy potential was all too obvious. They realized Japan's urgent need was for a *quick* victory, or a negotiated peace with a humbled and bloodied adversary. And to the oldest and wisest of them, even this possibility was in no way assured.

Most doubtful of all was the Commander in Chief of the Imperial Pacific fleet himself. As naval attaché in Washington, Admiral Isoroku Yamamoto had learned a great deal about the American people.

He had learned, first of all, to despise their navy. He thought of the typical American officer as a card-playing amateur, more concerned with the niceties of the social whirl than with the serious business of war. But he had learned, too, of the startling power of their industry, of the speed at which American factories could turn out anything and everything that struck the public fancy—and in an abundance that, turned to war-time needs, could well be disastrous for an enemy.

"Unless we win *quickly*," he said, "we will never win at all. And then, for His Imperial Majesty . . ."

He never bothered to hide, indeed he was proud of, his obsession for the safety of the emperor.

Once, as a young officer in the Russo-Japanese war, he had seen an enemy fleet appear unexpectedly outside Tokyo Bay. There had been panic in the streets. Angry mobs had attacked the home of the admiral whose duty it was to protect the Japanese shores. He had been one of the men who had charged into the stone-throwing, hysterical mob.

To avoid a repetition of such a morale-destroying event, Yamamoto had stationed a thousand-mile-long line of picket boats seven hundred miles from Japan's eastern coast. This warning system was supplemented by daily flights of long-range naval aircraft.

He sat now in the summer garden of a large house on the outskirts of Hiroshima, far from the bustle of this important military base, talking quietly with his friends and their ladies, while his hostess poured him tea. It was spring, and the cherry blossoms were in full bloom, their rich scent pervading the lovely garden. There was honeysuckle and trumpet vine and lavender, and beautiful red and yellow lilies everywhere. A small stream meandered lazily across the boulder-studded lawns.

The house itself was set back from the tree-lined street, roofed over in gray tiles, delicately curved up at the edges. It was built in the *Chaseki* style, its wings carefully placed to embrace the whole of the landscaped garden which was an integral part of the dwelling. It was heavily laquered both inside and out, with sliding lattices of oiled and polished teak and richly decorated rice paper. Dusty green trailing vines of pink and blue wisteria clambered everywhere in carefully modulated profusion.

He loved this garden. There was a high, curved

"drum bridge" made of oiled teak that arched from one side of the tiny stream to the other.

There was a gentle breeze coming up from the sea, bringing with it the myriad scents of the tiny islet they called Itaky-Shima, "the Island of Light." A lovely young woman was sitting in the shade of a beech tree playing the *samison,* the three-stringed lute. Her name was Kikuji, and she was as famous as she was beautiful, a geisha since her early apprenticeship at the age of seven.

Yamamoto was listening to the softly-cadenced voice of his hostess, an elderly and dignified woman in an embroidered silk kimono. He nodded gently from time to time as though in agreement with what she was saying. Actually, he was paying her no attention, masking his preoccupation with an occasional courteous smile, his mind far, far away. He was thinking of the growing might—and the growing anger—of the distant enemy. Only a few weeks before, the disturbing news had reached him that a task force from Admiral Halsey's 3rd Fleet had penetrated his protective lines of scouting vessels, undetected, and had struck at Marcus Island, a mere thousand miles from Tokyo. He deeply feared a raid on Japan itself, even though his junior officers scorned the possibility. He took little comfort in their arguments that carrier-based aircraft were limited in range, and that the danger was minimal.

The enemy's long-range, land-based bombers were now at a safe distance. His defensive perimeter to the south, where once there had been great danger, and to the east where the bulk of the enemy forces lay was twenty-five hundred miles and more from the Japanese mainland.

He brought his mind back with a conscious effort to remember his manners, and said, very quietly: "This is perhaps the most beautiful garden in all of Hiroshima . . ." He was watching the ducks at the base of the little waterfall, and was conscious of the pleasure his remark had given.

This garden had been designed by one of the great landscape architects, in the *gyo,* or intermediate degree of elaboration. Its style was known as *bunjin-zukuri,* or the "literary men's style," intended to promote the thoughts of the artist and the philosopher, with a guardian stone set in a tiny pond, and a worshipping stone in its foreground. A small portion had been set aside for the *roji,* or tea garden. The placement of the natural stones here, seemingly random, had been carefully pondered. The surrounding trees had been thoughtfully chosen to provide a subtle and constantly-changing graduation of foliage color. There were stone lanterns, tiny figures, and a small arbor. The laws of harmony, of direction, of the five elements, and of the nine spirits of the Buddhist pantheon, had all been combined here to bring the gentle, melodious qualities of peace together in one harmonious entity.

A short, muscular figure, he sat on the carpet laid on the grass and bowed his head politely as his hostess filled his delicate porcelain cup again. He turned his head in astonishment at the sound of a pounding on the heavy wooden gate that led to the garden. He heard a break in the soft lilt of Kikuji's *samison,* then the music went on again. The elderly lady had broken off her chattering and was staring at the gate, toward which a servant was hurrying in alarm.

Yamamoto saw the bolts thrown back and the gate opened. One of his junior officers was there, a round-faced, boyish-looking young man who brushed the servant aside with ill-disguised impatience and an absolute disregard of the demands of etiquette. He was Commander Yasuji Watanabe, and there was a grim, angry look on his face. He hurried through the scented garden, and Yamamoto rose to meet him. The young officer stood sharply to attention, saluted and said, his voice hoarse with emotion, "Forgive me, Admiral . . . Forgive me . . ."

The admiral handed the tiny porcelain cup to his hostess and stood there, cold and stern, his hands behind his back. The music had stopped, and he was conscious that several young children had appeared in the doorway of the house, giggling together as though this breach of protocol somehow contained the elements of humor.

Yamamoto said, his voice restrained and icy, "Well, Watanabe? What is it that brings you here?"

The young commander hesitated. He could not formulate the words. Finally he stammered: "Tokyo, Admiral. The Americans have bombed Tokyo . . ."

Yamamoto felt the blood draining from his face. He was conscious of the sudden silence in the garden. Dimly, he heard himself ask, "When?"

"Ten minutes ago, Admiral. Yokohama, Kawasaki, and Yokosuka were also bombed. There are also reports of attacks on cities to the south."

Yamamoto seemed frozen, unable to ask the question which was foremost in his thoughts. But Watanabe knew his admiral's fixation, indeed shared it. "His Imperial Majesty is unharmed, sir. I personally phoned the palace. The emperor is safe."

Yamamoto was visibly relieved. He turned to his hostess. "I'm sure you will forgive this intrusion? And accept my apologies for it?"

She inclined her head graciously. "Perhaps you would like to be left alone, Admiral? . . ."

He bowed slightly and waited for her to leave. Then he turned back to Watanabe.

"Damage?"

"Very little to Tokyo. The other cities haven't reported yet. But it seems probable that they, too, were barely scratched."

Yamamoto turned away, his eyes fixed on the offending sky. His voice was tinged with anger now. "But *how*, Watanabe? How did they penetrate our defenses?"

"With carriers, Admiral . . ."

"Carriers?" He was furious. "Carriers slipped through our picket line?"

"No, sir. They launched their planes from seven hundred miles out. B-25's."

"The B-25 is a land-based aircraft, Watanabe."

"Yes, sir," the young commander replied lamely. "An American army bomber. They launched twenty of them."

Yamamoto was in shock. *"Land-based* . . . How can that be?"

"No one knows, sir. Certainly no one could have foreseen . . . They came in at treetop level. They weren't even seen until they were over the city."

The admiral looked at the young officer as if he didn't, or wouldn't, believe it.

"It's true, sir," Watanabe said. "Intelligence has confirmed it."

There was a tense silence. The admiral said at last, "Very well, they've learned to launch B-25's from their carriers. But can they recover them? I think not. So where will they land? A suicide mission?"

"No, sir. No one on the General Staff believes that *kamikaze* is part of the American philosophy."

"Then where?"

"Perhaps at sea. They could rendezvous somewhere inside our picket line, ditch their aircraft in the water, and wait to be picked up by submarine."

"Possibly . . ."

"Or, more likely . . ." Watanabe hesitated.

The admiral looked at him sharply. "Yes?"

"There is the possibility that they may head for China."

"Yes," Yamamoto said. "Yes, a very distinct possibility. Have our troops on the Chinese mainland been alerted?"

"I'll contact the army General Staff immediately, Admiral."

Yamamoto turned away to stare at the sky again. "Tokyo . . . bombed!" His voice was heavy with bitter anger and Watanabe could feel the pain there.

He said quietly, "Sir, I understand your concern for the emperor's safety, a concern we all share, but . . ."

"You may speak freely, Commander."

Watanabe hesitated, then plunged ahead: "Sir, this raid is a blessing in disguise."

Yamamoto turned and fixed the young commander with a dangerous look. Only Watanabe's deep devotion to his admiral gave him the courage to continue. "The Americans have done us an invaluable service—and very little damage."

"What about the morale of our people, Watanabe?"

"Regrettably, there will be some—repercussions, sir. There's no question about it. But the important thing is that you have been proven correct."

Yamamoto gave his aide a questioning look. Watanabe continued: "The Americans have shown the General Staff what you have contended from the start. Namely, that our homeland is not invulnerable to attack."

"And you find comfort in that?" Yamamoto said caustically.

"Yes, sir. Because after today there'll be no more foot-dragging by the General Staff. Their opposition to Operation MI will end."

The Admiral's face softened almost imperceptibly and Watanabe could see that he was receptive, perhaps even hopeful despite the calamitous news he had just received. At length, Yamamoto sighed and said quietly, "Midway. You think they'll approve my taking Midway . . ."

"I'm certain of it, sir."

The admiral said, "Call a meeting of the General Staff as soon as possible, Watanabe. And come, we'll drive to Tokyo together."

He turned on his heel, and Watanabe, quietly elated, followed him across the garden and out onto the street where a long, black staff car was waiting.

A few hours later, word reached them from the Chinese mainland that a number of American B-25's had crash-landed near Nanchang. It was believed that the so-called Chinese patriots, whom the Japanese preferred to call bandits, were trying to take them to Chungking.

In Chungking there was to be a wild and glorious party for the survivors of the Doolittle-led raid. In Tokyo there was to be a great deal of soul-searching at the General Staff level. But the battle to take Midway was now inevitable.

2

Along "battleship row" at Pearl Harbor, the jagged outlines of the sunken vessels thrust their accusing fingers out of the bay, a grim reminder to a once complacent, overconfident nation. The easygoing camaraderie of its officer corps, characterized by Admiral Yamamoto as a socializing elite too preoccupied with their clubs to give serious attention to the war, had disappeared.

A new man had taken over CINCPAC Headquarters. He was Admiral Chester W. Nimitz, recently appointed Commander in Chief, U.S. Pacific Fleet and Commander in Chief Pacific Ocean Area. His first task had been to tighten ship.

Uniforms, now, were smarter and more aggressively correct. Salutes were edged with an overt display of discipline. There was a sense of direction, an air of urgency. The wounded giant was stirring and gathering his strength.

The navy-gray jeep sped through the simmering heat-waves which rose from the hot asphalt, its radio antenna whipping the air as it headed toward the huge concrete blockhouse. From the radio came the nasal twang of America's dean of newsmen, H. V. Kaltenborn.

"Lieutenant Colonel James H. Doolittle led the raid with a force of sixteen B-25's and an all-volunteer crew of airmen. Most of the planes carried three five hundred-pound demolition bombs and single incendiary clusters which were dropped on oil stores, factory areas, and on some of the military installations of Tokyo. A few planes went on to make minor strikes on Kyoto, Yokohama, and Nagoya, with one bomb hitting the Japanese aircraft carrier *Ryujo*.

"News of the raid has had a most heartening effect on American morale and the morale of our allies, while at the same time constituting a blow to the prestige of the Japanese."

Captain Matt Garth was at the wheel, a tall, angular man in his late forties, with a sharp, aquiline face and piercing blue eyes. His shoulders were squarely set, his waist kept slim by daily exercise. There was a look about him that, while not quite hostile, seemed to indicate an intolerance of human frailty, and more—an acute dislike for what he liked to call muddy thinking.

He was in a furious temper now. He snapped off the radio, swung the wheel hard over, and skidded to a stop at the blockhouse. Outside the ten-foot-high, barbed-wire-topped chain-link fence which encircled the blockhouse was a small guard station. It was manned by a young Marine lieutenant and two enlisted men. They were armed with tommy guns and were grinning as they watched Matt Garth climb out of the jeep and approach them.

Jubilation was the mood of the moment in Honolulu. In the background, Garth could hear the first sounds of the celebration that was to continue far into the night. It started with a workshop whistle, then another and another. The raucous honking of automobile horns joined in, followed by the wild hooting of ships in the bay.

The faces of the Marine guards summed it all up. At last America had struck back! It was about time we showed the Japs they couldn't shit on us and get away with it. This is only the beginning, by God!

Inside the guard station a radio was playing. Matt scowled as he heard Kaltenborn's voice again:

"At his press conference today, President Roosevelt was asked the following question. Quote: 'Mr. President, couldn't you tell us about that bombing? Where did those planes start from and go to?' He replied: 'Yes, the time has now come to tell you. They came from our new secret base at Shangri-La.' Unquote. Well, I suppose that's all we shall be told until the planes have at last reached a safe haven."

The young lieutenant snapped off a salute and said, grinning broadly, "You hear that, Captain? Doolittle clobbered Tokyo. First thing we've had to cheer about since December seventh . . ."

The captain cut him short. "Once in a while, Lieutenant, try *thinking*."

He was startled. "Sir?"

"I'm in a hurry, Lieutenant."

"Yes, sir." The young lieutenant was all cold efficiency again as he carefully studied Garth's credentials while the captain waited impatiently. He handed them back, saluted and gestured to the guards to open the gate.

Garth went inside, conscious of their eyes boring into his back. He crossed an open area to the heavy steel doorway of the blockhouse, where a modest little sign said, "NAVY COMBAT INTELLIGENCE." He pressed the buzzer. An observation port slid open and he presented his credentials to the Marine guard on the inside. More patiently now, he waited for the careful check, knowing that this was a vital part of the deadly game they were all playing. At length, the guard slipped the heavy bolts and let him in, saluting smartly.

Ahead of him was a short, vault-like hall terminating at the head of a steep, narrow stairway. Garth descended into the dimly-lit depths to a second steel door. He pressed the buzzer again. Mechanically, he thrust his credentials into the observation port when it opened for him, as though he were now part of this monstrous machine, waiting to be ingested by it like all the others who came here. He toyed for a moment with the fancy that the machine had a mind of its own, pulling into its mechanical intestines all who were unwary enough to approach it—a robot Venus's-flytrap with a particular taste for disgruntled navy captains.

At last the door swung open and he stepped into what was surely the untidiest room he had ever seen.

It was large, windowless, and crammed with battered desks, filing cabinets and tables. Every surface was covered with papers, files, reports, maps. Officers and enlisted men were milling around, filling the area with the blue smoke of cigars and pipes and cigarettes. Every square foot of the floor was taken up with boxes, crates, cartons, and piles of heavy reference books. There were suitcases used as file boxes, and old sea chests packed with folded maps, and orange crates filled with thick sheaves of papers held together with rubber bands and string. There was a shelf along one wall on which there was every kind of Oriental dictionary he could imagine, old and new, fat and thin—scores of them. And hanging on pins close by was a huge chart on which were inscribed all the ideographs of the Japanese language and the languages with which it was now, or was once, or was thought to be, or conceivably might have been, associated—Korean, Mongol, Turkic, Cantonese, Hakka, Mandarin, Swatow, Amoy, Wenchow, Ningpo, and Wu. There was even a detailed rendering of the ideographs into *Romanji,* an approximation of the Latin alphabet.

In the middle of the huge room, a beanpole of a man, wearing a rumpled red smoking jacket and bedroom slippers, was bending over a waist-high pile of folders stacked on the floor. He was dropping cigar ashes and muttering to himself as he searched among the papers, swearing gently and making little gestures of frustration.

He was Commander Joseph J. Rochefort, Jr. He swung round and straightened up clumsily as Garth approached. Grinning broadly, a wry, sardonic grin, he circled around the piles of cardboard boxes and thrust out a hand.

He said, "Well, I'll be damned. I was expecting some junior intelligence officer, and who do we get? Air OPS himself. An unexpected honor, Matt."

Garth took his hand. "The hell it is, Joe!"

Rochefort's grin hardly wavered. He cleared his throat and said, "Yeah . . . well, how's the boss?"

"Admiral Nimitz is just fine."

"Glad to hear it. My respects to the admiral and tell him that his Black Chamber creatures will soon be buried alive under enemy radio intercepts—"

"—if he doesn't get you out of this tomb and into decent quarters," Garth echoed. It was a complaint he was getting very tired of hearing, since there wasn't a damn thing he could do about it. Rochefort knew it and said:

"Forget it."

"I wish *you* would, Commander."

"Can the circus gorilla forget he needs a bigger cage?"

Matt Garth sniffed the air and said, "Speaking of gorillas . . . My God, it's raunchy in here! Don't you guys ever bathe?"

Rochefort grimaced. "Sure we do. Why, I had a bath myself only . . . What day is it today? Hell, must have been less than a week ago."

Garth shook his head disgustedly and said, "I have to talk to you, Joe. In private."

"Let me guess why. The admiral's worried about that estimate of Japanese intentions I sent him, right? Yeah, I thought so." He jerked a thumb. "In there."

There was a tiny cubicle in the far corner. As they moved toward it, Matt Garth stopped by the language chart and stared at it, and said, "Satisfy my academic curiosity, Joe. Can you speak *all* these languages? Or just one or two of them? Or is this just here to impress the top brass? A lot of bull?"

Rochefort chuckled. "I don't speak a single one of them, Matt. I can't even write half of them properly. But I can sure as hell tell you that if *nin* in Ga-on becomes *jin* in Kan-on, then it has to be *hito* in Japanese. Just a question of following the rules in linguistics . . . Like most things, it's relatively easy if you know how."

They went into the little room. Rochefort closed the door carefully and perched himself on a table littered with annotated cuttings. There was only one battered chair, to which he motioned his guest as he dug a fresh cheroot from his jacket and lit it. He exhaled and studied Garth closely. "I don't believe it's the boss who's got you pissed, Matt."

Garth gave him a withering look. Rochefort said, "Well, damn it, you look like a bitch weasel ready to bite."

Garth brushed at the cigar smoke Rochefort directed his way and glowered. Rochefort went on. "I should think Doolittle's attack would have you CINCPAC people dancing in the streets."

Matt Garth snorted and said, "Not by a long shot."

"We showed the Japanese their homeland isn't quite

as impregnable as they thought. You don't think that's good?"

"For Christ's sake, use your head, Joe," Garth said angrily. "That damned raid's going to boomerang. Our fleet's been clobbered, remember? We need *time*. Time to heal, to replace our losses." Garth paused, and made a visible effort to quench his anger. Then said quietly, "Joe, Admiral Nimitz thinks Yamamoto is going to jump right back at us."

"And you, Matt?"

"Me? I'm certain he's right. Pearl crippled us. But it made us fighting mad. Doolittle's raid must have made the Japs just as furious, but it did *not* cripple them. Everything we know about Yamamoto tells us he'll hit back, and *hard*. But where, Joe? That's what we have to know."

Rochefort slipped off the table and went to a large-scale map of the Pacific Ocean that was stretched across one wall. He squinted at it, puffed on his cigar, and said at last, "He'll use his carriers, his best weapon, so what we have to know is where they are and where they're going next."

"Brilliant thinking," Garth said caustically. "You ought to be on staff in Washington."

Rochefort chuckled, turned back to his desk, and found a large sheet of paper which he extended to Garth. "Here's a précis of the latest Japanese intercepts. I think you'll find it interesting."

Garth scanned the précis, his frown deepening. Rochefort stabbed at the map with his fist, dropping ash again, and said, "South of Rabaul. In the Coral Sea area. That's where they'll hit us next. We figure their target will be Port Moresby on Papua. The capture of Port Moresby would open up the northern coast of Australia to invasion. And there's damn little we could do to defend our Aussie friends." Rochefort paused and nodded his head as if to confirm his own thoughts. Then he said, "The Coral Sea. Everything points to the Coral Sea . . . and a big amphib operation."

"Are you positive, Joe?"

"Nope. This business is ninety percent supposition

and ten percent blind luck, you know that." He picked another large sheet of paper from among the litter on his desk, handed it to Garth and said, "Here's a list of the Japanese ships we *suspect* will be assigned."

Garth was visibly impressed, and concerned, as he studied the list. Rochefort resumed his perch on the edge of his desk and looked at the floor as if all the answers were to be found there. At length, he said worriedly, "But there's something else brewing, Matt. Something bigger . . . out our way."

"What?"

Rochefort shrugged and said, "I can still only guess."

Matt Garth exploded. "Goddamn it, Joe, you've cracked Yamamoto's staff-level code—and you can only *guess?* Good God, man, we need facts, not guess-work!"

Rochefort said mildly, "We prefer to call it analysis."

"All right, analysis. Just tell me one thing. How much in these intercepts can you *really* decipher?" There was a touch of sarcasm in his voice.

Rochefort was stung. He flicked his cigar ash onto the floor and said, "Well, the layman imagines that once we've busted a code, all we have to do is put it on the machine and reel it off, word by word. But that's not the way it works. We get a glimmer here, a flicker there. Once in a while, a missing piece falls into place. Sometimes, a whole week will go by when nothing makes any sense at all."

Garth's voice was hard. "How *much*, Joe?"

Rochefort grunted. "I told you, ten, maybe fifteen percent. When we're lucky."

"One word in ten. Great!"

"No, it's not. But it's all we have to work with."

Matt Garth went to the map and studied it. The line of Japan's advances was formidable. He said wearily, "All right, assuming something big *is* brewing out our way—and you've got no hard clues—what the hell do you have?"

"An increase in radio traffic between Yamamoto's staff officers."

Garth turned to face Rochefort, his disappointment, his impatience, evident. "That's all?"

"Could be significant," Rochefort replied quietly. "At least, I *feel* something's stirring."

Garth sighed and said, "I'll take this list of Japanese ships that are *maybe* heading for the Coral Sea. Admiral Nimitz might just send Jack Fletcher's task force down to investigate. Provided I can convince him that ten percent guesswork can deliver *something*."

Rochefort grinned and said mockingly, "On behalf of the Black Chamber code-crackers, I thank you, Captain."

Garth snorted and walked out, almost bowling over the young intelligence officer who was entering. His name was Wright and his glance followed Garth as he said:

"What the hell makes him so damned officious?"

Rochefort said, "How would you like the job of going back to Chester Nimitz and giving him your judgment on *us?*"

Wright looked around at the shambles they worked in. "Maybe we ought to think about cleaning this place up some day," he observed.

"Yeah. Some day. Anything in the new Yamamoto intercepts?"

"Just the usual crap, except for this." Wright handed his boss a slip of paper and continued, "It's a first-time mention of something called 'AF,' whatever that is."

Commander Joe Rochefort pondered over it. Somewhere in the deep recesses of his mind that combination of letters stirred a dim memory. But he couldn't bring it to the surface. "AF . . ." he muttered softly. "A . . . F . . ."

3

Matt Garth pushed the jeep hard through the midtown Honolulu traffic. "The poor dumb bastards," he thought, "honking their horns and grinning like baboons, as if they knew what the hell they were celebrating!" He swerved to miss a group of thoroughly drunk young soldiers who were cavorting in the middle of an intersection. "Where the hell are the MP's?" he muttered. "They probably think the war is over . . ." He stopped in midthought and laughed at himself. "Good God, you're in a foul mood. Let them celebrate. They'll pay later."

He cramped the wheel over and squeezed the jeep into a parking space outside a large, sprawling, navy-gray building, the entrance of which was guarded by a trio of heavily armed Marines. The sign over the big glass doorway read: "CINCPAC," navy hieroglyphics for "Commander in Chief, Pacific." It was the headquarters of Admiral Chester W. Nimitz and his staff.

Matt climbed out of the jeep and headed for the Marine guards, digging out the credentials he knew they would demand before they would admit him into his own office. A new contingent of guards was assigned to CINCPAC every week so that they never became familiar with anyone who had permanent duty on the admiral's staff. It was a simple security precaution calculated to prevent a careless wave-through of some unauthorized person who happened to look like one of the staff members. German spies had breached several staff headquarters in the European theater by waiting for a busy moment and a slipshod guard. Nimitz was determined it wouldn't happen at his headquarters.

The Marine private who took Captain Garth's credentials was barely nineteen, a lanky kid who probably didn't shave more than once a week. Matt was tempted to grin at the youngster's grimly serious expression. Instead he thought: "Look me in the face, son. Don't let the shoulder bars and the scrambled eggs on my visor distract you. At this moment, you're in charge."

As the guard returned the credentials and snapped a rigid salute, a voice called out: "Captain!"

Matt turned and saw a junior-grade lieutenant hurrying toward him from across the street. Pinned to his chest was a pair of gold wings, but no campaign ribbons. His uniform was rumpled and he carried a large parachute bag in which all his gear was stowed. His lean, tanned face was travel-fatigued and there was a sense of urgency behind the rather forced smile he mustered.

Matt responded with a spontaneous, unrestrained grin as the young flyer came on. He said, "Tom! When did you get in? Why didn't you let me know? My God, what a beautiful surprise!"

Tom's handshake was indifferent, almost perfunctory. "Last night, Dad," he said.

"Why didn't you write me you were coming? It's been too long, Tom. Far too long."

He was aware of the hesitancy. But he thought: "My God, my own son in uniform now!" He grasped him by the shoulders and said again, "Why didn't you let me know?"

The boy avoided the question. "I've been assigned to the islands, Dad. To Kaneohe."

"Great! Then we'll finally be seeing something of each other. You look great, Tom. Just great."

"So do you, Dad."

"Finally lost that puppy fat."

"A few years back."

There was an awkward silence. A vision of other days flooded Matt's mind. A fourteen-year-old, his body tanned but too plump, head bowed, eyes on the strings of the tennis racket he fumbled with, a reflective look on his face as he said, shyly, "Dad, why don't you and Mom get along?" Now he was leaner, fitter, and apparently more assured. But there was still that wary look on his face.

Matt Garth dropped his hands. "Kaneohe, huh? What squadron?"

"VF-8."

He nodded. "You'll like it there. Your CO was my wing man when we were flying off the *Langley* in San Diego. A guy by the name of Carl Jessop. A great guy."

Tom didn't respond. There was another awkward pause which Matt broke with a grin and said, "I heard you graduated top of your class. You that hot a pilot, or was the competition slow?"

"You'd probably grade them slow, sir."

"Hey. Come on, Tom!"

"Can we talk someplace?"

Tom's expression wilted his father's smile. "After all this time," Garth thought, "he's still as stiff-necked as ever. My God, can I ever reach him?" But he said, "Sure. It's lunchtime. All of a sudden I could swallow a bull moose. Hoofs and hide. If you'll butter his horns."

The boy's laughter was forced, hollow. Garth took the parachute bag, and tossed it into the back of the jeep. He waved Tom into the passenger's seat and thrust the miniature auto back into the frenetic Honolulu traffic.

The restaurant was small and somewhat dingy, but it wore its shabby look with a certain charm. The profusion of flowers in their ceramic pots, the occasional lei around the neck of a pretty young woman, the bright-patterned shirts of the "old islanders" and their soft cadenced laughter was a very welcome relief from the antiseptic steel and concrete bunker which the island had become.

They were led across the crowded room by a lovely girl dressed in traditional Okinawan attire. When they were seated at the cramped little table Garth said, "It's not much for atmosphere and it's always packed. But if you want fresh meat on this island you find an Okinawan restaurant. They've had the garbage-collecting concessions for as far back as anyone can remember. Ergo . . . they have a plentiful supply of pork."

A strikingly fat, ugly woman wearing an eye-bursting costume that looked like a circus tent approached, her radiant smile fixed on Garth. "Captain Matt! Please forgive the dreadful table. I did not expect you!"

"It's the same table I get when you *do* expect me," Matt said. Then he grinned and added, "It's all right, Yaechan. It was a surprise for me, too. I want you to meet my son, Tom."

Yaechan bowed, her beady-bright eyes appraising the young flyer closely. She said, "He is very pleasing to the eye. Like his father."

Tom was a little startled and Matt laughed at him and said, "She's a marriage broker on the side, Tom. You've just made one of her lists. Watch yourself."

Yaechan smiled and said, "The usual, Captain?"

"Please. And what'll you have, son?"

Tom sat uncomfortably on the edge of the chair, as though not anxious to stay too long. He shook his head. "Nothing, thanks."

"Come on. It's an occasion."

"Yeah . . . okay. A rum and coke."

Yaechan bowed and left to order their drinks. There was a tight little silence. Then: "I did phone you, Tom . . . the day you graduated. From Guam."

The young man nodded. "Yes, I heard. Sorry I missed your call."

"I guess your mother was there."

"Yes."

"How is she?"

"She says she's happy with her new husband."

"I'm glad."

There was a definite note of censure in Tom's voice as he added, "But you know Lisa. Her pride wouldn't let her say anything else."

Matt sighed and thought: "I wonder if I was that judgmental . . . that arrogant, when I was his age?" Then he said with a forced smile, "Yeah. She's a lady right out of the Victorian era."

His son was staring at him with a look which seemed to say, "You callous son of a bitch." Or maybe it was a look of pity. Matt couldn't remember the time when he first realized that he could no longer tune into his son's feelings. At some moment in the fifteen years of coldly calculated ego-mangling that featured his marriage to Lisa, the boy had turned inward for self-preservation. And who could blame him? Enigmatic. That just about summed up Tom's character.

Tom said brusquely, "Dad, there's something very important I have to tell you. I've fallen in love."

Matt forced a smile to cover his surprise.

"Well—great. Congratulations. Is she anyone I know? Someone from the old days? You always had them chasing after you, despite the puppy fat."

"No. You don't know her."

"Okay. When will I have the pleasure?"

Tom hesitated for a moment then spoke slowly and distinctly, "I've fallen in love with a Japanese girl."

For a moment, it seemed to Matt as though all sound in the bustling restaurant had ceased; he was only conscious that someone at the next table was drumming nervously with his finger, beating out a rhythmic tattoo that sounded like a galloping horse. And then the pretty young waitress was bending over the table and serving their drinks. And the sounds came back again, one by one—the tinkle of ice in glasses, the drone of voices, subdued laughter, automobile horns in the street outside.

Matt forced an amused little chuckle and said, "I know right where you are, Tom. When I was your age, I fell in love once a week, regularly. Each time it was more gut-clutching than the last. But, fortunately, there was always another pretty face, another sensational figure drifting by. And I was very easily diverted—"

Tom cut in. "Dad, I want to marry her."

"Marry a Japanese? . . ."

"I'm deadly serious about it."

"Tom, we're at *war* with Japan. Haven't you heard? There's no place these days for—"

"And I need your help."

Matt Garth stared at his son, noting the intense set of the jaw, the coldly defiant look in the ice-blue eyes. His mother's son, he thought, and there was a touch of bitterness in the observation. He said softly, "I damn well guess you do. And I'll give it to you in the form of some good, old-fashioned, sensible advice. Forget it, Tom. There's no possible way it can work out. Ever."

"No sir, I won't do that."

"Tom, for God's sake . . ."

He interrupted his father again, speaking very quietly and deliberately. "I'm in *love* with her, Dad. I'm going to marry her."

"Jesus Christ! . . ."

"I'm sorry if it sticks in your throat, but that's the way it's going to be."

Matt could feel the pulse in his throat pounding. He made an effort to hold in check the anger it presaged. "You're damned right it sticks in my throat. But not for the reasons you think. Hell, I did a four-year tour of duty in Hong Kong. If I hadn't loved your mother,

I'd have left her a dozen times for Asian girls. So don't give me that crap. I'm not a racial bigot, and you damned well know it." He gulped at his drink, and said, "But, my God, you've sure got a lousy sense of timing."

To his surprise, there was a slow smile spreading over his son's face. Tom said, "Meaning that you're going to help me, right?"

Matt sighed and said at length, "If I can."

"You know something, Dad? I never figured you wouldn't." Tom was laughing softly and Matt didn't know whether to feel like a sucker or complimented. "What's her name?" he asked.

"Haruko. Haruko Sakura."

"I assume she's at least—Japanese-*American?*"

"Yes, she is. She was born here, in Honolulu."

"How in the hell did you manage that? Training in San Diego—and getting involved with a Japanese girl in Honolulu. I thought this was your first time in the islands."

"I met her in San Diego. She's a student at San Diego State."

"But she's here now?"

"Her parents live in Honolulu. She wouldn't marry me without their consent, that's the kind of girl she is. So she came over here to see them." The boy paused and then said, "She was arrested the minute she stepped off the plane."

"My God, I need another drink."

He caught the waitress's eye and said, "The same again, miss."

Tom put his hand over the top of his half-empty glass. "Not for me."

A group of officers was sliding past their table. One of them clapped him on the back and said, "Hi there, Matt. How's it going?"

He said mechanically, "Fine, Jerry, just fine . . ." Then he turned back to his son. "What was the charge?"

"As far as I can find out, the FBI had some kind of a tip about her parents. You know how it is, every so-called patriot in the country wants to show what a great guy he is by turning in a Japanese."

"Listen, mister," Matt said, feeling his face flush with intensity. "There was never a war where hysteria didn't foul up a lot of innocent people. This one's no different. It stinks, what's happening to our Japanese citizens. But I suggest you remember that it's part of the dehumanizing that attends every conflict between nations—and knock off that self-righteous attitude."

"Sorry," said Tom, a little startled.

Lately, Matt realized he had become less and less tolerant of the people with the quick and easy judgments who responded to every crisis or circumstance with the same preconditioned, emotion-laden cliches, and looked at the actual facts of the situation later, if at all. His fresh drink came and he took a long pull, then said, "What else do you know about your girl?"

"Just that she was born here. And she's as loyal as either of us."

"That remains to be seen. Did you see her?"

"I tried. I went to the place where they're holding her. One of the so-called emigration centers. What a helluva name that is. It's a stinking jail! She wouldn't see me."

"Why not?"

Tom rubbed a weary hand over his face. "I don't know. I just—don't know."

Garth waited for the boy to get hold of himself. At length, Tom said, "I did find out one thing. They're on a list—Haruko, her father and her mother—scheduled to be shipped out to the mainland in a few days, the army duty officer told me."

"All right. I'll try to get the FBI report on her. Better write her name down for me."

"I already have. Here." Tom handed him a folded piece of paper.

Garth studied the name, aware that his son was watching him. "You wrote it down for me . . . You were pretty damned sure you could sweet-talk me into this, weren't you?"

"I figured you'd help me, yes."

"Okay. Just promise me you won't do anything stupid until I check this out."

"That's a deal."

Smiling now, the young man raised his glass. "Here's to you, Captain."

"To both of us, Tom." As Matt finished off his drink, the glass slipped and fell to the table, scattering ice cubes. He clutched his wrist as a sliver of pain shot up his arm and dissipated in his shoulder. For the first time his son noticed the ugly, deep scar across the back of his hand. Tom retrieved the glass and scooped up the ice cubes.

"You didn't tell me. Pearl Harbor?"

Matt Garth flexed his fingers and nodded. "Nothing to fuss about. Just a piece of Japanese shrapnel. Probably some of that scrap we shipped to them. Hell of a thing to figure you got shot by a piece of Chevy fender, isn't it? Now, how about some lunch?"

Tom said, "I'm starved."

4

As far as the eye could see in the darkness of the Pacific night, the great ships of the Japanese fleet lay at anchor in the rain which pounded Hiroshima Bay into a slate-gray slab. Surrounded by other battleships, heavy and light cruisers and sleek destroyers, was the huge dreadnought *Yamato,* flagship of Admiral Isoroku Yamamoto.

She was the largest ship ever built, and had been completed by the Japanese, under a veil of the strictest secrecy, the previous year. No warship in the world was more modern or efficient. She was eight hundred feet long, with a displacement of 72,200 tons, and she mounted nine eighteen-inch guns, as well as a vast number of antiaircraft guns. Her superstructure towered high into the night sky, her single funnel raked behind it. She was a ship of formidable power—the pride of the Imperial Japanese Navy.

There was a knock on the door of Yamamoto's sumptuous cabin. His steward, an aged, crimped-backed enlisted man, hurried to admit Commander Watanabe, Yamamoto's young aide, who said, "When you are ready, sir."

Yamamoto nodded and resumed dressing with the help of his steward. He was edgy tonight, worried about the staff meeting he had called. He anticipated some opposition, some debate over the battle plan he had proposed, but he expected to prevail. Yet there was this disquieted feeling, like a shadow hovering at the perimeter of his mind, just out of reach of his reason.

Watanabe was aware that his admiral's mood was clouded, but his own high spirits rejected it totally. He said, "Sir, I think you should know your flag officers are complaining."

Yamamoto gave him a steely look. The young aide beamed. "The General Staff in Tokyo is overwhelming them with cooperation. There's not a whisper of opposition to Operation MI."

"Indeed," the admiral said flatly as he fastened the last snap on his austere black uniform coat. In contrasting black were two wide and three narrow stripes on his right sleeve, and on either side of his collar, two gold bars embossed with three stars. This was the only insignia the admiral wore, despising as he did the western officer-corps' penchant for decorating their chests with a gaudy array of campaign ribbons, which he felt were boastful and beneath the dignity of a Japanese officer.

The steward scurried to open the door and the admiral stepped outside, Watanabe on his heels. As they strode down the long passageway, Watanabe laughed quietly. "General Doolittle would be appalled if he knew what his puny air raid will unleash on his countrymen."

Yamamoto said, irritated, "The briefing. How did they react?"

"Admiral Nagumo seems almost indifferent, sir."

Yamamoto gave him a bleak look. The young aide continued, uncowed, "He simply said his carrier pilots could carry out any assignments they were given. And why shouldn't he be confident, after his successes at Pearl Harbor and Ceylon?"

"Yamaguchi? How did he respond?"

"Admiral Yamaguchi is openly enthusiastic. He is looking forward to destroying the American aircraft carriers he and Nagumo missed at Pearl Harbor . . . Though I have the impression that he feels he should be in overall command of the carrier strike force instead of Nagumo."

Watanabe watched for some reaction in his admiral's face. He saw none and knew that Yamaguchi's ambitions would not be realized in this operation. He continued, "The only strong opposition comes from the officer who will command the invasion forces."

"Kondo . . ."

"Yes, sir."

The Battle Plot Room aboard the Yamato was the most modern command center afloat anywhere in the world. It was dominated by a huge table on which was a detailed plot of the Pacific, Japan at its westernmost edge, the Hawaiian Islands at its easternmost edge, and the Aleutian Island chain to the north. The legend "OPERATION MI," was printed in bold letters at the southern edge of the plot, and bright crimson arrows marked the sea courses of the various attack elements of "MI." Gathered around it were Admiral Yamamoto's flag officers, the most capable and experienced commanders in the Imperial Navy.

There was Rear Admiral Matome Ugaki, tapping impatiently on the side of his leg with his little cane. Vice Admiral Moshiro Hosogaya, gray-haired and studious. Rear Admiral Tamon Yamaguchi, aggressive, flint-eyed. Vice Admiral Chuichi Nagumo, stolid, aloof. And lastly, riffling through a thick sheaf of papers containing the details of the battle plan, was Vice Admiral Nobutake Kondo, heavy-set, outspoken, and at this moment trying to stifle his anger.

Kondo slapped the sheaf closed and glowered at the larger legend on the plot table: "OPERATION MI"! It seemed that everywhere he turned these days he was affronted with that symbol for folly. The scheme had alarmed him ever since the first obscure hints had been dropped. Now he detested and feared it. Now that it was out in the open, he was determined to stop it.

The objectives of this operation had been drawn in equally bold and uncompromising arrows. One of them, marked OBJECTIVE AO, was a bright red line which led straight to a painted circle enclosing the islands of Adak, Attu, Kiska, and Dutch Harbor in the Aleutians.

But it was the second objective that offended him the most: an arrow marked OBJECTIVE AF which struck out almost due west, thrusting toward the defensive perimeter of picket ships which Yamamoto had set up, and beyond it—to Midway.

He thumped the table with an angry hand and said scornfully, "It is regrettable that so much time and effort was spent on this plan. Because, in my opinion, it is doomed to failure."

Watanabe shook his head. "I must respectfully disagree, Admiral Kondo . . ."

Kondo overrode him with: "Midway! A speck in the middle of the Pacific. A repository of bird-droppings and sand-fleas!"

Watanabe said stubbornly, "If the admiral will permit me . . ." Kondo waved an impatient hand and the young aide continued, "Operation MI was conceived by the Navy's most brilliant strategist."

Kondo was conscious that Yamamoto, quietly sipping tea out of a tiny cup of egg-shell china, was almost ostentatiously paying him no attention. But he thought he detected something besides indifference in his commander's eyes. Was it the faint tarnish of doubt? One thing he did know, Yamamoto's attitude was too detached, and it encouraged him to go on. "We're all aware of Captain Kuroshima's authorship, Watanabe. But this time the God of Operations has given birth to a nightmare."

"Would you please explain, sir?"

"Explain? Isn't it obvious?" Kondo replied acidly. "The enemy can fly large numbers of long-range bombers from their airfield on Midway. Our carriers will be intercepted and destroyed before they can get close enough to launch an attack. How am I expected to get my troops ashore on Midway if the American airfield

and shore batteries are not first neutralized—smashed!"
He brought his palm down hard on the table. "It would
be suicidal!"

Vice Admiral Nagumo called Kondo's attention with
a small impatient motion of his hand. He was staring
at one of the long crimson-colored arrows on the
battle plot. It simulated a sea course which ran west-
southwest for a short distance, then veered northwest
into the mid-Pacific, finally slicing sharply south on
collision course with Midway Island. It was marked,
"FIRST CARRIER STRIKING FORCE" and represented
his flagship, the carrier *Akagi* and the carrier *Kaga,* with
their forty-two fighters, forty-two dive-bombers, and
fifty-one torpedo bombers; the carriers *Hiryu* and
Soryu, with forty-two each of fighters, dive-bombers,
and torpedo bombers, all under his Rear Admiral
Yamaguchi; and the screening group under Rear Admiral Susumu Kimura, consisting of the light cruiser
Nagara, twelve destroyers and five supply ships. It was
a powerful and highly mobile force, heavily-armed,
superbly trained and commanded.

He turned to look at Kondo. "I agree, Kondo. The
annihilation of Midway's defenses is vital to the success
of your landing operations. But I have just gone on
record that my carriers will accomplish whatever task
they are assigned. In this case, the obliteration of the
American airfield and shore batteries. I am surprised
that my statement made no impression on you."

Kondo was not mollified in the least. His tone was
cutting. "The enemy's land-based bombers—*land-
based,* Nagumo—have a range of at least four hundred
miles more than your carrier planes. Your ships would
be blown out of the sea before you could even
begin to spot your planes for launching."

"I think not." There was a deceptively mild smile on
Nagumo's face. "I took my carriers all the way to
Hawaii, where the risk was far greater. In spite of the
threat of their land-based bombers, I crushed the American fleet at Pearl Harbor. Four first-line battleships
destroyed. Four others badly damaged. Their Pacific
fleet almost ceased to exist, Kondo. And if I had not

allowed myself to be turned away from a second attack by my air group leaders, it would have ceased to exist entirely."

Kondo replied caustically, "They dissuaded you because of your own losses, which were scarcely negligible."

"Twenty-nine planes out of a total of three hundred and fifty-four? No, not negligible. But well worth the result."

"Agreed. But that was *then,* Nagumo, not *now.* A surprise attack with a carrier task force, before a formal declaration of war, is one thing. But this—" He gestured, exasperated, at the Battle Plot. ". . . A strike against Midway and the Aleutians, across waters scouted by enemy submarines—with two hundred ships and one hundred thousand men—"

Nagumo cut in, his voice husky now with an intensity which surprised everyone present. "Unfortunately, the American aircraft carriers were not at Pearl Harbor, as our intelligence predicted. This operation will give me the opportunity to engage them, Kondo."

Kondo grunted and turned away from the plot. There was a moment of silence. Admiral Yamamoto put down his teacup and got to his feet heavily. He could hear the pounding of the rain outside. His wounded hand was giving him trouble as it always did in the wet weather. He studied the battle plot, aware that the others were waiting for their commander to speak. He looked up and said, "Are there any other objections?" No one spoke. Yamamoto decided to force the issue. He turned to Ugaki. "Admiral, as my Chief of Staff, you should have something to contribute."

Somewhat reluctantly, Ugaki replied, "I have only one reservation, sir. Supply. It will be difficult to supply Midway after its capture." Then he smiled and added, almost lightly, "But if it proves too onerous, we can always destroy the installations and evacuate."

Kondo grunted again and said, "You've just proved the operation is totally pointless, Ugaki."

Yamamoto ignored Kondo, his glance falling on the scholarly Hosogaya. "What does my commander of the northern force think? Does the idea of taking these fly-specks in the Aluetians cause you any alarm?"

Hosogaya pondered the three arrows on the battle plot which were marked, "Second Carrier Striking Force," "Kiska," and "Attu." Each proceeded from the harbor at Ominato and, via separate courses, converged on the Aleutian Islands. He replied, "No, sir. However, an operation so large—so complex—I would like time to study and consider."

Yamamoto stiffened almost imperceptibly. "Time to study and consider," he echoed quietly.

Hosogaya glanced at the other flag officers and saw Yamaguchi nod his head in agreement. He continued, "Frankly, sir, it worries me. In a few days our Coral Sea operations will start—"

Yamamoto cut him short. "We have ample forces for both."

"Perhaps, sir. But it is no secret that the General Staff is not altogether enthusiastic about the Midway operation."

Watanabe interjected: "Tokyo has given its un-conditional approval of Operation MI, Admiral."

Hosogaya persisted quietly, "Nevertheless, I suggest we meet again. After the Coral Sea campaign. After the results of that operation are known to us."

Yamamoto did not answer him for a little while. Worried that his subordinates seemed incapable of keeping up with his own ambitions, he thought about the Coral Sea, an empty body of water which lay al-most three thousand miles to the south of Midway. The High Command had decided to extend the Japanese perimeter far to the south even before their many con-quests in Southeast Asia had been consolidated. Their strategy was to prevent any major counterattack from that direction while their attention was turned toward the east, where the bulk of America's forces lay.

The ultimate objective of this campaign was to take Port Moresby in New Guinea, because this was the only air base from which the long range, land-based bomb-ers of the Allies were still able to strike at the rapidly-advancing Japanese forces. Rabaul, in New Britain, had fallen to the Imperial Navy in January. It had provided them with a well-defended base that controlled the Northern Bight of the Coral Sea. But the southern limits of that sea were still under the control of the Americans and the Australians. Six groups of the Imperial Navy had been ordered south; some of them had left already; the others were at this moment preparing to leave.

First, there was the Tulagi invasion force, which was to move southeast from Rabaul, take Tulagi, and set up a seaplane base from which the huge Kawanishi flying boats could dominate the entire eastern reaches of the sea. This group consisted of a single large transport, two destroyers, and a number of mine-sweepers and submarine-chasers.

Secondly, there was the Nisima Island support group, comprised of two light cruisers, a seaplane carrier, and three gunboats. Its mission was to set up a second seaplane base at Nisima Island, from which to cover the sea's western reaches.

Thirdly, five transport ships loaded with troops, covered by a defensive screen of six destroyers together with a complement of mine-sweepers and mine-laying craft, were on their way toward Port Moresby itself, sailing round the eastern tip of New Guinea.

The fourth group was the covering force—the light carrier *Shiko* and four heavy cruisers, under orders to stand off Port Moresby and protect the invasion convoy.

Fifth—the two heavy carriers *Zuikaku* and *Shikaku,* carrying forty-two fighter planes each, escorted by two heavy cruisers, six destroyers, and an oil tanker, were detailed to intercept and engage any American carriers which might turn up and try to prevent the landing operation.

Lastly, there was the land-based air flotilla standing by at Rabaul, consisting of 150 naval aircraft, ready to be thrown into the combat wherever the commander thought necessary. With a range of 600 miles, these planes could reach out as far as Tulagi and to Port Moresby itself.

In the opinion of the Imperial General Staff, the

third of May should see the occupation of Tulagi, and the landings on Port Moresby would begin on the seventh.

Yamamoto sighed. The action in the Coral Sea was, indeed, to be a campaign of very considerable importance. But he was impatient for that quick victory, intolerant of letting the Americans get even the slightest breathing space in which to rebuild their shattered forces. For him, the vital strategy was to strike and strike again, to go on striking; to wear the enemy down, if necessary on a one-for-one basis, like chessmen manned off the board. Under this philosophy there could be no value in waiting. But he also realized that for such an enormously complex operation as "MI," he needed the wholehearted support of his flag officers. At present their reactions ranged from open hostility to ardent enthusiasm.

There was a bitterness weighting him as he said soberly, "Very well, gentlemen. We will meet again after the Coral Sea operation—at which time I will have more to say on the absolute necessity for striking the Americans at Midway Island. Good night."

Yamamoto left the room, followed by Watanabe, who made no effort to conceal his sharp disappointment from Kondo and Hosogaya. In a moment the others followed, leaving only the two dissidents behind them. Kondo picked up the heavy operation plan and hefted it under Hosogaya's face. His voice cracked with anger. "Do realize what this is, Hosogaya? A monument to Yamamoto's obsession for the safety of the emperor. Doolittle and his puny air raid have suddenly given credibility to a pointless, dangerous—"

Hosogaya cut in with a gesture. "Kondo, I want to study it before I decide." He bowed slightly and walked out of the room, leaving Kondo alone beside the huge plot.

Kondo stared at it for a long moment while his anger ebbed away, leaving in its wake a deeply troubled residue.

5

The PBY skimmed to a bouncing, spray-festooned landing on the choppy waters of Pearl Harbor. Twin engines bellowing, it headed for the ramp and labored up onto dry land. Almost before it came to a halt the cabin door was thrown open, steps were lowered, and Admiral Chester W. Nimitz was climbing quickly down, his aide, Lieutenant Commander Ernest Blake, behind him. He headed straight for the parking area at the edge of the seaplane base where his limousine and Matt Garth were waiting.

At the moment, however, Garth's attention was on another arrival. Joe Rochefort had just barreled up in a jeep and was hurrying toward him. He said breathlessly, "Gotta talk to the boss, Matt."

"No chance."

"It's *important.*"

"It will have to wait, Joe. I've got a major headache for the admiral already." He tapped the briefcase clutched under his arm.

"Coral Sea?"

Garth nodded. "A carrier battle. Yesterday."

"We get hurt? . . ."

Garth didn't reply, his attention going to the ramrod figure of Nimitz approaching.

The Commander in Chief, Pacific area, was a man of average stature, nothing particularly imposing about him. He was fifty-seven years old and his hair was a stark silver-gray color; but the spring in his step, the relaxed set of his shoulders gave the impression of a man much younger. As a young cadet Chester Nimitz had sailed the Far East in the USS *Ohio,* flagship of the Asiatic Fleet, then in the USS *Baltimore.* After the two years at sea required by law, he had been commissioned ensign. He advanced rapidly in rank and was promoted to rear admiral in 1938, to admiral in 1941.

A shrewd, no-nonsense Texan known for his leadership ability and his outstanding skill as a strategist, he was soft-spoken but as tough as a barrel of shrapnel fragments. His staff held him in awe and admiration, particularly his air operations officer, Captain Garth— whom Rochefort was pressing for an answer to his question.

"Matt, what happened?"

Garth turned back to the intelligence man and offered him a small consolation. "I can say this, Joe. You were sure as hell right about Coral Sea. That's where the Japs were, all right, every last ship on your list."

"Did they clobber us? They had a lot of first-line ships there . . ."

But Garth had turned away again and was snapping a salute. "Welcome home, Admiral. How was the flight?"

Nimitz grimaced. "Long and strewn with potholes, Captain." He moved straight past Garth and into the back seat of his limousine, saying, "Did Fletcher report yet?"

"Yes, sir. I have it here." Garth paused in the open door and turned to appraise the anxious look on Rochefort's face. He said, "Look, Joe, if it really is urgent—"

"It is."

"Then get in front. Wait'll I cue you in."

Garth climbed in beside the admiral and Rochefort hurried around to the front where the Marine driver leaned over and opened the door for him. He slid into the seat, staring fixedly ahead, wanting to light a cigar but thinking he had better not.

The car moved smoothly away and Admiral Nimitz slumped back wearily and sighed. "All right, Captain, let's have it. How did we do?"

Garth dug into his briefcase and brought out a report. He handed it to the admiral and said tightly, "I'm afraid we lost one of our carriers, sir. The *Lexington*. She was hit by torpedoes, and two eight hundred-pound bombs. The boiler rooms were flooded, but the engines were untouched. It looked for a while as though she might be saved. But she'd broken a fuel pipe, and a motor generator ignited the flames . . . She blew up, sir. She was abandoned late in the evening. She went to the bottom."

Nimitz said nothing. There was an awesome tension in the air. He read through the report carefully, his face grim, drawn. He said at last, "She was a damn good ship. How did the battle shape up?"

Matt said, "Well, sir . . . We started off evenly matched. Fletcher had two carriers. The Japs had two. They put about as many planes in the air as we did. It seems they spotted one of our oil tankers, the *Neosho,* and mistook her for a carrier, a mistake which sent their planes off in the wrong direction . . ."

He waited for the admiral to comment, but there was only silence, and that heavy-laden look on his face. He went on: "I'm afraid all the mistakes were not theirs. Admiral Fitch, on the *Lexington,* got word from one of his scout planes that two carriers and four heavy cruisers had been sighted. He launched ninety-three planes to attack them before he discovered that someone had fouled up—the message had been wrongly decoded. It should have read, 'two cruisers and two destroyers.' "

"He called off the attack?"

"No, sir. But he got lucky. His planes spotted a Jap carrier, the *Shoho,* only five miles off their course. They attacked her, scored seven torpedo hits, and thirteen bomb strikes." He looked at the admiral and said, "One thing we can congratulate ourselves on, sir. This was our first attack of the war on a Japanese carrier; and they sank her. We also sank a number of their smaller ships. Overall, sir, I'd say we broke even."

"Goddamn it," the admiral said, "we can't afford to trade the Japanese carrier for carrier. They started out with a three-to-one superiority."

He paused, weighing this deeply disquieting situation in his mind. Then he said, "With the *Lexington* gone, and the *Saratoga* laid up, that leaves us with—what? We've only got *Hornet, Enterprise,* and *Yorktown* left to counter Yamamoto's next move."

Garth handed the admiral another dispatch. "Admiral Fletcher's follow-up, sir. I'm afraid the *Yorktown* was damaged, too."

Nimitz seemed stunned. Then he asked, "How badly?"

"Very heavily, sir."

The silence was oppressive, as the admiral studied the follow-up report. In the front seat Joe Rochefort was turning round, gesturing to Garth.

Garth shook his head but Rochefort wouldn't be put off. Garth said grudgingly, "Admiral, Commander Rochefort has something urgent—he says."

Nimitz looked up, seeming to take notice of Rochefort for the first time. The intelligence man said, "It's about Objective 'AF,' sir. The meaning of 'AF.' "

The Admiral directed a questioning look at Garth, who explained quickly, "Since you've been gone, our intelligence listening posts have been picking up a lot of radio traffic between Yamamoto's flag commanders. What was just a stirring a week or so ago has become a rush."

Rochefort cut in: "Two references keep popping up, Admiral. Objectives 'AF' and 'AO.' 'AO' still has us stymied. But I think we've identified Objective 'AF.' It's Midway."

Nimitz shot a quick, disturbed look at Garth, who said cryptically, "He didn't hear it from me, sir."

Now Rochefort was puzzled. But before he could speculate further about the look that had passed between the admiral and his air operations officer, Nimitz said, "Go on, Commander."

"Yes, sir. Well—as I said, it had us stymied—until one of my men remembered an enemy intercept we decoded last March, after that fouled-up seaplane raid on Honolulu. The Jap pilot radioed his base that he was passing close to 'AF.' Admiral, we've plotted every possible course that plane might have flown from Honolulu—and the only land mass worth mentioning was Midway."

Garth made an exasperated sound and said disgustedly, "Joe, for God's sake . . ."

"All right, it's thin, I know that . . ."

Nimitz cut in, anger lacing his mild voice. "Thin, Commander? It's damn near invisible! If that's all you have to tell me, then you're wasting your time, which probably doesn't matter two hoots. But you're wasting mine, too, which does."

Rochefort's face turned the color of a boiled crab. He said stubbornly, "With respect, Admiral, I'm not wasting my time or yours. Because I've figured out a way to confirm the meaning of 'AF.' " He dug into his shirt pocket and extracted a scrap of paper torn from an envelope and scribbled on. Immediately, he wished he'd typed it up properly, but he hadn't, and that's all there was to it. He handed it to the admiral and continued, "If you'll have this flown to Midway, sir. It's a fake message—reporting Midway's fresh-water condenser has broken down. It should be transmitted exactly as written—and in the clear so there can't be any question of the Japanese operators getting every word."

Nimitz turned his attention to the scribbling and Rochefort saw a slow smile lighting the fatigue-lined face. He heard him chuckle, and then Nimitz passed the scrap of paper to Garth and said, "Captain, instruct Midway to include this in their housekeeping traffic tomorrow. And, yes, it should definitely be transmitted in the clear."

Garth read the scribbled words: "Fresh-water condenser broken down. Need urgent, repeat, urgent replacement." He looked up and saw Joe Rochefort grinning as the Admiral said, "Commander, you've made a gloomy homecoming almost bearable. Let's pray your little skunk trap works, because if Yamamoto *is* going for Midway next . . ." He paused and took in a deep breath as if to force back the weariness, then continued. "Well, you might as well know the secret the captain and I intended to keep from you and from everyone, for a while at least. I've just come from Midway. An inspection trip. And I can tell you we're not ready for Yamamoto. Not by a helluva sight."

Eleven hundred and forty-nine miles to the northwest in Midway's cramped radio shack, the high-powered transmitter gear stood like baleful-eyed robots among the banks of receivers which were spotted with hand-lettered signs identifying their monitoring assignments: Pearl Harbor, Cavite, Washington, Dutch Harbor . . .

There were thirty operators in the room, huddled over their keys, earphones clamped over their heads. One of them, Radioman, Third Class Dobrowski, was squinting at a dispatch that his chief radioman had just handed him.

Dobrowski was a gum-chewing draftee in his middle thirties, overweight, cursing a toothache, and wondering if he could face another session with the dentist. He also had a monstrous hangover from a night of beer-guzzling along the little prefab street that made up the island's entertainment center, such as it was.

He blinked at the dispatch and thought about how the damn beer tasted like cat piss and how he had tried to persuade a radioman in one of the PBY crews to sneak him in a fifth of real liquor from Honolulu. The bastard wanted thirty dollars. Dobrowski told him to shove it and his fucking gooney-bird airplane up his ass —sideways.

He made an effort to concentrate on the dispatch, scratched the top of his head and said, "Hey, Chief. Wait a minute."

The chief, a tall, laconic veteran from Oklahoma, ambled over and said, "What's the matter, Dobrowski? You can't read, is that it?"

Dobrowski showed him the dispatch and said, "Somebody screwed up. Read it! Shhhit! They're always screwing up around here."

The chief glanced at the dispatch and then at Dobrowski who said, with as much heat as his pounding head would allow, "It ain't broke down. Our fresh-water condenser is okay. I just come from there. Just a few minutes ago."

"Yeah, I noticed you were late relieving your watch again."

"Okay. But it's a good thing I caught this, right?"

"Wrong," the chief said acidly. "Send it."

Dobrowski spread his pudgy arms wide. "I just told you, Chief, our fresh-water condenser ain't broke down. We don't need no replacement."

"And I just told *you*," the chief said, dangerously.

Dobrowski shrugged. "Okay, okay, if that's the way

you want it. Ain't no skin off my ass. All I care, they can send us fifty replacements."

"Transmit in the clear and don't add any goddamn postscripts," the chief warned as he moved off.

Dobrowski glowered after him. Then he parked his gum under the console, fingered the other six pieces there, and began pounding out the message on his key.

6

The ships were anchored now in Hiroshima Bay, and a cool breeze was nudging the early-morning haze across the sea.

There were cormorants fishing near by, lunging their beaks into the water, coming up with small fish, then thrusting their long necks up into the air to enable gravity to help them swallow.

In the distance, Hiroshima itself lay in its island-studded bay, one of the most beautiful of all Japanese cities, and now one of the most important commercial and military centers of the homeland. There were three hundred thousand people spread out over its three thousand square miles, luxuriating this spring morning in the winds that blew softly over the water from the Island of Light, where the cherry blossoms were in full bloom, scattering their pinks and whites everywhere. Its streets were crowded with sailors but, nonetheless, the war seemed far removed; the town basked in its serenity.

But here, aboard the *Yamato*, the atmosphere was tense with repressed emotions.

The flag officers were gathered once more, this time in the wardroom. The long table was covered with various reports from the commanders in the Coral Sea; and they gave Admiral Yamamoto little comfort.

His carriers *Zuikaku, Shokaku*, and *Shoho*, with six heavy cruisers, four light cruisers, fifteen destroyers and a seaplane tender, had been ranged against two American carriers, the *Yorktown* and the *Lexington*, eight cruisers, and thirteen destroyers.

The Japanese morale had been extremely high, bolstered as it was by the knowledge that their Zero fighter planes were far superior to the slower and less maneuverable American F4F's. Over the long, rigorous months of their training, the pilots had been nurtured in their morale by the knowledge that the great Yamamoto himself believed that their part in this war, the part of carrier-born aircraft and their flyers, would be the deciding factor.

But now, one of them had disgraced himself, his comrades, and his whole service. A single scout-plane pilot had identified an American oil tanker as an aircraft carrier, a disastrous mistake. Every plane that could be mustered aboard the *Shokaku* and the *Zuikaku* had been scrambled and sent to the attack—bombers, torpedo bombers, and fighters. The tanker had been quickly set ablaze and its accompanying destroyer, the *Sims,* sent to the bottom. But a short while later when the *Yorktown* was sighted and correctly identified, there were no planes aboard the Japanese carriers to launch an attack. Worse, the Japanese carriers had been left defenseless against the seventy planes which took off from the *Yorktown* and the *Lexington.* Forty-eight reached their targets, and although the *Zuikaku* had found refuge in the thick gray mist of a rain squall, three bombs hit the *Shokaku* and put her out of action, while the *Shoho,* which took thirteen bombs and seven torpedoes, was sunk in flames.

The Japanese took severe losses: the carrier *Shoho,* a destroyer, and three smaller ships sunk. In addition the *Shokaku* had been heavily damaged, seventy-seven planes lost and one thousand seventy-four men killed or wounded. And they had been compelled to turn back the invasion force headed for Port Moresby.

The Americans had lost the carrier *Lexington,* the tanker *Neoshu,* and the destroyer *Sims.* The *Yorktown* was heavily damaged and sixty-six planes were lost, five hundred forty-three men killed or wounded.

In spite of the numerical superiority they still enjoyed, there was one consequence of the Coral Sea campaign that weighed heavily on the Japanese: they had lost so many of their best pilots that neither the *Zuikaku* nor the *Shokaku* would be able to take part in the attack against Midway.

Admiral Yamaguchi was late because his personal barge had developed engine trouble on its way to the *Yamato*. Now he was hurrying down the passageway to the wardroom where two Marine guards were posted. As they snapped to rigid attention, Watanabe stepped out of the door and saluted his superior.

Yamaguchi asked, "Have they started yet?"

"A moment ago, sir . . . when Captain Kuroshima arrived."

Yamaguchi showed surprise. "Kuroshima! . . . So the God of Operations deigns to commune with mere flag commanders."

Was it an implied criticism of Operation MI through its creator? Watanabe wasn't certain, but coming from Yamaguchi who had been a proponent of the plan, it was disturbing as well as unexpected. He said carefully, "Admiral Yamamoto felt the author of Operation MI could best defend it."

"We'll see," Yamaguchi replied curtly.

The admiral slipped into the wardroom and took a seat at one end of the long table with the other flag commanders, Nagumo, Hosogaya, and Kondo. At the other end were Yamamoto, his Chief of Staff, Ugaki, and the young, brilliant, icily confident Captain Kameto Kuroshima.

Kondo was on his feet, speaking to Yamamoto with even more urgency than at the last meeting of the flag officers. "And even if we are totally successful, what have we gained? An island of dubious strategic value which your own Chief of Staff has admitted will be impossible to supply—"

Ugaki cut in, *"Difficult* was the word I used, Admiral Kondo. Difficult to supply."

Kondo ignored the correction and continued to address Yamamoto, who seemed more than ever aloof and circumspect. "Sir, it is my urgent advice that Operation MI be abandoned."

He sat down heavily and Ugaki, who was chairing the proceedings, said, "Hosogaya, at our last meeting you were the one who asked for more time to study and consider . . ."

Hosogaya cleared his throat nervously and replied, "I agree with Admiral Kondo. Abandon MI. Or at the very least, postpone it. There is a critical need for more officer training, especially at the staff level. And pilots. Particularly pilots. We lost many combat veterans at Coral Sea."

"Plus seventy-seven planes!" Kondo interjected. "The *Shoho* sunk. The *Shokaku* heavily damaged—"

Hosogaya put a hand on the shoulder of the overwrought Kondo to silence him, then appealed directly to Yamamoto. "Sir, there simply are not enough pilots ready."

Captain Kuroshima smiled gravely, his tone quietly tolerant as if explaining the obvious to respected but none-too-bright elders. "Coral Sea also cost the enemy many pilots—and *two* carriers. So the balance of force remains the same—heavily in our favor."

Ugaki shifted his attention to Nagumo who appeared, as usual, to be almost disinterested in the debate. This was the officer through whom he expected to bury once and for all the doubts and fears of the dissidents. He said, "Nagumo, the entire operation depends on your carriers. Are you being sent into battle ill-prepared?"

Nagumo hesitated for a moment. Surprisingly, he seemed ill-prepared for the question. At length he said, "It is . . . always desirable to have more time . . . more training. What commander ever thinks he is totally prepared for battle? Especially one of this magnitude. Our . . . Coral Sea losses were serious. Particularly in combat-experienced pilots. Still . . . as Captain Kuroshima has observed . . . the balance of forces remains heavily in our favor . . ."

There was a long silence, everyone expecting Nagumo to follow up on what they thought was a preamble. It wasn't. It was his entire statement. Hosogaya and Kondo exchanged puzzled looks. Yamaguchi was staring at his senior carrier commander with open disbelief. Fleetingly, he wondered if the losses at Coral Sea had spiked Nagumo's confidence in the invincibility of Japanese carrier power. Before he could enlarge on the thought, Ugaki was speaking to him. "Yamaguchi, you'll be commanding two of the four carriers under Admiral Nagumo. Do you think you'll be ill-prepared?"

"No," Yamaguchi replied without hesitation.

It was the answer Ugaki had hoped for, indeed, required to put down the dissidents. But then Yamaguchi continued. "Nevertheless, I am now convinced that Operation MI should be postponed. The plan is seriously flawed."

Ugaki was stunned. He glanced quickly to Kuroshima and saw the young "God of Operations" shift slightly in his chair, but his bleak, self-assured expression remained fixed.

Yamaguchi continued bluntly, "As it stands, our carrier task-force commander will have no direct access to enemy radio intercepts, because of the inadequate antenna system aboard his flagship . . ."

Kuroshima smiled slightly as he interrupted. "All important enemy radio intercepts will be relayed to Admiral Nagumo from our listening posts in Tokyo and Kwajalein."

"Across thousands of miles of ocean, Captain Kuroshima? I think not." Yamaguchi turned to Yamamoto and continued, "There is only one way to cure the problem. This ship—your flagship—has the most powerful radio equipment in the fleet. Sir, you must operate directly with the carriers." He shifted his glance back to Kuroshima and added with a definite note of disdain, ". . . Not three hundred miles in the rear as the captain's plan decrees. Further, I urge the admiral to take personal command of the carrier strike force."

It was a startling, almost sacrilegious suggestion. Nagumo obviously resented it. His face turned a gray, chalky color as he waited in stiff silence for Yamamoto to respond.

Yamamoto did not answer immediately. Although he was often irritated by Yamaguchi's brash aggressiveness, he respected the young admiral's shrewd mind; so he weighed the suggestion carefully. Perhaps it was only fitting that he should take personal command at the front line of the battle. What other flag officer held his conviction about the vital necessity of Operation

MI? Kuroshima's opinions sprang from his vanity as the creator of the plan, and the pliant Ugaki was so used to echoing his admiral's every thought that he had almost lost the capacity for independent judgment. That left the dissidents and Nagumo, who had obviously lost some of his self-assurance since their last meeting.

Perhaps a little less cocksuredness would be an asset for his carrier commander, Yamamoto thought. It would tend to make him more vigilant, more wary. On the other hand, it could very well cause Nagumo to be over-cautious at a critical moment in the battle.

It was an agonizing decision to make, and the only factor he could find to favor one conclusion over the other was Nagumo's rigidly strained expression. Yamamoto realized that to relieve him of his command would cause Nagumo an irreparable loss of face. So he did not respond to Yamaguchi's suggestion; he simply permitted Kuroshima to have the final word.

"Sir," Kuroshima said, "I am confident there will be no communications problem."

Yamamoto got to his feet and the others quickly arose, too. "Gentlemen," he said, "before I hear any further comments from you, I want Captain Kuroshima to explain the details of his plan. But first we will refresh ourselves with tea and sweet cakes and some less serious conversation." There was a smile on his face which was calculated to relieve the tension which had so quickly become dangerously stifling. He was pleased to see that it had its intended effect. Even Kondo seemed willing, for the moment, to put aside his angry apprehensions.

Watanabe went to the door and summoned two stewards in from the passageway. They hurried to the far end of the wardroom and drew aside a painted screen behind which was a table laden with a variety of delicacies created to tempt the most jaded palate. Tea was served and the flag officers engaged in polite conversation, carefully avoiding any reference to the matter that had brought them aboard their Commander in Chief's flagship.

Yamamoto circulated among his flag officers, waiting for just the right moment to make an off-the-record statement which he felt was vital to their understanding and acceptance of the Midway operation. He decided that Kondo would be his sounding-board. "Kondo," he said, "you remember when certain militants put a price on my head?"

"Yes. The Black Dragon Society . . . because you spoke out for peace."

"Ironic, isn't it, that now I find myself cast in the role of the prime mover in this war?"

Yamamoto was aware that the other officers had turned their attention to him. His smile faded and there was a grim set about his mouth as he continued. "Despite our victories, I still oppose this war. My fear for the emperor's safety deepens with each success. Some of you, I know, feel that I am ruled by that fear. I can't deny it. But I am also compelled by another fear."

He paused, permitting their curiosity to peak before going on. "While I was a young engineering student at Harvard College," he said, "I had the opportunity to hitchhike from one coast of America to the other. I was enormously impressed by the size and the industrial capacity of the country. Later, when I returned to Washington as a naval attaché, I found the giant even stronger. More awesome, gentleman. Believe me, America's industrial might will crush Japan."

There was a rustle of shocked reaction from Yamamoto's flag officers.

Yamaguchi was the first to find his voice. "Surely the admiral is not serious . . ."

"Indeed I am, Yamaguchi. Utterly, unequivocally serious. America *will* defeat us—*if* we allow her time. *Time* is our greatest enemy. Our only hope is that one massive, lightning stroke will bring us a quick victory."

In the stunned silence that followed, Yamamoto watched the faces of Nagumo, Kondo, Hosogaya and Yamaguchi, the men on whose battle skills and judgment the fate of Japan would rest. Their expressions told him only that they were gravely troubled. He waited for one of them to speak, to challenge his statement. No one did. He put down his teacup and nodded to Watanabe.

"If the admirals will follow me," the young aide said, "We will proceed to the battle plot where Captain Kuroshima will brief us in more detail."

Kuroshima leaned across the battle plot and laid the tip of his pointer on the broad bay at the northern extremity of Japan's main island, Honshū. "Here," he said, "Ominato in the Bay of Mutsue Wan, this will be the starting point for Admiral Hosogaya's thrust. It will proceed due west until it has cleared the southernmost tip of Hokkaido, at which point it will split into two columns. The northern force under the admiral himself will proceed in a northeasterly direction, and the second carrier striking force under Rear Admiral Kakuta will continue due east. The first of these two forces will divide again when it reaches the island of Etorofu in the Russian Kuriles, the Attu force bearing to the north and the Kiska force bearing slightly to the northeast as indicated here. You will note, gentlemen, that Admiral Kakuta's second carrier striking force will make a wide, wide sweep out into the middle of the Pacific Ocean before turning north to attack Dutch Harbor in the Aleutians, and that Admiral Hosogaya will approach Attu and Kiska, in the same chain, from the southwest. Once the Aleutian Islands are approached, it is expected that mist and fog will obscure the fleet's movements. This is all to the good, because we fully expect that by then the American spotter planes will have discovered the twin thrust of these two columns, and will have correctly identified their targets as somewhere in the Aleutians. It is our hope that they will regard these islands as our primary target and, thus, Admiral Nimitz's attention will be drawn away from our true objective. In other words, gentlemen, this is a diversionary tactic intended to draw off at least a part of Nimitz's forces."

He waited for any objections, looking over the grimly fixed faces that were watching him. When there was no immediate response he went on:

"Now. The main force will depart from here, from Hiroshima. It will steam between Kyushu and Shikoku and into the Philippine Sea. It will consist of the first carrier striking force under Admiral Nagumo, whose flagship will be the carrier *Akagi,* accompanied by the heavy carriers *Kaga, Soryu* and *Hiryu*—the latter two under the command of Admiral Yamaguchi. The main force —the First Fleet—under Admiral Yamamoto will follow a parallel course, and will consist of this battleship, the *Yamato,* which will serve as the combined-Fleet flagship, and the *Nagato* and the *Mutsu,* with the light carrier *Hosho,* the light cruiser *Sendai,* twelve destroyers and two seaplane carriers, one of which, the *Nigshin,* will be carrying six midget submarines and two motor torpedo boats. The Second Fleet, also out of Hiroshima, and the Midway occupation force out of Guam, will be under the command of Admiral Kondo. He will have the battleships *Kongo* and *Hiei,* the heavy cruisers *Atago, Chikai, Myoko,* and *Naguro,* the light cruiser *Yura,* and the light carrier *Zuiho* with twelve fighters and twelve torpedo bombers. He will also have eight destroyers, four supply ships, and the repair ship *Akami.* He will also command the support group under Rear Admiral Kurita, with the heavy cruisers *Kumano, Suzuya, Mikuma,* and *Mogami,* with two destroyers and one supply ship. Additionally, he will command the Seaplane tender group under Rear Admiral Fujita, consisting of the seaplane carriers *Chitose* and *Kamikawa Maru,* with one destroyer and a patrol boat. He will also have under his orders the transport group under Rear Admiral Tanaka, which comprises the light cruiser *Jintsu,* and twelve transports carrying five thousand officers and men for the occupying force, together with ten destroyers, four patrol boats carrying assault detachments, and one oiler. All these forces, except the Aleutian force, will converge, as indicated here, on Midway."

He put down his pointer and took a long, deep breath. "As you can see, gentlemen, we have marshaled a very considerable force for this battle, indeed the largest armada the world has ever seen. Certainly the most powerful. We will employ more than two hundred ships, seven hundred aircraft, and one hundred thousand officers and men."

Kuroshima stroked the length of the pointer with his

thumb and forefinger, like a billiard champion preparing to make a brilliant shot. He continued, "This is how I expect the battle to develop. When the northern force, under Admiral Hosogaya, strikes here, in the Aleutians, the commander of the American Pacific Fleet will be forced to respond. He will send at least part of his already depleted forces to counter the invasion of Attu and Kiska Islands—and to protect Dutch Harbor, which we will bomb."

Watanabe interjected, "A diversion . . . to keep Admiral Nimitz's attention away from our main objective."

Kuroshima glanced at the enthusiastic young aide and said, "I've already made that point, thank you, Commander." Then he went on. "Nimitz will not realize that it is Midway until twenty-four hours later when Admiral Nagumo's carriers strike the island—and destroy the American planes and shore batteries."

"That's when you move in, Kondo," said Yamamoto, "with your invasion forces."

Kuroshima disliked sharing center stage with anyone, but he realized that Yamamoto's deep fervor and the zeal of his young aide would have to be tolerated. He took a slow breath and continued. "Nimitz will be forced to respond again. He will have to commit the balance of his fleet—most certainly his carriers—to repel the invasion."

"But it will take at least forty-eight hours to reach Midway," Watanabe said. "*If* he gets through our submarine screen."

"If he does," Kuroshima went on, "you'll be free and waiting for him, Admiral Nagumo. You'll have the advantage of position and at least a two-to-one superiority in carriers."

"And four or five times the number of screening vessels Nimitz can muster," Watanabe added.

Kuroshima continued. "Should Nimitz divert any of his Aleutian-bound ships to Midway—Admiral Yamamoto waiting here with his fast battleships, three hundred miles to the rear, will be in a perfect position to intercept them."

"Or if necessary," Watanabe beamed, "join Admiral

Nagumo in mopping up the remnants of the enemy fleet."

Kuroshima put down the pointer and waited for comment from Yamamoto's flag officers. It was Yamaguchi who spoke: "All of this assumes that the American fleet will be guarding the Hawaiian Islands when we strike."

Kuroshima answered with a tolerant little smile. "What alternative does Nimitz have? He's crippled and on the defensive. He must deploy his remaining strength around his most valuable Pacific base."

The answer was too easy, too pat: Yamaguchi looked at Yamamoto. "Sir, we must make certain where the enemy fleet is before we strike. I propose that we send two long-range flying boats from Kwajalein to French Frigate Shoal, refuel them by tanker submarine and fly them on to Pearl Harbor the next day. Let *them* report whether or not the American Fleet is actually there."

Kuroshima decided to throw Yamaguchi a bone. "A very wise precaution indeed, Admiral. We'll call it Operation 'K.' Does the Admiral have any other thoughts?"

Yamaguchi remained silent. Kuroshima turned to Watanabe and said, "Now I believe Commander Watanabe has something to contribute . . ."

Watanabe picked up a file and extracted a glossy photograph of a dour-looking American with the stars of a Vice Admiral on his collar. He passed it to Kondo and said, "We believe that Nimitz's carrier commander will be Vice Admiral William F. Halsey, the one they call the 'bull.' He's aptly named. He's tough, courageous, aggressive, and above all, impetuous. He has very little of that caution which is so necessary when the enemy's true intentions are masked by diversionary tactics such as have just been described."

Kondo was frowning darkly. He looked at Watanabe. "It seems to me, Commander," he said, "that you are putting a great deal of faith in your estimation of Admiral Halsey's character."

Watanabe nodded. "Perhaps, Admiral. But let me tell you something about this man. He has arrogated to himself a slogan which indicates the key facet of his character: *'Hit hard, hit fast, hit often.'* As I said, an impulsive, aggressive man. Let me cite some examples. The task force which attended General Doolittle on his ridiculous raid on our homeland was under Halsey's command. Admittedly, he succeeded in penetrating our defenses to within eight hundred miles of our shores—but for what? For a raid that knocked down a few flimsy houses, and cost the enemy dearly. Again, impulsive and aggressive. He was responsible for the carrier attacks on the Gilbert and Marshall Islands, as well as the raids on Wotje, Kwajalein, and Marcus Islands, and Wake—again, taking enormous risks for very little military advantage. I might add that at the time of Pearl Harbor, Admiral Halsey was returning there from delivering planes to Wake. He launched all his planes in an attempt to locate our raiders. He failed completely. He never found even one of them. He's brave and a good carrier commander. But I repeat—the key word is impetuous. He's the kind of man whose reactions can be predicted with an extraordinary degree of accuracy. Thus, when the Americans discover what our real objective is, we expect Halsey to come rushing to the aid of Midway headlong into the jaws of the trap we will have ready to spring on him."

Again, Yamamoto watched the faces of his flag commanders, and saw no enthusiasm for Watanabe's prognosis. They were, in fact, openly skeptical, especially Kondo. He decided the time had come to reveal to them the simple, unadorned core of the Midway battle plan. He took a deep breath and said, quietly, "Gentlemen, the enemy is still unprepared and outnumbered. His fleet, particularly his aircraft carriers, *must* be lured into battle at Midway and destroyed. America will then have no significant naval force left in the Pacific—and so will be compelled to negotiate for peace."

He did not wait for comments or reactions, but continued, his voice growing firmer, more controlling. "Operation MI will proceed exactly as planned. It will not become the subject of further debate. Any officer whose conscience prevents him from accepting the command assigned to him may now decline it. There will be no question regarding that officer's motives or honor."

He waited. Nobody spoke. To his surprise, he found he was deeply moved by their trust in him. He said gravely, "I thank you for your loyalty, gentlemen."

He knew the battle for the battle was over, and that now the battle itself would begin. Just as he had planned it.

As the admiral's launch skimmed across the placid waters of Hiroshima Bay, Yamaguchi stared out to sea. Hosogaya was standing at his shoulder and Yamaguchi could sense that his colleague's thoughts were deeply troubled. "You're still not convinced, Hosogaya," he said.

"Wrong. We will win a great victory—provided one thing."

"What is that?"

"That the Americans do exactly what we expect of them."

7

All of them, officers and enlisted men alike, had left their posts the moment one of the cryptographers had yelled, "Hey fellas, I got one! We got it again . . . 'A . . . F' . . ."

They had watched the machine at work, watched the deft movements of the pencils over the code books, excitedly watched the flipping of pages and the pressing of buttons that would flash their yellow lights and throw the translations, garbled still and out of context, up onto the tiny screen.

Garth was detached from them, listening only half-consciously to the bedlam of their voices. He was sitting on a desk in a far corner of the Intelligence Black Chamber with his feet on a pile of crates, studying the papers he had picked up earlier in the day.

Among them were photos of a graying old man and

his wife in conventional Japanese clothes, and a picture of a young girl with wide, slanted eyes and a frank and open smile, her long black hair cascading around her shoulders. She wore a neat white blouse and a bright aquamarine sweater and contrasting skirt. She was looking into the camera happily as though the picture were being taken by someone she loved dearly.

Garth thought she was very beautiful indeed. There were other photos of her, too, not so flattering, taken with a long-focus lens: of her stepping into a Japanese market on a narrow San Francisco street; getting off a bus; posting a letter at a mailbox; looking into a store window and adjusting her dress; talking to another Japanese girl at a football game; handing a package to a young man in a dark suit . . . They gave the impression that the subject had been totally unaware that someone was following every move she made, snapping off pictures from whatever hidden point of vantage he could find.

Matt read the long report through for the third time, and waited for the fuss at the table across the room to die down. Rochefort was in there somewhere, in his red velvet smoking jacket, hunched amid that mass of sweltering bodies. When the noise suddenly increased in tempo and volume, Matt looked up; someone had thrown a sheaf of papers into the air and Rochefort was yelling: "That's it, what did I tell you?"

He slid off the desk and watched the heap of human flesh opening up to reveal Joe Rochefort, with Wright beside him, grinning broadly and waving a piece of paper. Everyone was congratulating everyone else, hugging shoulders, slapping backs, shaking hands . . .

Rochefort crossed the room to him, dropping cigar ash everywhere, and said, beaming: "There it is, Matt! The bastards fell right into our little skunk trap—claws, hide, and brush!"

He held up the sheet of squared paper on which the ideographs had first been rendered into *Letinji,* then dotted with lines and arrows and parentheses to indicate their probable sequence, then annotated with their code-book references, and finally translated into their finished form.

He read it out loud, grinning: *"'AF is having trouble with its fresh-water condenser . . .'"* He laughed and said, "Do you know what this means, Matt? It means that they intercepted our message. It means that 'AF' is definitely Midway. I told you, just a question of fitting all the little bits and pieces together. A question of patience."

Garth looked at his watch. It was almost midnight. He said, "The old man likes to get to bed at a reasonable hour whenever he can, but for this—he'd want me to wake him."

He reached for the telephone and said to the operator, "This is Captain Garth. Get me Admiral Nimitz, at his home, right away."

He waited, and when he heard Nimitz's sleep-thickened voice at the other end he said, "Sorry to disturb you, Admiral, but I thought you'd want to know. Commander Rochefort has just deciphered a dispatch from the Japanese listening station on Kwajalein to Yamamoto's staff in Hiroshima. I'll read it for you, if I may."

He took the paper and read out the message, slowly and clearly: *"'AF is having trouble with its fresh-water condenser.'"*

He heard the admiral's reply, grave and restrained: "Well, I guess that clinches it, Captain. Give my compliments to Commander Rochefort. And be in my office at oh five hundred. I'm calling in the whole staff."

"Yes, sir."

He heard the click of the Admiral's phone, and put down the receiver. "He sends his congratulations, Joe. Add mine, for what they're worth. See you."

He eased his way through the crowd, climbed the steep stairs, walked down the maze of concrete corridors into the cool, dark night. He climbed into the jeep, wheeled it around, and headed for the assembly and repair plant, a huge and complex factory, blacked out now but still leaking flashes of light from the welders at work inside.

The shop was packed tight with aircraft, not an inch of unused space anywhere. As he entered, Garth grimaced at the cacophony that assaulted his ears—electric hammers, screeching lathes, pounding machinery of every description.

Garth weaved his way to the workbench that lay across the north wall where the lieutenant in charge was sweating over a mass of blueprints and a heavily-annotated file. There were seven electric bomb-arming switches laid out before him on the bench, in varying stages of disassembly. The officer snapped off a salute and said, not waiting to be asked, "Still testing, Captain. They're not right yet, I'm afraid."

"No? What the hell's wrong with them, Lieutenant?"

The lieutenant shrugged; he was very worried. "Some snafu in the circuitry; we're trying to track it down."

"In the design, or in the manufacture?"

"We don't know. We'll find out, I guess, but . . ."

Garth interrupted him brusquely. "Well, either get them working—and I mean one hundred percent reliably—or else rip 'em out of every SBD in every squadron. Is that clear?"

"Yes, sir."

As Garth turned away he saw Tom standing in the doorway across the cavernous building, searching for him among the maze of ailing aircraft. He caught the boy's eye with a wave of his hand and they moved to meet each other. Under the wing of a PBY he shook his son's hand and shouted, "Let's get out of this infernal racket. How the hell they work in here I'll never know." Tom nodded and said something that Garth couldn't hear as they made their way back to the door and stepped outside.

The relative quiet was a distinct relief. They walked a few yards in silence, then Tom threw his father a quick glance and said, "You got the report from the FBI?"

Matt nodded. "I got it. It wasn't easy, and I'm—maybe I'm sorry I did. It's not exactly encouraging. Over here."

He found a door in the darkness and they went inside to a brightly lit corridor. Matt pulled the report from his briefcase, handed it to his son and asked, "Did you know that your Haruko belonged to those Japanese patriotic organizations?"

Tom was sifting through the report, an incensed frown on his face. "Sure I did. I saw some of their literature in her apartment. But it doesn't mean a damn thing . . . just a lot of propaganda sent out by—by—"

"By whom?"

Tom gestured vaguely. "You know. The kind of stuff that's always being shoved around. Hell, Dad, every creep in the States has surfaced and gone into the streets agitating for something. I don't think she even bothered to read that garbage."

"Garbage to you and to me, maybe. But subversive to the attorney general."

The boy flushed. "It doesn't mean a thing, for God's sake!"

"Tom, look at it from the government's point of view. I talked it over with my FBI contact. He feels— they all feel that Haruko wasn't telling the truth about her reason for suddenly appearing in Pearl Harbor."

"She came here to get her parents' consent to our marriage. I told you that."

"And I told them it's part of her culture. But in their book that only makes it worse, more damning."

"Why?"

"Because it points her up as more Japanese than American. And these days that's all she needs."

Matt could sense his son's tight fury; he felt he had to keep talking to dissipate Tom's anger. "Listen to me. You've got to look at it from their angle, or we'll never get anywhere. Their first responsibility is the country's security. They're definitely *not* going to give much thought to the claim that she's in love with a brand-spanking-new navy flyer. It simply makes the whole bloody mess look more suspicious."

"But it's the truth, for Christ's sake! . . ."

"I know that! Damn it, Tom, you're not *listening* to me!"

They were shouting at each other suddenly, and Matt realized he had to hold himself in check. He said, more calmly, "Their viewpoint is this: A Japanese-American woman comes to Hawaii, leaving her studies, just a few days before the attack on Pearl Harbor. They make a routine visit to her state-side apartment, and what do they find? A lot of subversive literature. What are they going to do? Forget about it? They have to take some sort of action! They *have* to! Surely you can't blame them for that!"

Tom said stubbornly, "I sure as hell can! And I can sure as hell straighten them out, too . . ."

Matt cut him off. His tone was stinging and edged with impatience. It left no room for further argument. "You'll keep your mouth shut. And you'll leave this to me."

Tom stared at his father, stricken and angry with himself for showing it. He thought of all the times, when he was a young boy, that this same man had ended their differences with that same tone. Matt realized what was flashing through his son's mind and was instantly sorry. But the damage was done. Old attitudes had surfaced and taken control. He could only continue, more quietly now: "You came to me for help. Do you want it or not?"

For a moment Tom held his silence. He broke it with a question. "I don't have any alternative, do I?"

Matt heard the door slam behind him. He jammed the report into his briefcase and began to swear, vehemently, uselessly.

To his surprise, he found the admiral and Lieutenant Commander Blake were already there. He checked the clock. It was only a quarter of five. He saluted the admiral and said, "Good morning, sir. Sorry I wasn't here ahead of you."

Nimitz said easily, "The meeting's at oh five hundred, Captain, you're in good time. I'm just taking another look at our battle plot."

The huge chart of the Pacific Ocean was dotted with little flags that represented the widely-scattered ships of the fleet. He saw that Task Force 16, consisting of the carriers *Enterprise* and *Hornet*, was very close to Pearl Harbor, heading into port, and that Task Force 17, the *Yorktown*, was far out in the area of the Gilbert Islands, midway between the Coral Sea and Hawaii.

Commander Blake saw him frowning at it and said, "The *Yorktown*, it's got us worried, Matt. The *Enter-

prise and *Hornet,* they're due in harbor tomorrow, no problem. And the rest of Admiral Halsey's task force should be in by morning. But the *Yorktown*'s more severely damaged than we thought. She's listing badly."

"What's her speed?"

"Barely fifteen knots. And she's leaking oil. Badly."

The admiral looked up from the plot and said to his aide, "How soon do we expect her to dock?"

Blake sighed. "By the seventeenth—if a Jap submarine doesn't spot the oil slick she's trailing and track her down."

"Has Admiral Fletcher radioed in his repair list?"

"Yes, sir. It just came in. And it's a long one."

He took several sheets of paper from the file he had tucked under his arm and handed them to Nimitz. The admiral studied the list in grim silence, then he said to Blake, "Get this over to the yardmaster right away. Tell him I want every workman he can muster standing by to board her the second she docks."

There was a knock on the door, and Nimitz said, "Come."

One of the staff officers, Lieutenant Wold—a slight young man with a perpetually harried look—entered. "Sorry to disturb you, sir. I'm afraid that sharpshooter from Washington just landed on us."

Nimitz glanced at the clock in mild surprise. Wold said, "He came straight from his plane, sir. Says he's returning to Washington on the next flight out."

"Evidently he intends to make short work of us," Blake remarked. "Who did they send?"

"Captain Vinton Maddox."

Blake swore. "Maddox! He's a goddamned scalphunter."

Nimitz was smiling, bemusedly. He said to Wold, "See that he's thoroughly briefed, Lieutenant."

Wold said, "I've already done that, Admiral."

"Including Rochefort's latest intercepts?" Nimitz turned to Garth and added, "It came through after you left the Black Chamber last night, Matt. Show it to him, Blake."

Blake handed Garth the intercept and said, "It's guaranteed to blow your mind."

Nimitz turned his attention back to Wold who said, "Yes, sir, I showed him the intercept. He almost choked on it."

Nimitz chuckled. "I can well imagine he did." He looked at Garth who was staring at the intercept with an incredulous expression. "It's quite a net-full, isn't it?"

"Yes, sir!" Garth breathed.

Blake said again. "A scalp-hunter! Admiral, why don't you let the captain and me handle him. It would give us a lot of pleasure."

Nimitz shook his head. "No. He's come a long way and he's entitled to a crack at me personally." He turned to Wold. "My compliments to Captain Maddox, and tell him I'm ready when he is."

"Yes, sir," Wold said.

He went out and returned a moment later with a rather youthful looking officer, tall, lean, craggy-faced with the kind of smile that can charm or intimidate with equal ease. Now, as he stood straight and correct, the smile was carefully respectful, indeed, deferential.

Wold said, "Admiral, this is Captain Vinton Maddox."

"It's a pleasure, sir," Maddox said.

"All right," Nimitz said bluntly. "Let's get right down to it, shall we, Captain?"

The smile scarcely faltered. "Certainly, Admiral."

He looked calmly at Blake, and then at Wold and at Garth, as though sizing them up individually, gauging their worth. It was an old trick he had learned: *when dealing with the tough ones, let them hang for a minute, you regain the initiative.*

He turned back to Nimitz. "Well, sir—I'm sure you're aware of Washington's opinion about this Midway invasion business."

There was the slightest touch in his voice, not of scorn, but of amusement, as though "the invasion business" were a lot of nonsense.

Nimitz refused to take the bait. "Yes. They think it's an enemy ruse."

Maddox nodded. "An elaborate phony, Admiral."

"Go on."

It was Maddox's turn to feel discomfited; he didn't like the ball to be so firmly in his grasp if he could avoid it. He was conscious that Blake, and Wold, and Garth were all watching him, waiting for him to say the wrong thing. "Could we speak in private, sir?"

Nimitz nodded easily. "If you'd feel more comfortable." He gestured at the others, and reluctantly they left the room.

Maddox opened his thickly-packed briefcase and took out a bundle of files. "Sir, these are our copies of the relevant radio intercepts from your intelligence unit under—Commander Rochefort, is it?"

"As you well know, Captain. Joe Rochefort, he's a good man."

"Yes, of course. But there are rather a lot of them, aren't there?"

"There are indeed. And very detailed."

"And this one that your Lieutenant Wold just handed me. Detailed. Too damned detailed, Admiral." He flashed a carefully respectful smile.

Nimitz felt himself getting irritated but he smiled back and replied, "I think not, Captain. The operation Yamamoto has in mind requires that kind of detail. There's nothing slipshod about the Commander in Chief of the Imperial fleet. I knew him . . . when he was naval attaché in Washington. He leaves nothing to chance, believe me."

"I understand he had quite a reputation as a poker player."

"It was well earned. But if you're thinking of making a comparison between a game of cards and what we're engaged in now, please spare me."

Maddox realized it was not going to be easy. He said quickly, "That was not my intention, Admiral." He paused, letting Nimitz hang for a moment. Then he said with barely disguised patience, "Sir, do you remember what happened just prior to December seventh?"

"Are you referring to the fact that the Japanese flooded the airways with fake messages?"

"Very similar to these . . . yes, sir. These could be carbon copies of those messages. Admiral, Washington is convinced that Yamamoto is feeding you this hurricane of data to cover up his real intentions."

"That's a very definite possibility."

"Well then, sir, how can you still insist—"

The admiral cut him short, firmly and courteously, but in a tone that clearly said he would brook no further argument on the point. "Because it's my judgment that this information is factual. That's what the estimation of an enemy's intention is always about, Captain Maddox—judgment. I'm convinced that Yamamoto's target is Midway. And I am acting on that assumption, the assumption that my judgment is not failing me."

Maddox tried another tack. "Sir, if you're wrong . . . if you send our carriers into a Japanese ambush, the West Coast and the Hawaiian Islands will be left wide open for invasion."

"Yes, I'm fully aware of that."

"Then, sir, shouldn't the war college doctrine rule? 'Decisions must be based on what the enemy *could* do, not on what he will probably do.' "

Nimitz cut in. "I'm fully aware of War College doctrine, Captain."

"Of course, sir. Excuse me." Maddox could see that he had touched on the dilemma which, despite Nimitz's outward conviction, was troubling him. But with a man of Nimitz's caliber there was the ever-present danger of overkill, so he kept his silence and waited.

At length Nimitz said, "Captain, what you're saying —what Washington is saying—is that the safe play is to defend the home folks first?"

Maddox replied softly and with emphasis, "With respect, sir, it's the *smart* play."

Nimitz ran a hand over his chin. "Captain, if we surprise the enemy—catch him where he doesn't think we'll be—we can drive him back three thousand miles. And keep him there until we're ready to take him on in his own front yard."

Maddox did not lose his smile but his voice turned coldly official. "Sir, I have been instructed to convey Washington's deep concern for the safety of the West

Coast and of the Hawaiian Islands. That is—if you insist on pursuing this Midway invasion theory."

Nimitz fixed him with a cold and piercing look. "Captain Maddox, perhaps you'd enlarge on that for me. Is Washington *ordering* me to stay on the defensive? To defend against a possible attack here and on the West Coast?"

"No, sir. My instructions are simply to *consult*. No, I have no such orders for you, Admiral."

"Good. I'm glad to hear that." Nimitz crossed to the door, opened it. Immediately, Blake was there in the doorway. The admiral said deliberately, "Commander, declare a state of Fleet Opposed Invasion. Target: Midway Island. Issue the order immediately."

There was a gleam in Blake's eye. "Yes, sir. Immediately."

He hurried out, but Matt Garth was close behind him, standing there in the doorway he had vacated, an expression on his face that indicated trouble. He said, "Admiral, may I see you alone, please?"

Nimitz turned to Captain Maddox. "If you'll excuse me, Maddox . . . Hope you have a good trip back."

He headed out after Garth, and when the door had closed behind him, Garth said grimly, "A message for you, sir. I didn't think you'd want to receive it in Maddox's presence."

He held out the message for Nimitz and said, "Admiral Halsey is beached. In hospital. They don't know what it is yet. Could be it's not too serious."

Nimitz read the message through and scowled. "Captain, if you knew Bill Halsey as well as I do, you'd know how much he despises hospitals. If he's gone anywhere near one, it's not only damned serious, it's probably critical."

He handed back the message and moved to the window, to stare out over the waking city. "Bill Halsey. The one man I *can't* do without."

Garth said, "There are a lot of very competent men on the flag officers' roster, sir . . ."

"Yes. But it's what will happen to morale that worries me, Matt. More than any other officer, Halsey is responsible for lifting a thoroughly whipped fleet off its backside. After the pasting we took here on December seventh, that took a helluva lot of doing." He sighed and turned back to Garth. "Well, there's one thing he can still contribute. He can recommend his replacement."

Lieutenant Wold was hurrying toward them along the corridor. He said to the admiral, "Commander Rochefort's waiting in your office, sir. He says it's important—urgent—that he speak to you or to Captain Garth immediately."

Nimitz nodded and he and Garth followed Wold to the admiral's office.

Rochefort's thin, angular face was drawn, his eyes inflamed slits from too little sleep and too much cigar smoke. As Nimitz and Garth entered, he stashed the stub he had been chewing and said, "Admiral, I've got some bad news."

Nimitz said wryly, "This is the day for it, Commander. Go on."

Rochefort spread his hands in a hopeless gesture. "The Japanese have changed their JN25 code—the code that's been giving us all of Yamamoto's plans."

Nimitz said heavily, "How long before you can unravel their new system?"

Rochefort shook his head. "God knows, Admiral. It took us the best part of seven years to crack JN25. Of course, now we know the way their coding works, and that's one helluva leg up. And we'll be working on it day and night, nonstop, the best men and machines . . ."

The admiral cut him short. "How long, Commander?"

"A month. Maybe two."

"In other words, from here on we're in the dark. We know Yamamoto's going to hit Midway, but we'll have to guess the day and the hour. Is that about the size of it?"

"That's the size of it exactly, yes, sir. I'm sorry."

Nimitz fell silent for a long time. He turned away and stared at the large map of the Pacific area which hung behind his desk.

Garth waited. At last he broke into the admiral's

brooding. "Sir? Do you still want those fleet orders issued?"

Nimitz replied tightly, "I hope they've already *been* issued, Captain. The target—is Midway."

8

When Vice Admiral Chuichi Nagumo came aboard his flagship, the carrier *Akagi,* he was greeted by unrestrained euphoria on the part of his officers and men. Even in the waters surrounding the great ship, that jubilation had manifested itself in the astonishing array of small craft that had turned out to wish the fleet well. Myriad boats were crowded together with thousands of flags waving to the chant of voices raised in never-ending shouts of *"Bonzai . . . Bonzai . . . Bonzai!"* There were flowers floating on the water, great masses of scarlet and yellow hibiscus, and pink cherry blossoms, and garlands of bougainvillea in purple and orange and red—a striking contrast to the great gray warships massed in the harbor like waiting thunderclouds, thick black smoke pouring from their stacks. An awesome total of seventy vessels, the armada included five aircraft carriers, two seaplane carriers with their midget submarines hidden in their holds; eleven huge battleships; eleven cruisers; thirty-one destroyers; nine supply ships, and one repair ship plus many support vessels.

Aboard their respective ships were the Imperial Navy's most able and experienced commanders: Yamamoto, Nagumo, Yamaguchi, Abe, Kimura, Kondo, Takasu . . . These were the men who had forged Japan's navy into one of the most powerful war machines the world had ever seen.

And this was only part of the massive invasion force that had been assembled for the assault on Midway.

Altogether, Admiral Yamamoto had under his command two hundred ships and seven hundred planes, manned by one hundred thousand officers and men; the total tonnage of these ships exceeded one million and a half, an enormous numerical superiority over the opposing American forces.

Most importantly, the Japanese had a three-to-one edge in the all-important aircraft carriers alone. It was always the carriers that were in the forefront of Japanese naval strategy; how else could a war be won when its battles had to be fought thousands of miles from Japanese shores?

And given this superiority, as well as the known excellence of the Japanese pilots, the splendid capabilities of their highly-maneuverable Zeke, or Zero, fighter planes, who could doubt the outcome of this particular battle?

Admiral Yamamoto's only fear was a negative one. There were moments when he wondered, as he studied the combat records of the enemy admirals, whether or not they would dare challenge so powerful a force. He had learned a bitter lesson in the Java Sea and the Sundai Strait, when he had sent Nagumo against the hastily-assembled British Far Eastern fleet under Admiral Sir James Somerville. Hoping to repeat his success of Pearl Harbor, Nagumo had steamed toward Ceylon. Somerville's ships were not only heavily outnumbered, they were so old as to border on obsolescence; and after losing his two cruisers, the *Dorsetshire* and the *Cornwall,* Somerville had wisely decided to withdraw. The frustrated Nagumo wasted four precious days trying to find him.

And now, once again, the dangers inherent in such overpowering might were apparent. Would the enemy, once he had ascertained the strength of the assault, choose not to engage it, but instead to withdraw and bide his time? It was always a possibility.

Aboard the flagship *Akagi,* the skipper, Captain Taijiro Aoki, was pacing the bridge impatiently, awaiting his admiral and trying not to show the tremendous excitement that was consuming him as well as his officers. He was aware of Admiral Yamamoto's desire for a negotiated peace; but to him, the Battle of Midway would attain a different, more exciting goal; it would open up the long and indefensible American Pacific coast, and bring about not peace, but conquest.

He heard someone below shout, "Attention!" And then Vice Admiral Nagumo was moving onto the bridge. He was accompanied by the erratic, brainy strategy expert, Rear Admiral Ryunosuke Kusaka, a sly sort of man who always seemed preoccupied with his own thoughts.

Aoki saluted and said, "Welcome aboard your flagship, sir. This is a great day for all of us."

"Yes, it is indeed," Nagumo replied. "This is Admiral Kusaka. He will be my Chief of Staff. Captain Aoki . . ."

"We have served together before," Aoki said.

As the two men exchanged polite bows, Nagumo got the fleeting impression that Aoki was not one of Kusaka's admirers. But this was not the time for such idle speculation. He looked around and said, "Where is my air operations officer? Where is Genda?"

Aoki shook his head. "Commander Genda is in sick bay, Admiral."

Nagumo frowned. "Genda in sick bay? . . ."

Aoki nodded. "I'm afraid so, sir. He has influenza. It is quite severe."

Nagumo stared at him in dismay. He had been counting heavily on Genda, and the news was very disturbing. "And how long, Aoki, before he's back on duty?"

"According to the doctors, a week, possibly more, sir."

"But by then the battle will be underway!"

"It may be less, Admiral. But the doctors—"

Nagumo said sharply, "See that he gets every attention. I don't like the idea of beginning this operation without my best air commander. I don't like it at all."

"Yes, sir," Aoki replied. Then he added, hesitantly, "Sir, we have another sick bay casualty. Commander Fuchida. He came down this morning with acute appendicitis. They're operating now."

Nagumo was choleric. "Fuchida, too? Impossible!"

"I'm sorry, sir . . ."

Nagumo turned away and stared out at the bay and the small boats which were circling his carriers like jubilant calves around a mammoth female finback. He stood there for a while, scowling, drumming on the handrail with agitated fingers. He said at last, "Have you given any thought to his replacement?"

Aoki said promptly, "Genda suggests a veteran torpedo pilot aboard the *Hiryu,* sir. Lieutenant Joichi Tomonaga."

Nagumo nodded morosely. "Well, if Genda says he's good enough . . . I'll want to see this Tomonaga as soon as possible." He turned to Kusaka and said, "Fuchida led my first air strike against Pearl Harbor, and Genda planned it. Now they're both out. Both of them! It's a bad omen, Kusaka."

"An inconvenience, sir," Kusaka said with a faint smile. "We'll manage."

There was the faintest note of disrepect in his voice, but Nagumo was too preoccupied with his gloom to catch it. He was wondering just how competent Tomonaga really was. He finally concluded that it was not an easy matter to win the approval of a man like Genda, so perhaps, after all, he could rely on him . . .

None the less, the loss of two of his key officers weighed heavily on him. His apprehension was acute, as though the first blow had been struck against him even before he left port.

Was it, indeed, an omen?

With an effort he thrust his fears behind him, and said brusquely, "When you are ready, Captain. Midway—is waiting for us."

Captain Aoki gave the first words of command, and the great fleet weighed anchor and slowly, ponderously, began the voyage that would lead it to its destiny.

The *Akagi* led the way out of port, three other huge ultramodern carriers behind her. The battleships followed, flanked by the destroyers which took up their protective stations, some in the lead, boring their way through the blanket of small boats that miraculously opened up a path for the line of great ships. Immediately they took up new positions alongside the armada, their helmsmen and passengers cheering wildly, the bright flags waving, the garlands of blossoms tossing with the cadence of the waves. More than three hours passed before the last warship steamed out of Hiroshima Bay, leaving all the exuberance and the tens of thousands of prayers for victory behind.

The great armada's course was, first, southeast, and then due east; then east northeast. It would skirt the Bonin Islands, then Sulphur Isle (which later would become better known as Iwo Jima), and Marcus Island, the scene of Admiral Halsey's daring raid, which the Japanese called *Minami Tori Shima*. Soon part of the convoy would speed north to support the diversionary action against the Aleutians, the main force following it for some distance to bolster the impression —should it be trailed by enemy submarines—that the Aleutians were indeed the main target.

This was a cat and mouse game, a carefully calculated effort to mislead the American into rushing desperately with all or most of his forces to protect a target that was never really threatened. When the enemy had committed himself, Nagumo's carrier force would make a sharp turn to the southeast and swoop suddenly down on an unsuspecting Midway.

But one question had to be answered. The enemy fleet, according to all intelligence reports, was still nursing its wounds behind the safe and now-alert defenses of Pearl Harbor, eleven hundred miles to the southeast of Midway.

Or was it?

The question was crucial. There was no sense to the cat and mouse game if the cat did not know where the mouse was.

Yamamoto had sent a reconnaissance probe to find out—a sop thrown to the doubting Rear Admiral Yamaguchi. Now he was thankful that he had ordered the giant Kawanishi flying boats to confirm the intelligence reports.

Like Admiral Nimitz, Admiral Yamamoto sometimes had his moments of misgivings.

9

The moon was high in the slate sky, and in the clear, bracing air of the shoals the night-time visibility seemed to stretch into infinity. It was the kind of night that elated the silent stalkers and alarmed their intended prey.

Anchored in the precarious safety of the small lagoon at French Frigate Shoal was a U.S. seaplane tender. Below in their blacked-out mess hall, the men on the midwatch were passing their off-duty hours in trivia. There was a four-handed cribbage game going on in one corner with the usual kibitzers offering unwanted advice to the players. The dog-eared comic books were being reread for the umpteenth time and a Honolulu broadcasting station was playing a dreamy Jimmy Dorsey record.

The crew was bored, restless and disquieted. The repairs being made in the bowels of the engine room of their squat tender made it a sitting duck for any enemy warship that might be prowling the chain of tiny volcanic islands which formed a 1,500-mile arc from Pearl Harbor to Midway.

Snatches of conversation drifted around the room as though borne on the blue clouds of tobacco-smoke.

"Hey, I tell you about that snatch I met in Pearl? Hair right down to her fanny, and black! . . . Like a raven's ass. Said she was eighteen but her sister told this other guy I was makin' liberty with that she was barely sixteen."

"Jailbait, you stupid bastard."

"Listen. If they're old enough to bleed, they're old enough."

"Christ! Will you deal the fucking cards?!"

"Hey, you guys hear the one about the preacher and the hundred-dollar whore?"

"Shit! Not *that* one again! . . ."

"You hear what the lieutenant said about the Japs bombing San Francisco?"

"Son of a bitch is full o' crap. How the hell they gonna bomb San Francisco?"

"I'll tell you how they do it. They got midget submarines, with midget planes on board, and they surface, see, and the midget planes take off with midget bombs . . . "

"Yeah, and midget pilots . . . "

"Deal the *cards,* for Christ's sake! . . ."

On deck a seaman lookout was searching the silvered surface of the water, turning his glasses from time to time on the sky.

He was startled when the Officer of the Deck tapped him on the shoulder; he had not heard the approach.

The lieutenant said: "Anything, Miller?"

He shook his head. "Just miles and miles of water is all, Lieutenant." He snugged the windbreaker closer around his neck and asked: "How long before we get underway again, Lieutenant?"

"Why? Some place else you'd rather be?"

"Yes, sir. I can think of a hundred places I'd rather be. You ever been in the blackland prairies, Lieutenant?"

"Where the hell are the blackland prairies?"

"Up from the Red River to the Rio Grande. Me and my dad, we got four hundred acres of melons there, cantaloupes, honeydew, watermelons . . . We got a Stone Mountain grows to fifty pounds. Far as you can see, fifty-pound watermelons lying there on the ground. How far from here to Tokyo?"

The lieutenant was startled by the non sequitur. He said: "Three thousand miles, sailor. Why? You looking for action?"

"No, sir. I'm lookin' to get home in one piece. Did you know Nimitz comes from Texas?"

"*Admiral* Nimitz to you, sailor."

"Yep, son of a bitch comes from Texas."

The lieutenant ignored the response and moved on. Miller turned his attention back to the water. He tried to visualize it as a field of watermelons, but couldn't. It was calm, flat and desolately empty, broken only by a rippling ribbon of silver where the water reflected the luster of the moon. A quick series of *plops* startled him. He jerked the binoculars up, then relaxed as he saw the phosphorescent bodies of flying fishes skimming over the surface of the lagoon.

He thought: "My God, in less than a month the old man'll be hiring the Mexican pickers to harvest the early melons. I won't even see the crop this year."

The Japanese submarine, an I-class tanker, lay at periscope depth outside the inlet to the lagoon exactly four hundred and forty yards from the American seaplane tender. She was the I-125, and her skipper was Lieutenant Commander Toshitake Ueno.

Face pressed to his periscope, he was studying the American ship intently. He snapped his fingers at his executive officer and said: "The recognition charts, Akita. Quickly."

Akita had anticipated his skipper's need and handed him a thick, loose-leaf binder which contained the silhouettes of every warship, enemy or friend, known to be in commission. Ueno riffled through the pages, stopping at the Auxiliary Vessels heading. He put his finger on a particular silhouette, checked his periscope again and said, at length: "Yes . . . yes . . . It's an American seaplane tender. No question. Take a look, Akita."

Akita peered through the periscope and said excitedly: "Four hundred and forty yards, Captain. We can send her to the bottom in three minutes. Two torpedos, that's all we'll need."

The Japanese were using torpedoes powered with oxygen fuel; they left no telltale bubbles on the water to give away their presence. Akita was thinking: *the first amidships, the second to the stern, an easy target . . .*

Ueno regretfully shook his head. "No, we can't do that. They'd still have enough time to send out a radio alert."

Akita pointed to the silhouette. "Then let's surface, sir. If we shoot off her radio mast the moment we break water . . ."

Ueno cut him short: "Not even a pistol shot. Our orders are quite specific. We are to wait here for two reconnaissance seaplanes on their way to Pearl Harbor. We're to refuel them and return immediately to our base, undetected."

"Then, Captain, I suggest we radio for new instructions. Our superiors should know there's a sleeping goose here, waiting to have her bowels reamed."

Ueno shook his head. "We are also ordered to keep strict radio silence. Apparently the high command is determined that the enemy gets no possible hint of this reconnaissance operation." He put his forehead against the periscope again, took a long look and sighed: "No, Akita, we'll have to let her sleep the night, unmolested. No doubt she'll be gone by morning."

But by morning, the American tender was *not* gone. All night the submarine lay there, and all night the seaplane tender lay there, too, quite oblivious of the danger off her port bow.

All night, too, Commander Ueno had maintained his constant vigil at the periscope.

A cool, very capable submarine veteran, he was not easily angered, but now he raged to himself: "Still lying there, like a pig floundering in the mud!"

Akita tapped him on the shoulder. "We've just picked up a radio message from Kwajalein, sir. Our reconnaissance planes took off two hours ago." As his skipper frowned over the message, he added: "Captain, we can't just sit on this reef and watch them land in the enemy's lap."

Ueno turned his attention back to the periscope, and he wondered if just possibly he *could* surface and shoot out the tender's radio before she could flash a warning of his presence. His orders were quite explicit about avoiding enemy detection; but avoidance of detection might also be interpreted to mean the concealment of his presence from the enemy high command, not simply from a single American vessel. But if he failed, if an alert was transmitted before he could send her to the bottom . . .

Akita, who was consulting the data appended to the tender's silhouette, interrupted his brooding. "Sir, that tender has four gun tubs, each mounting a quadruple

Bofors 40-mm antiaircraft gun. Also six 50-caliber machine guns, and perhaps a 37-mm cannon. Those Bofors can saturate the skies. No Kawanishi would have a chance against such fire power . . ."

Ueno motioned impatiently. "I can see that for myself, Akita." He straightened from the periscope and said more cooly: "You're right. We can't just sit here. We'll have to risk it."

"Torpedoes, sir? Or shall we surface?"

"Neither. We'll break radio silence . . . and ask for instructions. See to it immediately."

Akita was obviously disappointed, and he did not bother to hide the fact from the captain. "Yes, sir," he said coldly.

Ueno returned to his vigil at the periscope. There was a distinct possibility that the enemy tender itself would pick up his radio message; he wondered if he should dive immediately after it was transmitted and await a depth-charge attack. He decided not; the waters were perilously shallow here.

When Akita returned from the radio room, there was a perplexed look on his face. He held out the decoded instructions to his skipper and said: "This doesn't make any sense, sir. We've been ordered to retire, undetected."

Ueno could not credit his hearing. "To *retire?* But that's impossible!"

"I radioed Kwajalein to repeat their orders. The confirmation came back immediately."

"I can't believe it . . ."

"Why didn't they give us another rendezvous? There are dozens of hidden shoals to the south where we could refuel the Kawanishis safely. Necker Island is ideal."

Akita continued to voice his dismay: "The whole operation scrubbed! . . . It doesn't make any sense at all."

"We have our orders, Lieutenant. Slow astern at periscope depth. Clear to four thousand yards, then take her down."

Slowly, silently, the submarine began to ease off.

Soon, it was clear of the shoals and sank into deeper water, a gray steel fish bloated with aviation gasoline which it would never deliver.

10

The internment center on the outskirts of Honolulu was a disgrace.

Approaching it, Matt Garth stared in dismay at the huge, decrepit warehouse sagging at its beams and seeming to indicate that everything about it was doomed to extinction—including those quartered inside it.

The building was once beach-white, but the paint was now old and grimed and peeling everywhere. The asphalt yard, reflecting the oppressive heat of the midday sun, was vast and encircled with new and forbidding galvanized-mesh fencing, shutting it off from the rest of this lovely island as though it were a leper colony.

He turned to his escort, a pudgy young army second lieutenant, barely out of OTC, and said: "You mean to tell me that people actually live in there?"

The young man replied in a matter-of-fact tone: "Just Japs. No white people."

Garth said nothing. His lips were tight with anger.

One of the guards saluted and rolled back the massive warehouse door and they went inside, to find a cavernous, dimly-lit building which had been divided by random sheets of plywood into tiny numbered cubicles. There were hundreds of Japanese-Americans, some in traditional clothes—the older ones—and some in occidental dress. They all had one thing in common: there was a desolate but patient look on all their faces as they sat on upturned wooden boxes, or strolled, or simply stared at the peeling paint of the warehouse interior. No one was talking; it was as though their indignity could not be verbalized, but only suffered.

The lieutenant stopped at a closed door: "Here we

are, Captain. The Sakura family. They're collaborators."

Matt Garth said coldly, "Thank you, Lieutenant. I'll find my own way back."

"You bet, Captain."

The lieutenant saluted smartly and moved off. Garth waited for him to turn a corner and then knocked quietly on the door to the cubicle. It was crudely stenciled with the figures 329.

In a moment, the door opened and he was face to face with the girl his son loved.

She was a lovely slip of a girl in her early twenties. There was a properly respectful look on her face as she bowed politely and said in a low melodic voice: "Please come in, Captain Garth."

He followed her into the tiny room. She did not close the door.

Three army cots, a single wooden chair, an upturned packing case which served as a table, and a broken crate for use as a wardrobe occupied most of the floor space. Two middle-aged Japanese in Oriental dress got to their feet and bowed solemnly as Garth entered.

Haruko said simply: "My parents, Captain Garth. Tetsuro and Sada Sakura. This is Tom's father . . ."

Garth nodded. "How do you do? . . ."

Haruko remained in the doorway. "I expect you will want to talk to me in private, Captain. My parents will understand."

"Ah yes, please . . ." Suddenly feeling very ill at ease, he nodded at the two grave-faced parents and followed Haruko outside.

The warehouse floor was as big as a football field and forested with exposed, rusted, iron poles which supported the sagging roof. A detail of soldiers was pushing a food cart along, hammering brusquely on cubicle doors, calling out impatiently: "Chow time, open up . . . Come on, move it."

As they walked along the long corridor between the countless cubicles Haruko said, very sure of herself: "If I embarrassed you just now . . . and I believe I did . . .

please forgive me. I wanted you to meet my parents. I wanted you to see for yourself that they're not really much of a threat to our national security."

Garth shrugged. "I never imagined that they would be."

"Then maybe you'll speak to the people who print those stories and cartoons picturing all Japanese as snag-toothed and bloody-handed."

"War and truth are rarely compatible, Miss Sakura."

"And I shouldn't be bitter about it, is that what you're saying?"

"No. I didn't say that . . ."

She interrupted him angrily, a sudden flush of temper inflaming her face. "Damn it, I'm an American! I don't see what makes *us* different from Italian-Americans or German-Americans."

Her outburst surprised him; her simple, unerring logic left him without an adequate response. All he could say was: "I . . . know how you feel . . ."

She went on, incensed and trying to hold back her tears. "I try to understand the panic my country is feeling . . . and the hunger for revenge that puts my parents and me and all the other Japanese-Americans behind barbed wire. But damn it, I'm a loyal American! . . ."

There were tears in her eyes now, tears of pain and humiliation.

He said gently: "Would you like to sit down?"

"No."

He sighed. "Well, in that case . . ."

He hardly knew how to begin. He said quietly: "Let's talk about the FBI report on you and your parents. I've seen it. I'm afraid it doesn't make very good reading."

She said tartly: "Did you expect a reasoned intellectual discourse?"

"No, I expected what I got—a point of view that is meant to justify what's happening."

"And it does?"

"Not in my view, no. But I can understand that it would theirs."

"You make the distinction between *you* and *them* very easily."

"I came here to help you, Haruko. I wish you'd remember that."

She didn't sound as though she had meant it very strongly, and he said again: "To help you, and to help Tom. I promised him I'd do what I could, and . . . It seems to me that I have to fight with him, with you, with everybody else."

She was not in the least mollified. "There's a war, so everybody has to fight."

"Not with our friends, Haruko."

"No, I suppose not."

Her mood changed quickly, and she smiled at him.

"I'm really quite a nice person, can you believe that? And this time I mean it. I really am sorry. Put it down to . . . to the strain of just . . . just being here. Can you forgive me?"

"Of course. May I ask you a few questions?"

She nodded. "Yes, please do. Anything you want to know. I have absolutely nothing to hide."

"Good. Then I'm sure we'll manage somehow."

It was still not going to be easy. He took a long, deep breath. "Your father was frequently seen entering the Japanese consulate in Honolulu."

"Is there any reason why he shouldn't? He has old friends there, and he cares about his friends. Perhaps that's part of the Oriental heritage."

"*Touché* . . . But there was a little edge to that remark, wasn't there? Have you forgotten already?"

"Forgotten?" She was genuinely surprised. "Forgotten what?"

"That I came here as a friend."

She touched his arm. "No, I haven't forgotten. And I'm grateful, truly I am. It's just that . . ." She broke off, frowning.

He looked down at her. "Just what?"

She said slowly, a little break in her voice: "It's not only what's happening to me. I'll survive it one way or another. But for my parents . . . they just sit there all day and stare at nothing, do nothing. It's painful to watch what's happening to them. It's painful to realize that it's happening to me, too, the insidious approach of . . . How can I put it? Of dispassion? We're becoming completely disinterested in what might happen to us. For the first few days, it was all a matter of anger, and anger is easy to cope with. But now . . . it's become disinterest, as though we don't really care any more."

Matt could think of nothing to say.

After a few steps in silence, Haruko continued: "So if I sound . . . short-tempered, at least that's better, isn't it, than the state of mind I'm so worried about? If this were to go on much longer, and you were to come to me just a few weeks later, I'm quite sure I'd be saying: 'Go to hell, Captain Garth, I just don't give a damn.' But I'm not saying that. Instead, I'm fighting you, yes, I know it . . . But that's better, isn't it?"

Matt nodded gravely. "Yes, I think you are absolutely right. So let's get back to that FBI business, shall we?"

"All right, let's do that."

"There's one thing the FBI seems very worried about. Those Japanese patriotic organizations. It seems that you belong to some of them. I hope that's not really true."

"But it is! My father enrolled me when I was born, and out of respect for him, I never wanted to resign. But I never played any active part at all in . . . in whatever it is they do. I don't even *know* what they do! As far as they are concerned, I'm just another Japanese name, one of thousands on whatever lists they have. It doesn't mean a thing."

"And what about the newspapers they found in your parents' home? The Japanese newspapers?"

She said scornfully: "Some copies of the *Prairie Shinbun*. It's published in Wyoming! My father has deep emotional ties to Japan, of course he has; he was born there. But even he thought the *Prairie Shinbun* was a ridiculous propaganda sheet. He scarcely ever read it."

Garth said swiftly: "Then why did he subscribe to it?"

"Because he was raised in the tradition of the rice cakes."

"The tradition of the *rice cakes*? I'm afraid my knowledge of Japanese customs isn't quite up to it."

She waited until they turned and started back again, down the interminably long hall.

Haruko said slowly: "It was in Japan, in the sixteenth century . . . There was a very lowborn boy named Hideyoshi, who rose to become a very famous general under the sponsorship of the ruling shogun of the time. Without the shogun's favor, you must understand, he would have remained poor and insignificant all his life, but with it . . . he became a strong and popular soldier, so popular that the shogun decided he was a threat to the shogunate itself. So he sent the general a gift of rice cakes. And they were poisoned."

"And so? . . ."

She was smiling still. "The general knew they were poisoned; he'd already been warned. So what do you think he did?"

Not waiting for his reply, she went on: "He knew they were poisoned, but out of politeness and respect toward his benefactor, he ate them. Quite deliberately, you understand. That is what we call . . . the tradition of the rice cakes. My father was once greatly indebted to the man who publishes the ridiculous *Prairie Shinbun*."

"I see."

It all made a certain sense, but he wondered if he could convince the FBI. Here, the slight, lissome figure, the olive skin and the large and lovely slanting eyes gave a touch of reality to an attitude that, anywhere else, he would have found hard to understand himself.

He said: "There's one thing that puzzles me. Tom says you came to Honolulu to get your parents' permission to marry him."

"Yes I did."

"But you didn't tell that to the FBI. You told them nothing of your reasons for coming here."

"No, I never mentioned Tom's name to them. Of course not."

"But why? You left them wondering what might have prompted you to come here at all, to interrupt your studies . . ."

She interrupted him again. "I didn't want to implicate Tom. I thought it might harm him, too."

"I see. One last question. He came to visit you here, and you refused to see him. Why?"

She looked at him, a questing, quizzical look. "Can't you guess?"

"I can understand that you might not want him to see you in a place like this, but I don't think it's a very good reason."

"It's not the reason at all, Captain."

She was biting her lip, tense, withdrawn into her own thoughts. He waited. She said at last, avoiding his eyes: "I just didn't know how to tell him . . . to tell him that my parents will not give me their approval of the marriage."

He stared at her. "For God's sake . . . do you accept that? Certainly you intend to make up your own mind . . ."

"No, I can't do that. I cannot disobey them. I will not disobey them," she added softly.

"But goddamn it, this doesn't make any sense at all! You started this conversation by telling me at great length that you're an American. Now you're saying, in effect, that you're really an Oriental."

She looked at him, meeting his eyes head on. He went on: "Haruko, in this day and age young women just don't allow their parents to dictate whom they can or can't marry."

She replied with tight anger: "Perhaps you're right. Perhaps I'm more Japanese than I thought, Captain Garth."

"You're really making it difficult for me to help you. We're back to quarreling again."

She made a visible effort to overcome the tempest of emotions which seemed to compel her to deliberately antagonize this man who had come to her aid. At length she replied quietly: "No. I don't want to quarrel with you."

He took hold of her shoulders and swung her around to face him. "Haruko, what can your parents possibly have against Tom?"

"It's not Tom that's the problem. It's simply that . . . I have been forbidden to marry outside my race."

He threw up his hands in dismay. "I don't believe it!"

"And I want you to tell Tom for me."

"No!" He found he was shouting at her. He calmed down a little and said: "I can't do that, Haruko. I'd rather he didn't know that we talked at all."

She frowned, staring at the ground.

He pushed his point home, a minor victory in her silence: "He's at the Kaneohe Air Station, Haruko. Send for him, please."

She looked up at him and held his eyes for a moment, and then, without another word, she turned away abruptly and hurried back to the bitter confines of her family's cubicle.

11

Vice Admiral William F. Halsey was never the sweetest-tempered man in the world, and now, as he lay in bed with calamine lotion smeared all over his body, he was like a bear with a fishbone stuck between his teeth.

A gruff, hardbitten man, just turned sixty, he had learned how to fly a plane, and had been designated a naval pilot when he was fifty-two years old. After serving part of World War One in Ireland, he had assumed his first command, of the *Benham*, in February 1918. Two months later he had taken command of the *Shaw*. Both were destroyers, and for his services aboard them he had been awarded the Navy Cross with the citation:

For distinguished service in the line of his profession as CO of the USS *Benham* and the USS *Shaw*, engaged in the important, exacting, and hazardous duty of patroling the waters infested with enemy submarines and mines, in escorting and protecting vitally important convoy of troops and supplies through these waters, and in offensive and defensive action, vigorously and unremittingly prosecuted against all forms of enemy naval activity.

The key word was . . . unremittingly. This was the major clue to his charactor, an impatience to be up and at them, to hit, as he liked to say, hard, and fast, and often.

In April of this year, his task force had escorted the carrier *Hornet* on the Doolittle raid, and soon he would be searching out the Japanese and hitting them at Guadalcanal, the Bismarck Archipelago, in the Palaus, the Philippines, Formosa, Okinawa, and the South China Sea; in Manila Harbor, at Leyte, Mindoro, and Luzon. By the end of the war the forces under Admiral Bill Halsey would have accounted for the destruction of an incredible 2,804 enemy planes, 148 Japanese combat ships and 1,598 merchant ships, and 195 locomotives.

Hit hard, hit fast, hit often . . .

But now, his wrath was directed against the good Lord up there, not so good any more, for having put him in hospital just at the time when the enemy was out there waiting for him in the kind of force that had never been seen before on the high seas. He was in a foul temper.

The spacious hospital room was cool and quiet. On the table beside the immaculate bed was a pair of heavy naval field glasses. Admiral Nimitz, grinning at his friend's discomfort, was sitting in the Windsor chair, his long legs crossed, his cap on his knee.

Halsey said furiously: "Goddamn it, this damn itching is driving me crazy! All those medics seem to know how to do is smear me all over with this god-awful paste!"

Nimitz chuckled. "When they get up enough nerve to come near you, you mean."

A nurse poked her head in the door, a look of nervous apprehension on her face. She glanced quickly at him and said: "All right, Admiral? Anything you need?"

She hardly waited for the gruff shake of his head before she was out again, and Nimitz laughed and said: "They're all scared stiff of you, Bill."

Halsey growled: "They should be. Yes, I guess I'm a son of a bitch of a patient, but . . . A skin disease! Of all the stupid, goddamn useless things to get laid up with! Like a schoolboy getting into puberty! It's driving me nuts, Chet."

"Bill, this is one time you *have* to think straight. I need your advice . . . if you can stop bitching for half a second."

"Me, bitching?! You never met a sweeter-tempered bastard. What's on your mind?"

"Fletcher's docking the *Yorktown* right now—"

Halsey cut him short. "Why the hell aren't you down there to meet him, Chet? That crew's done an impossible job bringing that cripple home. You ought to be there to tell 'em so."

Nimitz replied patiently: "I'm not there because I've got more important business . . . here. With you. Bill, I've got a hard decision to make. A vital one."

He got to his feet and moved to the window where he could look out across the lush green hospital lawns to the harbor beyond. Halsey waited in silence.

At length Nimitz said: "I'd like you to recommend your own replacement." He turned to face Halsey and the explosion he was certain was imminent. It didn't come. Instead, Halsey said mildly: "Yeah . . . I figured that was why you were here."

"You know? . . ."

"Hell, yes, I know. The damn quack doctors have been trying to keep it from me, but I've got a spy on their staff. She's a red-headed nurse, Chet. Makes me wish I wasn't married, wasn't so damned old, wasn't so god-awful ugly and had a full head of hair." He chuckled. "Quite a sack full of miracles I'd need, uh?"

Nimitz just shook his head and grinned at his irrepressible friend. Halsey went on: "The official prognosis is that I'll be laid up for at least two months." He laughed and added: "You were supposed to break the news to me, uh? The medics didn't have the guts."

"Something like that, yes."

"Well, relax. I'm not going to fight you. I'm too damn sick, Chet. God, I hate being sick!"

Nimitz was visibly relieved. He smiled and said: "You're sure as hell full of surprises, Admiral."

"Yes, sir." Halsey grinned. "Now what was that advice you wanted? I'm loaded with it. All good. But don't expect me to accept any of yours in return."

Nimitz let his smile die, then said bluntly: "Your replacement . . . I have to name him immediately."

Halsey did not hesitate. "Ray Spruance. The best possible man for the job, Chet."

Nimitz was shocked. "Spruance! Goddamn it, Bill, he's a cruiser skipper! I need someone who knows planes, knows what they're all about."

Halsey said again, patiently: "The only man for the job, there's no one better then Ray. Yes, I know; he's never served a day on a carrier . . ."

Nimitz interrupted: "And he's junior to a hell of a lot of other flag officers . . ."

"But he *knows* carrier tactics. In fact, there's damn little he doesn't know."

Nimitz shook his head. "Go back to his training, Bill. World War One. What was he? Inspector of Machinery! Fire Control Officer!"

"You asked for my recommendation, Chet."

"Yes, I did . . ."

Halsey waited a moment for his old friend to cool. Then he went on:

"He was second in command in the Marshall Island operation, and at Wake Island . . ."

"I remember. He did a good job . . ."

"More importantly, he was *my* second in command at Marcus Island. The tactics we used there were his, Chet. Not only mine."

Nimitz thought about it for a long time.

He said at last, ruefully, "I can just picture Washington's reaction if I hand over the *Enterprise* and the *Hornet* to a cruiser skipper! Especially with all the static I've been getting about going out to look for the Japanese at Midway."

"Ha! They're on to you about that, are they? I thought they'd be. Sons of bitches!"

"They think Yamamoto's been feeding me a lot of diversionary crap, trying to lure me away from where he doesn't want me to be."

"What they think doesn't matter a goddamn. You're in command. What do *you* think?"

Nimitz grinned. He said bluntly: "I believe that Joe Rochefort's boys down in the Black Chamber have laid Yamamoto's plans out on the table for me to take a good hard look at. I believe he's going to hit Midway, and by God, I'm going to hit him there with everything I've got. I tried to convince Washington that I'm right, but . . ." He shrugged and shook his head.

Halsey said: "Well, the answer to that problem's in your own words, recorded for the benefit of posterity."

"Oh? What's that?"

"You once told me, Chet . . . 'When you're in command . . . *command.*' "

Nimitz got to his feet. "Well, history's going to be made, Bill, one way or the other. Either we knock Hell out of the Japs at Midway . . . or we lose the fleet. There's nothing in between."

In his nighttime office, Admiral Nimitz was buried under the paperwork that he hated so much. It seemed to him that the wartime effort was producing almost as much paper as ammunition, and he was impatient with it, knowing that it had to be done and that if it was to be done right, then he had to take care of an immense amount of it himself.

Lieutenant Wold knocked and entered. "Sorry to interrupt you, sir . . . Admiral Fletcher is here."

Nimitz shoved the papers across the desk with a sigh of relief. "Good, show him in, Lieutenant."

He got to his feet as Fletcher came in, and shook hands with him warmly, and said: "Welcome home, Jack. And congratulations on bringing in your cripple."

"Black Jack" Fletcher was fifty-seven years old, an easygoing man who thought of himself as much a diplomat as a fighting man. He was calm, reserved, and studious.

"Thank you, sir. We got lucky. Could have easily finished up on the bottom."

Nimitz glanced at the *Yorktown*'s damage report. "Looks like you took a lot of punishment out there."

"A hell of a lot more than I thought any ship could take and stay afloat." Fletcher grinned and added: "But we're home now . . . . and ready for some liberty and leave. Lot's of it. My crew deserves it, Chet."

But Nimitz remained silent as he studied the fatigue-etched face of the man across the desk.

"We don't have much time, so I'll give it to you fast. I expect you heard already, Halsey's beached. He's in the hospital, and he won't be leaving for quite a while. I'm sending you out again, Jack. In seventy-two hours. Back to sea."

"Seventy-two hours? What's my new ship?"

"The same one. The *Yorktown*. You've got three days to get her into full combat readiness."

Fletcher stared at him. He said, shocked: "The *Yorktown*? In three days? Chet, it'll take at the very least *three months* to get her back into commission."

"Seventy-two hours. That's all the time I'm giving you."

"But it's impossible!"

"It's got to be done, Jack."

"Mind telling me *how*, Admiral?" Fletcher asked heatedly.

"The yardmaster knows what has to be done. He'll have men swarming over the *Yorktown* stem to stern, three shifts, twenty-four hours a day. If he needs more men, he'll get them . . ."

"*Skilled men?* If you mustered every skilled shipfitter in these islands you still couldn't do the job you're demanding—"

Nimitz cut in and continued calmly:

"I'm giving Ray Spruance Halsey's command. He'll be taking the *Enterprise* and the *Hornet* to sea tomorrow. You'll follow, in the *Yorktown,* forty-eight hours later."

Fletcher said, aghast: "Ray Spruance? He's a cruiser commander! . . ."

"But he knows carrier tactics. He proved that, at Marcus."

"He's not even a flier . . ."

"Well, he sure as hell can't learn to fly by tomorrow, can he?"

Fletcher was very worried. He looked at his old friend and said quietly: "I hope to God you know what you're doing, Chet."

Nimitz nodded. He said mildly: "I usually do, Jack. I usually do. If I'm wrong this time . . . we stand a good chance of losing the war, don't we?"

"Yes, sir, a *very* good chance."

Nimitz was silent for a moment as he struggled against the specter of his ever-present doubts. Then he looked at Fletcher and said: "Do you realize that if we lick the Japs at Midway it will be their first major defeat since the Chinese knocked hell out of their expedition to Korea three hundred and fifty years ago? It's when you stick your neck out that you run the risk of getting it wrung. And that's sure as hell what they're doing at Midway . . . sticking their necks out. So, let's wring it."

Fletcher couldn't help grinning with a sort of fascination. It was like watching a sidewinder carefully coiling to strike a victim many times its size.

Nimitz continued: "The *Yorktown will* be ready, Jack. Now let's take a look at the battle plot. I want you to see what you're up against."

They went down the long corridor where the Marine sentries were standing stiffly to attention, and into the plot room, where Ray Spruance was waiting for them, carefully masking his unease.

Fletcher went to him at once and shook hands. "Congratulations, Ray. I'm very glad about this, I hope you are, too."

Spruance gestured helplessly. "Me? I'm still in a state of complete shock."

Matt Garth was there, too, and Fletcher nodded to him. "Good to see you again, Matt. We missed you at Coral Sea."

Nimitz said: "Well, you've got him for this one, Jack.

Matt's going out with you on the *Yorktown* to join your
air operations staff."

"Good, I'm glad."

Matt said slyly: "And we're sailing in seventy-two hours, remember?"

Fletcher nodded. "How can I forget?"

The battle plot had been set up on a huge table in
the center of the room, a gigantic plaster model of the
Pacific Ocean in relief, the volcanic islands and the
reefs dotted about and carefully annotated. Nimitz took
his pointer and indicated the position shown for the
Japanese fleet; heading east from Hiroshima Bay.
He tapped at it and said:

"This time we're up against the biggest force the enemy has ever sortied, more than two hundred ships, the
majority of them sailing out of Hiroshima. The main invasion force, we believe, will sail from Guam and Saipan.
They'll have a four-to-one superiority—in numbers.
Yamamoto himself is commanding. We know when,
and from where each unit sailed. We know their ini-
tial course. They're shown here on the plot. But we do
not know what changes they'll make in their courses,
or where they'll rendezvous . . . or *when* they'll strike.
We don't even know from which direction they plan to
hit us, but my guess is it will be from the west. However, there's no intelligence to support that. It's just a
guess."

He hesitated. "If I were Yamamoto, I'd sure as hell
want to hit as soon as I got within striking distance,
rather than go chasing around to the east side of Midway, worrying all the time about being spotted by our
air and sea traffic to and from Hawaii. The element of
surprise is very important for him. And that means
speed. That, in turn, means he has to hit as soon as he
can." He paused again, then said gravely: "Now, I
have to tell you that Washington thinks this whole Midway thing is an elaborate ruse on the part of the Japanese to cover up their real intentions . . ."

He saw the sudden alarm on Fletcher's face, and
glanced quickly at Spruance; the dark, narrow eyes
were thoughtful, waiting.

He went on: "*I* think Washington is wrong."

"So, Ray, assuming that I'm right, what counter-moves do you suggest?"

Spruance promptly ran the tip of his finger on a northwesterly direction from Pearl Harbor.

He said without hesitation: "I'd take my carriers on this course. Lie in wait for Nagumo's carriers here, to the northeast of Midway."

A long, shallow arc halfway between Midway and Hawaii, fencing off the two islands from each other, was drawn on the battle plot. It was marked: "JAPA-NESE SUBMARINE CORDON." Nimitz pointed to it and said: "What about the enemy's submarine picket line?"

"We'll have to go straight through it. That's the only way we'll get there on time."

Nimitz looked up at Spruance thoughtfully, the pale blue eyes bright and alert. He said, puzzled: "You'd wait northeast of Midway? . . . Why not head north-west and hit them head on?"

Spruance looked Nimitz straight in the eye and re-plied quietly: "Because there's just a chance that Wash-ington is right, sir."

Nimitz was disturbed. He felt Fletcher's eyes on him, watching him closely. Nimitz said: "You think Hawaii or the West Coast could be Yamamoto's real target?"

"It doesn't matter, sir . . . provided I'm in a position to cut him off if he moves west, or . . . if his target *is* Midway . . . to bushwhack him."

The answer pleased Nimitz very much. He shot a look at Fletcher, who nodded his approval with a slight little smile which seemed to say: This cruiser skipper will do just fine, Admiral.

Nimitz said: "All right. Jack, you're senior. You'll take overall command when you two join up."

Fletcher said dryly: "If the battle's not over before we get the *Yorktown* glued back together."

Nimitz's reply was abrupt: "The *Yorktown will* be at sea in seventy-two hours." Then he said more cooly: "I don't need to dwell on the fact that Yamamoto outweighs us in every department. Your three car-riers and a handful of escorts are all that stand be-tween the enemy fleet and the American coastline."

He paused, waiting for comment. There was none.

He went on: "Now, about the point of rendezvous for the *Yorktown* and Ray's two carriers . . . what shall we call it?"

A voice from behind him said: "Point Luck, sir?"

Nimitz turned to face his young aide, Lieutenant Wold. He looked at him sharply, then said: "That sounds like a prayer, Lieutenant. But . . . I must admit, it's damned appropriate. Point Luck it is. Now, Captain Garth will read your orders. Matt . . ."

Garth produced a sheet of paper and read from it. "In carrying out the task assigned to you, operational plan number 29-42, *Enterprise* and *Hornet* will be governed by the principle of calculated risk, which you will interpret to mean the avoidance of exposure of your force to attack by superior enemy forces without good prospect of inflicting, as a result of such exposure, greater damage to the enemy."

Garth handed each of the admirals a copy of their orders and Nimitz said: "Any questions about your orders, gentlemen?"

"No, sir," they replied.

"Good. Ray, any thoughts about your course to Point Luck?"

Spruance said: "If Yamamoto is already at sea, we don't have time for anything but a beeline under flank speed, Admiral." He leaned over the plot and chalked a straight line from Pearl Harbor to a spot northeast of Midway where he made an "X" and scrawled: Point Luck.

Admiral Bill Halsey was out of bed and standing at the window where he was trying to focus his field glasses on the shipyards beyond the hospital grounds. There was a palm tree dead center in his view, and the damn thing kept swaying like a hula skirt in slow motion. He muttered: "Son of a bitch! . . ." Then he shouted: "Nurse!"

To his surprise, the door opened immediately. He turned to roar out an order and found himself looking into the mild, tanned face of Admiral Ray Spruance.

"Ray! . . ."

"Bill . . ."

Spruance was looking at him as if he was deciding whether or not to send for a couple of orderlies and a straitjacket. Halsey suddenly felt foolish and realized what a ridiculous figure he made in his skimpy hospital gown with all the chalky-pink lotion smeared over his skin, head to toe. He felt obliged to explain: "I was just about to ask the nurse to go out there . . . I mean, to have somebody go out there and chop down that Goddamn tree. It's blocking my view of the shipyard . . ."

Spruance kept staring at him. "How do you feel?"

Halsey padded back to his bed and climbed in. "Great. Can't sleep. Can't eat, just spend twenty-four hours a day scratching at myself. You ever have an oatmeal bath? Don't."

Spruance kept staring and Halsey waved him to a chair.

"Sit down, for Christ's sake, and stop gawking at me."

"Bill, I haven't got much time. I just came by to thank you for recommending me to take over your task force. Then I want to ask you a question—"

"No need to thank me," Halsey replied brusquely. "Now what was your question?"

Spruance said it with an absolutely straight face: "Did the itch go to your head?"

Despite the discomfort it caused him, Halsey cracked a grin. "Stop underestimating yourself. Any skipper who could keep all those cruisers and destroyers alongside my carriers from one end of the Pacific to the other is definitely the man for the job."

Spruance said quietly: "Thanks. I think. But Nimitz is not so certain as you seem to be."

"What the hell makes you think that?"

"I'm a cruiser sailor, Bill. That's my specialty."

"So? . . ."

"We're so different, you and I."

"Be grateful for that."

"Will I be able to pull it off as well as you could have?"

Halsey scratched furiously at his stomach: it was giving him hell. He said between groans and snorts:

"Listen. The only thing I can tell you is to play it the way *you* feel it—not the way you think *I'd* have played it. Go to sea—find Yamamoto—and chew his ass. Now that's all there's to it."

Spruance nodded and smiled gravely. "All right, Bill. I'll do just that. Thanks again and good-bye for now—"

He extended his hand. Halsey almost took it, but jerked back at the last instant and roared: "You damn fool! You want to catch what I got? You want us to lose the son of a bitch war?!"

Spruance grinned, flicked a little salute, and went out to take over his new command.

12

The Japanese fleet had run into heavy fog soon after it entered the open waters of the central Pacific, and it was causing Admiral Yamamoto grave concern. His ships could not use visual signals—the kind least likely to be intercepted by the enemy—to keep in their carefully-planned formations, and on their correct courses.

The fog had come down unexpectedly, blown in from the northeast.

Above it, Yamamoto's spotter planes could look down only on a dense, clammy mass that smothered the water like a gelatinous shroud, beneath which their shipmates were groping, completely hidden. A hundred warships in close and perilous formation forced their great prows through the dark water, maintaining their positions only by the expertise of the navigators. The awesome fear of collision was on everyone's mind.

The Imperial weather bureau, never the most competent of prognosticators, had indicated clear skies and excellent visibility all the way to the target area. But now the fleet was crawling ahead at reduced speed, which would be difficult to make up if, and when, the fog ever cleared.

From the beginning, a certain perverse fate seemed to dog the Imperial Navy.

First of all, in spite of the fact that the crews had been supplied with heavy winter uniforms to bolster the myth that their objective was the Kurile Islands in the frigid North Pacific, it seemed that all of Japan—certainly Hiroshima—knew that the real target was Midway. There had been many leaks in the elaborate screen of security that Yamamoto and his staff had flung around the operation, sometimes of an almost incredible nature.

Frequently, among the *bonzais* shouted by the thousands who jammed the Inland Sea in their small boats to give encouragement to the men on board the great warships, had been heard the word *"Midway."*

And worse, only a few days before the sailing, a routine, administrative question concerning a problem of the most trivial nature, had been sent over the radio in the *clear*. It was the bureaucratic query: Where should the mail be forwarded for the men aboard the armada?

And the question had been answered, also in the clear: *Midway* . . .

So much effort had gone into planning the deceptive appearance of a major strike to the cold north; yet *everyone* seemed to know the truth about the real objective.

If the simple fisherfolk in the Bay of Hiroshima knew, if half of the country's population was waiting for Midway's capture, could it be that the enemy was still unaware of what was happening?

American submarines were known to be operating off the coast of Japan, shadowing the movements of the Imperial fleet. Although, thus far, they had refrained from attack, because their mission was simply to track and report on the disposition of Yamamoto's warships, the danger of a wolf-pack torpedo attack, such as the Germans were employing to ravage Allied shipping in the North Atlantic, was always there. Yamamoto was so keenly aware of it that he had adopted a circular formation with Rear Admiral Kimura leading the way in the flagship of his screening force, the *Nagara,* with four carriers behind her surrounded by two wide circles of screening cruisers and destroyers.

The great convoy was zigzagging its way on a generally southeastern course at a speed of eighteen knots, driving into the dark wall of thick fog in which the mournful sounds of the warning horns seemed to lose all their identity.

Without visual help, and visual signals, there was no way of knowing if the fleet was still in its formation, if the destroyers were maintaining their correct positions. Each time a vessel swung round to port or to starboard, there was simply no assurance of any kind that another vessel was not immediately in its path.

And how, in this murk, could anyone hope to see any telltale signs of the shadowing submarines? Where were they?

How could the scouting planes ever hope to see *anything* down there?

It was a miracle that they were able to take off from their carriers at all; a greater miracle—a result of their rigorous training—that having taken off, they could be recovered.

The danger of collision was appalling; imminent chaos seemed almost certain; and when the moment came for the scheduled splitting up of the convoy into its varied arms, Admiral Nagumo, commanding the first carrier striking force, decided on a reckless gamble that could have been disastrous. He broke radio silence with the *Akagi*'s low-powered radio transmitter in order to signal the other vessels of his first carrier striking force to change to the final course that would take them directly to Midway. Fortunately, luck was with him. The vital message was not intercepted by either the American land-based monitoring stations or by the enemy submarines which were believed to be shadowing the Imperial fleet.

But the good fortune of the Japanese armada was diluted by a number of foulups. For some reason, news of the scrubbing of the reconnaissance mission to Pearl Harbor by the Kawanishi flying boats had not yet been passed on by Tokyo, and Yamamoto was still under the impression that he would soon be armed with the certain knowledge of the whereabouts of the American aircraft carriers.

In addition, Yamamoto was positive that the *Yorktown* was so badly damaged, if not actually sunk, that she could not possibly take part in the battle for Midway.

Yamamoto was operating under a cloud of ignorance as murky as the fog which shrouded his vessels. On board the *Yamato,* he prowled the battle room like a caged animal, listening to the murmured reports of the staff officers as they moved the model ships on the plot table. Overhead, the drone of the escorting planes was reaching him even here. They were flying so low that they seemed to be brushing the superstructures of the great ships.

He stopped and stared at the models, wondering if the various elements of his fleet were actually in the positions and on the courses plotted. Far out on his left flank, Hosogaya's northern force had split into its triple attack groups, one heading for Attu, one for Kiska, and the third making a wide sweep to the east before turning north for the final dash to Dutch Harbor. He noted that Nagumo's first carrier striking force had just made its third course change to east-northeast, precisely on schedule and that Kondo's occupation force was well on its way from Guam, together with the cruiser and destroyer force of Rear Admiral Kurita's support group.

Everything, it seemed, was as it should be. Despite the foul weather, despite the prowling enemy submarines, despite the appalling lack of security, and despite his ignorance of the whereabouts of the American aircraft carriers.

But was it? Actually, he had no certain knowledge that anything he saw on the elaborate battle plot was accurate.

Surprise was one of the key elements in the battle plan which the young, erratic "God of Operations," Captain Kuroshima, had conceived. To assure that surprise, the entire armada was sailing under strict radio silence. Positions, speed, course changes, fuel consumption, weather information—none of these vital facts could be transmitted by his captains to each other or to their Commander in Chief; nor could he contact them. Each of them was entirely on his own, with only a set of orders for guidance.

A flash of regret crossed Yamamoto's mind. He remembered when Operation MI had first been handed to him by Kuroshima. He had questioned the necessity of absolute radio silence in the vast reaches of the Central Pacific. He had felt the risks outweighed the possible advantage of surprise. But Kuroshima had been adamant, and in the end Yamamoto had conceded the point. Now he doubted the wisdom of that concession.

Suddenly he was aware that the sounds of patroling spotter planes had receded into silence. He turned to Watanabe and asked: "The *Hosho* . . . Is she still sending up her air patrols?"

Watanabe nodded. "Yes, sir. They're fanning out now, looking for a break in the weather."

Yamamoto stared at the plot for a moment and then said: "It's a little difficult to believe what I see here, Watanabe—that all our skippers have held exactly to their positions and courses in this filthy weather."

"Our navigators are the best in the world, Admiral. I have no doubt that the situation is precisely as the plot shows."

"And is your optimism shared by the other officers?"

"It is indeed, sir. And down to the lowest enlisted rating."

Watanabe could see that his admiral still had reservations and it disturbed him. He said: "With respect, sir, we have not acquired the habit of defeat. Our entire history, with a few rare exceptions, is one of victory piled on victory."

Yamamoto kept his silence as he turned away. Watanabe hurried to open the door for him, glancing at the admiral's disquieted expression. Yamamoto caught his young aide's anxious look and smiled. "I'll be in my cabin, Watanabe. Have the steward send in some tea."

"Yes, sir."

Watanabe closed the door behind him and rang for a steward. Then he moved back to the battle plot and studied it, and wondered just what was there that seemed to be distressing his Commander in Chief so deeply.

As he pondered the plot, a young officer began moving submarine models onto their screening stations—a sweeping picket line half way between Pearl Harbor and Midway, lying directly across the route on which Nimitz would have to send his aircraft carriers when he learned that Midway was the real target of the Imperial fleet.

Watanabe heard a second young officer say in a low tone of voice: "That can't be. Our submarine screen isn't due on station for another twelve hours."

"No. Tonight. Look at the timetable." The first officer indicated an entry on the operations timetable, and the second officer asked: "Did they confirm that they have reached their stations?"

"They can't. Like the rest of us, they're under radio silence—" Then he grinned and added pointedly: "Until one of them sights the American fleet coming through."

Huddled in his greatcoat, Admiral Yamamoto paced the flying bridge of his flagship, the *Yamato,* the most powerful battlewagon in the world. The tea he had taken in his cabin had soured his stomach, and the miasmal fog which still enveloped his ship served only to deepen his disquieted mood.

Watanabe waited nearby, ready to spring to his admiral's command, and wishing for some order or errand which would take him away from the funereal atmosphere of the flying bridge. But none came and he tried to content himself with thoughts of Kure, his home on the southwest coast of the lustrously beautiful Hiroshima Bay. He saw himself crouching opposite his father, balancing precariously on the skeletal bamboo framework of their long raft from which were hung hundreds of flat cages containing growing oysters. His father was hauling up one of the cages and muttering that in the seven years which it took for an oyster to produce a pearl of suitable size and quality to be of any value, he would have raised and lowered its cage half the distance to the nearest planet. Then his father had looked up and flashed him a smile through teeth broken in the early years of brawling with fellow pearl farmers over the choice raft locations in the bay.

He recalled that day when he opened a mature oyster, which looked no different or more promising than the hundreds of others they had harvested, and found a pearl of such size and exquisite beauty that he was unable to call out to his father. And he remembered the almost reverent look on his father's face as the old man gently lifted the gem from the flesh of its host.

Watanabe's reverie was broken by a movement inside the bridge house. A communications officer had rushed in and handed Kuroshima a dispatch. Through the moisture-streaked window he saw Kuroshima scan it and frown, obviously troubled by its contents. Then the "God of Operations" straightened his uniform and came out onto the flying bridge, his expression icily composed.

Kuroshima saluted and handed Yamamoto the dispatch, saying, "A dispatch just picked up from Tokyo, sir. They report a sudden increase in coded radio traffic at Pearl Harbor. Especially among patrol planes."

Watanabe was alarmed. He said: "Patrol planes! . . . The kind of communications that go with a big fleet movement."

"Or a big training exercise," Kuroshima replied flatly.

"Perhaps," Watanabe conceded. "But if Americans have discovered our intentions—"

Kuroshima cut in: "Unlikely. Highly unlikely, Commander."

Watanabe turned to Yamamoto who was still pondering the meaning of the dispatch. He said, "Nevertheless, Admiral, your carrier strike force should be alerted. Admiral Nagumo should be warned."

Without hesitation, Yamamoto said: "See to it, Captain Kuroshima." Then he turned back to his brooding at the rail.

Kuroshima hesitated, an argument on the tip of his tongue. But he decided against openly opposing his admiral's orders and returned to the communications officer, who was waiting inside the bridge house. Kuroshima dismissed him: "No action."

The communications officer couldn't believe he had heard correctly. "Sir? . . ."

"We can't risk breaking radio silence. In any event, our carrier strike force undoubtedly picked up this information directly."

"But, Captain, if they didn't—"

Kuroshima cut him short, his crisply officious tone closing the discussion. "Whatever the Americans are up to, our reconnaissance flying boats will tell us the moment they overfly Pearl Harbor, which should be any hour now."

"Yes, sir." The communications officer saluted and left the bridge. Kuroshima crumpled the dispatch and buried it in his pocket.

13

Haruko Sakura was walking slowly along the inside of the high wire fence surrounding the detention area. On the other side, hands thrust into his pockets, head down, Tom Garth was pacing with her, grappling with the intolerable pronouncement she had just made. The words had been simple and straight to the point. He could reject them. He did reject them. But it was her cold, flat tone which had stunned him to the point of speechlessness.

When he finally was able to respond, he shook his head and said: "I just don't believe it, Haruko. You're too damned independent to take 'no' from your parents, or from anybody else."

She would not meet his eye. "It's the truth, Tom. They will not allow this marriage. I have to obey them . . ."

"But why, for God's sake? In one breath you tell me you're a one hundred percent American, and with the next you're saying you have to respect honorable parents' wishes . . ."

There was an edge of derision in his voice and she

shot him a startled look. He was instantly contrite. "I'm sorry. But you don't have to obey anybody."

She did not reply and he went on: "Okay. They'll be upset . . . angry with us, but they'll get over it. Believe me, they will. I wish it could be different. I don't want to offend them any more than you do, but this is *our* life we're talking about, not theirs."

He tried to catch her eye but she would not look at him. He went on, miserably, his words seeming hollow and terribly inadequate. "Look, I understand that they bring part of their culture with them. They should. I accept that. But *they* have to accept part of ours, too. And freedom for a twenty-three-year-old girl to decide her own future is one of the things they have to get used to."

"No, Tom. They can not. They will not."

"Then they'll have to live with it, because I won't give you up, Haruko."

She was very distraught. "You'll have to. There's enough Japanese in me still to . . . to compel me to respect their wishes."

He said angrily: "I don't buy that for a second. It's bullshit."

She answered in a low, taut voice: "They'll be . . . sending us to the mainland soon. I'll stay in a camp there. I'll never see you again, and that's the way it has to be."

"No, it doesn't have to be that way. No!"

"I'm sorry, Tom, I had . . . I had a wonderful feeling of . . . of hope. But it's gone now, all gone."

She still would not look at him. It was as though there were other barriers between them as well as the heavy mesh of the wire. He stopped, forcing her to stop, too. He gripped at the fence and said angrily: "There's something else, isn't there?"

She was trying not to cry. "No, nothing else. Except . . ." He looked at her, waiting, and she stumbled over the words, letting them come out fast and incoherently: "Except that . . . Since I've been here, Tom, cooped up like an animal, I've begun to realize . . . there's . . . there can't be any future for us, any future at all . . ."

"There *has* to be . . ."

"No! It's changed me, Tom, changed me completely. If you could see the way the guards look at us, the suspicion on their faces, the contempt they have for us, the hatred . . . It's forcing me apart from everything American, forcing me to wonder about my own country, wonder how its people can be so . . . so hateful. I'm no different than I was six months ago, when I had so many Caucasian friends! . . . But all that is changed now, and it's changed me too. I feel it! I know that even if I were to get out of here, if we could still . . . still go ahead with our plans, we'd have this terrible hatred and suspicion all around us, and what sort of life would that be for us?"

He was shocked. "As the wife of an American naval officer . . ."

She interrupted him. "That would only make it worse, for you."

He let the tension drain out of him, and said quietly: "All right, let's accept the fact that it won't be easy for either of us. Is that reason enough for us to break up?"

"Yes. It has to be." Her voice was very small.

"Then look at me."

She could not. She said miserably: "I wish you'd go now. Please, Tom? . . ."

"Look at me."

She still kept her face turned away. "Please go, Tom?"

He said stubbornly: "When I hear you say you don't love me."

She took a long, deep breath. "All right. I don't love you. It was a mistake and it's all over now." There was a terrible catch in her voice.

"To my face. Your eyes on mine, Haruko."

The tears were welling in her eyes, and he said angrily: "Tell me to my face, damn it!"

He saw her shaking her head, her eyes still averted. Then she turned slowly to look up at him and tried to speak, but the words would not come; there were only the tears, now tracking down her face.

She clutched at the fence and tried to fight them

back. She could not, and he reached a finger through the mesh and touched her cheek, very gently.

And suddenly she was throwing herself against the mesh, reaching out toward him, trying to get her arms about him, pressing herself against his body, trying to kiss him, crying openly now with bittersweet relief.

He said: "My God, you scared me . . ."

And then, they were both laughing, like a pair of carefree children.

The Officers Club was bright, and cheerful, and noisy.

It was as though once the heavy blackout drapes were drawn, the world out there, the world of anxiety, of tension, was effectively dismissed and replaced by the pleasures of rest and relaxation.

Commander Carl Jessop, in from Kaneohe, was with a group of other senior officers at the end of the bar, a large bourbon and water clenched in his hand. He was gesticulating with it, a trifle unsteady on his feet, though he'd only had four drinks all night.

He was saying, addressing anyone who would listen to him: ". . . and you know? I've been away from base . . . what is it?" He checked his watch. "Less than twelve hours, and I'm already beginning to feel antsy. Can't get it out of my head that my exec doesn't know what side is up, that everything's falling apart, and here I am getting drunker by the minute. Oh, I've got a helluva long way to go yet, but sweet Jesus Christ, I'm gonna get there before this night is over—" Jessop's roving eye fixed on someone across the room. His face lit up in a big, watermelon grin. Matt Garth had just come in and he was delighted to see him. He hurried to meet Matt, his hand outstretched. He said: "Hey! . . . *Matt!* For God's sake! . . ."

"Carl! How are you? What're you doing off your station?"

"How am I? Shitty. I'm fifty-three and trying to celebrate the fact. It's my birthday, I regret to say."

Matt grinned. "Well we all have that problem. Once a year, on the average. Why don't we find somewhere to sit. Your deck's rolling."

Jessop lifted his glass. "It sure as hell is, Matt. Would you believe that this is my first R and R since Pearl? Honest to God."

"I'll tell the admiral you're unhappy."

"And overworked, old buddy."

They found seats at the end of the long bar, and Jessop said, sighing, remembering: "Listen, right now I'd swap every one of these damned stripes for the days when we were aviation cadets together."

"My God, that was a century ago!"

"Sure as hell feels like it, especially when I've had a belt of fuddle water. Can't hold it the way I used to, Matt. I get sloppy. Sentimental. Used to wanna knock knuckles with the nearest shore patrol, or play grab-ass with the nearest female. Remember?"

"Indeed I do. In my nightmares."

"Well, didn't we manage to stay out of the brig, old buddy? Uh? Didn't we?"

"Barely."

Jessop stared at his glass, then finished it off, and passed it over the bar for a refill. He turned to Matt and laughed suddenly. "Hey! Remember that blonde with the beauty mark between first and second base?"

Matt joined the laughter and said: "I'll never forget her as long as I live. Which one was that?"

"The one who thought an endless belt was a night out with a navy man . . ."

"Ah, that one. Yes I remember her. In my worst nightmares."

"Yeah, and if I hadn't hauled your dumb ass out of that courthouse, you'd have married that broad."

"Funny, I thought *I* hauled *your* ass."

"Well now, maybe you did at that . . ." Jessop roared with laughter.

The bartender was splashing drinks into their glasses. Matt raised his. "To your fifty-third, Carl."

"Yeah. Fuck you, too." Jessop grinned sourly as he clinked glasses with his old friend.

"How do you like it down there in Kaneohe?"

"Liked it a helluva lot better when you and I were flying together, Matt, off the old Langley out of San Diego. But . . . well, we've got a lot of bright young kids coming in . . . Your son is one of the best of the crop, Matt. I've assigned him to VF-8 Squadron."

"How's Tom behaving, Carl? He always bucked discipline when he was a kid."

"No problem. He's four-oh."

"That's good to hear."

Suddenly Jessop seemed to realize what they were talking about and the grin slipped from his face. He looked back over his shoulder, as though seeking to assure himself of privacy. He lowered his voice and said: "Matt, I've been meaning to get in touch . . . about Tom . . . and this . . . ah . . . girl he's got himself involved with. I mean . . . how do you feel about it? You know . . . this Jap?"

Matt felt himself stiffening; he stared at Jessop coldly, and Jessop threw his arms wide, mistaking the look, and said: "Well, it's no secret. You must know. For God's sake, he's told the whole damn squadron! Christ, he's only a kid, but you'd think he'd have sense enough to keep quiet about a thing like that, wouldn't you?"

Matt said, his voice like an icicle: "I've met her, she seems to me to be a very fine girl . . ."

"What do you mean, a fine girl? For Christ's sake, Matt!"

"Okay. She's a Japanese-American. And it's giving her a helluva lot of trouble just now."

Jessop grunted. "What else? People aren't going to forget December seventh very damn soon."

"We're talking about an *American* citizen, Carl, whose heritage happens to be Oriental . . ."

"Japanese."

"Yes, but she's as loyal as any of us. I'm sure of it. And she's being given a thoroughly bad time by all the . . ." He broke off. "By everyone."

Jessop growled. "You didn't answer my question. How do *you* feel about it?"

Matt did not answer. He was waiting for the anger to die down. And looking at the scowl on Jessop's face he knew that it would not, not yet, anyway. He finished his drink and said quietly: "I have to run, Carl. I'll see you."

He got to his feet, and Carl Jessop gripped his arm and said: "Hey, the scuttlebutt says you're shipping out with the *Yorktown*."

"It does? What the hell ever happened to that phenomenon they used to call security?"

"Hell, Matt, a guy's got to know when his friends are shipping out. Is it true?"

Matt sighed, the anger dissipating. "Yes, it's true. We're just about ready to sail."

"Ready to sail? That's not what I hear. They say the poor old *Yorktown*'s going to be three months in dry-dock, maybe more."

"You'd be surprised what a tough old bastard Nimitz is. What he wants, he gets. And he wants the *Yorktown* out, like yesterday."

"I wish him luck. And I'm gonna envy you, Matt . . . *if* you get her out to sea before the war's over."

His infectious grin was there again, and Matt grinned back at him. "Yes, I guess you will." He said again: "Gotta run."

"Well, keep your dumb ass outta drafts, uh? Remember, you don't have me around to save it for you."

"That's going to concern me a lot."

"And don't worry about your boy, old buddy. I'll look after him."

Matt nodded. "I'd appreciate that, Carl. Just see he doesn't get into too much mischief. Thanks."

He pushed his jeep hard through the early evening Honolulu traffic, heading for the dry-dock where the badly mauled *Yorktown* was being refitted. In the bowels of the giant carrier, he found Admirals Nimitz and Fletcher with an engineering officer—a worried, exhausted man named Delaney. They were making their way through the maze of the engine room, and he looked around aghast at the amount of work that was still to be done.

There were workmen toiling at dozens of different tasks, laboring elbow to elbow in the cramped spaces. It was difficult to believe that so many jobs could be tackled in the same time and space . . . and in the heat and the noise. The temperature was up around a hundred and twenty and the racket from the jackhammers and the riveting was unbelievable.

He followed the two admirals around as they inspected the progress of the work. Nimitz and Fletcher were nodding their approval, pleased with the way it was going, shouting over the deafening cacophony, straining to make themselves heard.

Delaney yelled, cupping his hand to his mouth: "Three of the boilers are still out of commission Admiral. The yardmanager says he'll need another two days."

Nimitz yelled back: "You tell Mr. Gillette that I expect him to finish tomorrow at oh-six hundred. By that time, I want every workman off the ship. I want her ready to sail. Oh-six hundred, Mr. Delaney. Understood?"

"Yes, sir."

They walked in single file along a narrow gangplank, and made their way up the long ladders to the decks above them, where the welders were closing up the great, gaping bomb holes. It was good to breathe fresh air again, to escape from the monstrous roar of the jackhammers. They found they were still shouting, an automatic reflex.

Worried, harried, Delaney saluted. "Anything else, Admiral? If not . . . I'll get back below."

"That's where you belong, Mr. Delaney."

"Yes, sir."

Delaney hurried off, and Nimitz turned to Fletcher, he said crisply: "I'm sorry about those three boilers, Jack. It's going to slow you down. But if you clear Pearl by oh-seven hundred, you'll still make your rendezvous with *Enterprise* and *Hornet* before Yamamoto hits Midway."

"Agreed."

"You'll have only one hour to get underway. We've got to give Gillette every minute we can."

"Then one hour will have to be enough."

"Good, that's what I like to hear." Nimitz shot out a hand. "I wish you good luck. And good hunting."

"Thank you, sir."

Nimitz turned to Matt. "And you too, Matt. See you back here soon."

"Aye, aye, sir."

Matt saluted, and stood by the rail to watch the admiral leave. All he could do now was wait.

14

The last of Yardmaster Gillette's welders and ship-fitters were dragging their heavy cables and gear off the great carrier when the young flyers posted to duty aboard the *Yorktown* began arriving, carrying their parachute bags and other luggage. They were all in their early twenties, with faces as scrubbed and fresh as their uniforms. They were told that their quarters were not ready yet: there was still frantic cleanup activity belowdecks. But they were already beginning to feel that they were a part of this giant carrier, rising like a phoenix after it's miraculous escape from disaster.

Matt Garth was watching the gangplank, mentally recording the personalities of the youngsters, watching for alert eyes, for eager looks, for that decisive walk and bearing which evidenced pride and confidence.

He was astonished when he recognized his son Tom waiting in the line to present his credentials to the OD. He hurried toward him.

Tom saluted smartly and said, with biting politeness: "Nice of you to take the time to see me off, Dad."

Matt took him by the arm and drew him away from the others, out of earshot. "Tom, what the hell are you doing with this air group? Your squadron isn't due out for another month!"

Tom gave him a bitter smile. "You're asking me, sir?"

"Yes, I'm asking you!"

"My orders, sir."

"Your orders? Let me see them."

He held out his hand. Tom took them from his pocket and handed them over, standing stiffly at attention and waiting. Matt read through them.

He said tightly: "When did you get these?"

"Just in time to pack my gear and get aboard." The smile was there again, sardonic and mocking. "You're not really surprised, are you? Your old buddy Carl Jessop could hardly wait to have me transferred. All it took was one phone call. There's nothing he wouldn't do for you, is there?"

Matt was stunned. "Tom, I didn't know . . ."

The boy interrupted him hotly. "The hell you didn't! You wanted me shipped out before I could . . . how did you put it? Before I could do anything stupid. Like keeping my girl from being sent to the mainland . . . to prison! So, your old pal Jessop obliged."

Matt kept his voice low. "Tom, for God's sake, I had nothing whatever to do with it!"

"You didn't speak to him? . . ."

"Yes. At the Senior Officers Club. It was . . . it was a chance meeting. I hardly mentioned your name. I just asked if . . ."

He broke off, remembering. All he could do was raise his hands helplessly and keep talking, knowing that his explanation sounded lame and contrived. "Tom, listen to me, for Christ's sake! I saw Jessop, yes. He's here on R and R. I did what any father would. I asked him to keep an eye on you. Sure, he'd been talking about . . . about you and Haruko, and I guess mistakenly thought that . . ."

Tom interrupted him, savagely: "Forget it, Dad. The damage is done. You've succeeded in stopping me from doing anything stupid. And that's all you've wanted all along, isn't it?" Saluting stiffly, he said with finality, "I have to report to the OD now, sir. If you'll excuse me."

He turned on his heel and walked away.

Matt watched him, a feeling of acute pain at the pit of his stomach. He stood there, deep in thought for a long moment, wondering how he would be able to reach his son again. His mind thrashing for an answer, he remembered an old friend who might just be able to help. It was a long shot, and maybe foolish, perhaps even dangerous. But he made up his mind instantly, went to his cabin, picked up the file on Haruko, then hurried past the waiting line of young flyers and on down the gangway. He caught a shuttle out to the main gate and jumped into one of the taxicabs waiting there. As he sat back in the seat, he thought about his old friend—the only man who could help him now.

But was he still his friend?

Once they had been quite close; but that was many years ago. They had drifted apart, and his old Annapolis classmate was an admiral now, with a reputation for being tough and mean as a cornered weasel. He tried to think of how best to phrase the question he would ask, but when the cab drove up outside the building of CINCPAC Naval Intelligence, he still hadn't worked it out. He paid off the cabbie, took a deep breath and went inside.

The Head of Naval Intelligence, Admiral Harry Pearson, was stuffing a briefcase full of papers to take home to work on during the evening.

Matt stared at him in surprise; he had aged. The eyes were still as sharp and as shrewd as ever, but the face was deeply etched with lines of apprehension and fatigue, the lips tighter than he remembered them, the set of the jaw more firm and jutting.

But Pearson was obviously both surprised and pleased to see Matt. He grasped his hand warmly, as though he, too, were looking for friendship in a world that was suddenly devoid of it.

He said, beaming: "Hey there, Matt. For God's sake! . . . How the hell are you?"

"I'm fine, Harry. And you? You look great, just great."

"Bullshit. I look lousy. I feel lousy. I am lousy. This bloody job is a killer, Matt."

"I guess you have got your hands full . . ."

"And then some, Mister. Believe me. Say, I hear you're up for another stripe and a command to match it."

Matt smiled and shrugged. "I'll believe it when it happens."

"Take it from me, it's true and you deserve it. Oh, I've followed your career. I like to keep an eye on my old classmates, even if I don't see much of them anymore."

"It has been a long time, Harry."

"Too goddamn long. Listen. I'm on my way home. Gotta pile of work to plough through, but there's no reason why we can't stop for a drink someplace and snow each other about how good the old days were. Uh? What do you say?"

He was moving like a cyclone, sweeping up papers from his desk and thrusting them into his dispatch case.

Matt shook his head. He said, very carefully: "I'm sorry, Harry. I'd like that very much. But by the time I've finished what I have to say, I've a suspicion you're not going to feel like taking me for a drink."

Pearson grinned. "Bad as that, is it? Well, say on. I've got a mighty tough hide, or I wouldn't be in this stinking job."

Matt perched himself on the edge of the desk. "No good beating about the bush, I guess. Harry, I'm going to have to do something I've never done before. At least, not since we left Annapolis. I'm going to have to ask you a favor."

Pearson spread his hands wide. The smile was wide and inviting: only the eyes seemed out of kilter—wary, expectant, more than a trifle suspicious. "Is that all? Well ask away, Matt. A favor? Lord knows, I owe you a few, if only from the old days."

Matt dug into his briefcase and pulled out the FBI report he had shown to Tom. He held it out for Pearson and said steadily: "It's an FBI report. One of their enemy-alien reports, Harry."

Pearson stared at him. "And how did *you* get your hands on it, Matt? Those things are top-secret."

Matt shook his head. "Never mind how . . . I got it."

There was a moment of silence. The atmosphere had changed. The smile was still there, but it was no longer open and frank; not forced, exactly, but no longer genuine either.

"Matt, I could find out easily enough."

THE BATTLE OF
MIDWAY

THE STARS

**Charlton Heston as
Captain Matt Garth**

**Henry Fonda as
Admiral Chester W. Nimitz**

**James Coburn as
Captain Vinton Maddox**

**Glenn Ford as Rear Admiral
Raymond A. Spruance**

Hal Holbrook as
Commander Joseph J. Rochefort

© UNIVERSAL PICTURES

Toshiru Mifune as
Admiral Isoroku Yamamoto

© UNIVERSAL PICTURES

Robert Mitchum as
Commander Carl Jessop

Robert Wagner as
Lt. Commander Ernest Blake

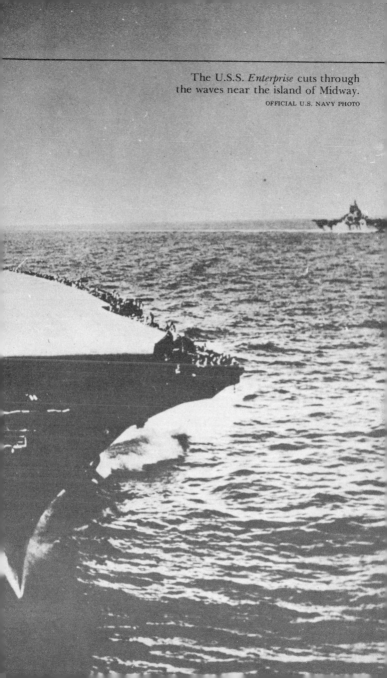

The U.S.S. *Enterprise* cuts through
the waves near the island of Midway.

OFFICIAL U.S. NAVY PHOTO

SBD Dauntlesses in attack formation.

A squadron of Devastator torpedo bombers waits for take-off from the deck of the *Enterprise*.

The sky above Midway is filled with TBF Avengers.

June 3, 1942:
U.S. Marines land on Midway Island.
OFFICIAL U.S. NAVY PHOTO

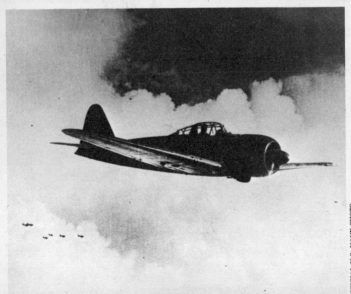

A Japanese Zero seeks prey.

OFFICIAL U.S. NAVY PHOTO

Japanese planes successfully bomb Midway.

Flak fills the sky as the battle continues.

A wisp of smoke marks the end of this Japanese plane.

The U.S.S. *Hornet* is attacked by
Japanese torpedo planes and dive bombers.

The U.S.S. *Yorktown* is bombed.

Fires ravage the *Yorktown*'s decks
as firefighters, without enough
water pressure to fill their hoses,
watch hopelessly.

The maimed *Yorktown* lists forlornly.

A Japanese cruiser of the *Mogami* class,
demolished by the planes of Task Force 16.

June 4, 1942:
the U.S.S. *Yorktown* goes down.

The Japanese carrier *Akagi* maneuvers
in circles to confuse her pursuers.

June 6, 1942:
an American F4F returns to its
flight deck after the battle has been won.

OFFICIAL U.S. NAVY PHOTO

"Don't, Harry."

Pearson held Matt's eyes. He was acutely aware that something was coming that neither of them was going to like. He opened the file and studied it quickly, flipping the pages over and shaking his head in disbelief.

Finally, he growled: "I can't understand how you managed to get your hands on it . . ."

Matt said calmly: "I've been through it word for word. It's everything the bureau's got on an American citizen named Haruko Sakura—and her parents. There's absolutely nothing detrimental there to any of them."

Pearson stared at him in utter dismay. He dropped the file down on the desk, and he let his anger explode. "You're way out of line, Matt! This isn't your department, and that makes it . . . *tampering*. What are these people to you?"

"Someday, maybe, the girl will be my daughter-in-law."

Pearson's voice was like tempered steel: "I wish I hadn't heard that, Matt. But I did, and so I'll tell you. It's not only tampering, but it's also pressing a superior officer to take highly improper actions—for personal reasons. Good God, can't you see how serious that is?"

Matt gripped the edge of the desk with both hands and leaned across to Pearson, his voice taut and husky with the feeling of outrage welling up in his throat. "Improper action, hell, Harry! I've studied that report. I've checked it twenty ways from the middle! Those people are no more a threat to our national security than . . . than your pet Airedale!"

There was a long, oppressive silence. Then Matt said quietly: "Help me, Harry. Please?"

Pearson went over to the window and stared down at the busy street. He said slowly: "Do you know what I hear from Washington, Matt? I'm not supposed to tell you, and if I didn't think you knew already, I wouldn't. But the word is that you're just on the brink of getting your own carrier command. Did you know that?"

"Yes. Yes, I'd heard."

"And you're willing to sacrifice that . . . for this?"

"If I have to, yes."

"Because . . . and you must know this, too. I'll have to report this request of yours."

Matt's voice was very steady. "Yes, I know that. That was a risk I had to take."

"A very considerable risk, in view of the damage it can do you! And you were still prepared to go out on a limb like this?"

"If I don't help my son, I'll lose him. I lost my wife . . . and I'll lose him, too. Believe me, Harry. Forever!"

Pearson said impatiently: "Your request *has* to go into your record, and I can't, offhand, think of *anything* more likely, more certain, to jeopardize your whole future."

He swung around. "Your whole future, Matt! Up in flames because of some goddamn nonsense over a Japanese girl! Over a suspected collaborator! It can destroy you!"

"I'm aware of that."

"A carrier command means so little to you?"

"It means everything in the goddamn world, of course it does! But my son . . . he's got to come first."

Pearson threw up his arms in a gesture of futility. "I can't believe this! You're actually putting your career on the line by asking me to take action that you know bloody well is highly improper. And worse, you're presuming on our friendship, goddamn it, to get this underhanded little piece of business done. I won't have it, Matt!"

Matt made one last desperate attempt. "You know . . . that I'd never ask you to do this if it were for me personally, you must know that. I'm asking . . . because it's for my kid. Hell, Harry, I'm *begging!*"

Pearson turned away again.

He let out a long, long sigh. He said reluctantly: "All right, Matt, I'll investigate. Now get the hell out of my office. And you're right, I don't feel like buying you a drink."

"Thank you, Harry."

Pearson said nothing; he wouldn't even turn around.

Matt Garth went out, and made his way back to the *Yorktown*.

15

The admiral's cabin on board the flagship *Yamato* was somewhat larger than he thought necessary, but it was beautifully fitted with furniture of the finest piled teak that reflected the yellow light of the lamps, and he found great pleasure merely in contemplating the chiaroscuro of light and dark there.

He sat in the special chair that had been brought on board from his house in Hiroshima, and sipped his favorite green tea, and thought calmly and rationally about the coming battle.

The fog had cleared, and the weather was bright and calm. And the great convoy was moving on to its destination, all the ships once more in visual contact with each other, all in their assigned positions and speeding now on a course that was roughly northeast.

Nagumo's first carrier striking force was on a parallel course, eighty miles to the northwest of his own line of ships, and word had been received that Kondo's occupation force was well on its way from Guam, heading almost exactly northeast, together with Kurito's support force; both these columns were exactly on schedule; soon they would be swinging east for the final drive on Midway.

The minesweepers from Saipan had already passed the danger area, the waters around Wake Island where American submarines were known to have moved in, and were now swinging to the northeast to meet up with the other two convoys.

Yamamoto's doubts were beginning to disappear. Now that the battle was near, he was beginning to feel the exhilaration that was so prevalent among his junior officers and enlisted men.

He had just finished his second little cup of green tea when Watanabe came hurrying in. He saluted and said: "Admiral . . . Captain Kuroshima respectfully requests that you come to the battle room as soon as it's convenient."

Yamamoto got to his feet. He was studying Watanabe's boyish face, wondering whether the concern there meant that Kuroshima's news was bad. He decided he would not ask him. He said quietly: "I'll come at once, Watanabe."

He hurried out with his aide and went quickly down the long gray passageway to the battle room.

Captain Kuroshima, frowning, was staring down at the plot. An aide was erasing a line that went from Kwajalein to French Frigate Shoal, and as the admiral came in, the captain saluted and said: "I'm afraid we have some rather puzzling news, sir."

The aide was removing the little models of the Kawanishi flying boats and the tanker submarine. Yamamoto looked at the captain and said sharply: "Operation K? What went wrong?"

Kuroshima said coolly: "We have just received a dispatch from Tokyo. The overflight of Pearl Harbor by our seaplanes has been canceled."

"Canceled!" He could not believe it. "But why?"

Kuroshima shook his head. "It's not very clear, but it seems . . . there was some question that they might be discovered. There was an American vessel of some sort at the shoals."

He still could not hide his dismay. "And if there was? Couldn't they have moved to Necker Island? Or to Nihoa? Or to Gardner? Who gave the orders for cancelation?"

"Presumably it came direct from Tokyo, sir."

"And they couldn't have consulted me first?"

Kuroshima gestured. "An answer from us would have meant breaking radio silence, Admiral."

Watanabe saw that the admiral was furious, and he knew what he was thinking.

He said slowly: "The message was sent directly to us, Admiral, to the flagship. The urgent question, therefore, is . . . did Admiral Nagumo also pick it up?"

Yamamoto turned for the answer to Kuroshima, but he kept his silence, preferring to let Watanabe make his argument first, knowing what the aide's advice would be.

Watanabe went on: "Sir, you will recall Admiral Yamaguchi's concern about the *Akagi*'s inadequate radio antenna system . . . and his advice that your flagship, which has the most powerful radio equipment in the Imperial fleet, operate directly with Admiral Nagumo's carrier strike force . . ."

"Yes, yes, Watanabe . . ." Yamamoto said impatiently.

"Sir, because we picked up Tokyo's warning, does not guarantee that Admiral Nagumo did."

Yamamoto threw up his hands. "Then Nagumo will assume that Operation K is going forward as planned. If he hears nothing . . . he will assume that the result of that operation is positive—that the American fleet is safely out of the way in Pearl Harbor."

"Where our latest intelligence reports," Kuroshima said, "have placed it."

Yamamoto snapped: "What intelligence reports? Have our submarines sighted the American fleet in the past twenty-four hours?"

"No, sir, they have not."

"Then we're back to where we were when we left port. We don't know if they're in Pearl Harbor, in the Solomons, in the Coral Sea . . . We have no idea where they are."

"With respect, Admiral, there's no reason to assume that . . ."

Yamamoto said angrily: "There is *every* reason to assume that! Our security, from the very beginning of this operation, has been abominable! There wasn't a single person in the whole of Hiroshima who did not know exactly where we were heading! And if the Americans know, too, then instead of our laying a trap for them, they might well be setting a trap for us!"

Kuroshima stuck to his guns. "My original argument, sir, was that Nimitz is crippled and on the defensive. Therefore, he *has* to stay close to his most valuable base, the Hawaiian Islands."

"That argument, Captain, was made *before* our security broke down," Watanabe interjected.

"It was, indeed. But suppose we assume that Nimitz has agents in Hiroshima, and that they reported everything they saw and heard on the day our fleet put to sea . . . he still can't be certain that it was not an elaborate ruse, that the fleet is not headed elsewhere. To the Hawaiian Islands. Or to the Pacific Coast of America. Sir, Nimitz is not a reckless man. He would never send his carriers away from the protection of his long-range, land-based bombers to chase a spy rumor thousands of miles into hostile waters. No, sir, he will wait until the provocation is too great to resist . . . until we attack Midway."

Yamamoto, conscious of Kuroshima's tactical brilliance, was listening to him carefully.

Kuroshima continued: "And when Nimitz responds to our challenge, he will send his most reckless and daring carrier commander . . . Admiral Halsey . . . the kind of foe we can quickly trap and annihilate."

Yamamoto had always been uneasy about the premise that Halsey was certain to rush headlong into disaster at Midway. He said: "You are very certain of Halsey, aren't you, Captain?"

"Indeed I am, sir. I have insinuated myself into his mind. Our profile on him is as complete and detailed as it could possibly be. I know the way he thinks. I know the way he works. I know his weaknesses and his strengths. I know the man totally."

Yamamoto sighed and studied the plot. At length, he said: "If you are correct, Captain Kuroshima, it won't matter whether nor not Nagumo knows that Operation K has been scrubbed. Nevertheless, I would feel easier if we could alert him."

"We must not break radio silence, Admiral. We must not risk letting the enemy know where we are. The element of surprise is one of the most important aspects of our strategy. Just as it was at Pearl Harbor."

Yamamoto nodded. Kuroshima was right, of course. He was right about Nimitz's lack of offensive options and about Halsey's temperament.

But, despite the logic of everything Kuroshima had said, Yamamoto was only partly mollified as he returned to his cabin. And Watanabe, reading his beloved admiral's mind, was deeply disturbed.

Not so Kuroshima.

Satisfied that the cancelation of the French Frigate Shoal operation was nothing more than a nuisance, he turned his attention back to the battle plot.

The mighty convoys were still on their allotted courses. There had been no report of enemy submarines or spotter-plane activity. The central South Pacific was theirs, and theirs alone.

He was satisfied that in its entire immensity, it would soon *all* be theirs.

At CINCPAC headquarters in Pearl Harbor, the battle plot under the tense and meticulous scrutiny of Admiral Nimitz was very much like the one that Admiral Yamamoto was using, but representing, with its miniatures, the opposite side of the picture.

The two plots were like two chessboards, each hidden from the other, on which the pieces were positioned, as the two master players made their deductions, their estimates, and their guesses about the enemy's moves.

Here, on the American board, Admiral Spruance's Task Force 16, the *Enterprise* and the *Hornet,* was halfway to the pinpoint on the chart that had been designated as "Point Luck." Admiral Fletcher's Task Force 17, the *Yorktown,* was making a beeline for the rendezvous to the northeast of Midway, its crippled boilers working overtime to maintain the highest possible speed.

Commander Blake was carefully covering the plot at Midway with a transparent plastic overlay on which had been drawn a search plan to cover a massive arc some seven hundred miles in radius, and embracing the whole of the area to the west of the island through which a Japanese fleet would have to pass.

Blake said: "Here's our best shot, sir. An air search involving twenty-one PBY's. Each plane will fly a spoke seven hundred miles out and cover a sector of eight degrees. That gives us a one hundred and eighty-degree look at anything coming at us from the west. And it still leaves an excellent flanking area northeast of Midway for our carriers."

Admiral Nimitz leaned on the table with both arms, worrying about the 900-mile Japanese submarine cordon that lay outside the search area, a line of them running south from French Frigate Shoal for some four hundred miles, and northeast of them for another five hundred.

He said growling: "You'd think they owned the goddamn Pacific Ocean."

But the area to the west of Midway showed another cordon, a cordon of American submarines waiting for the approaching enemy fleet. Their orders were to lie low and track the Japanese. And with twenty-two twin-engine Catalinas flying their search sectors daily . . .

Nimitz straightened up. "It's a good cover. Have Midway put it into operation immediately."

16

Nearly three thousand miles out into the Pacific Ocean from the nearest stretch of United States continental coastline, somewhat closer to Tokyo and over a thousand miles from the major defenses of Honolulu and Pearl Harbor, the men on Midway Island were digging in for the coming assault.

Barbed wire was being strung along the beaches, great coils of it around the entire perimeters of the twin islands. Bulldozers were piling up huge mounds of sand everywhere. Sandbags were being filled and stacked for revetments. Marines were digging foxholes, scooping out gun emplacements, stringing field telephone wires, setting up communication equipment in the command posts.

The island was a bomber's dream, with every available square foot of land put to use. Hangars, fuel dumps, ammunition dumps, gun emplacements—all were crowded in, cheek by jowl. Every target was dangerously close to all others, and with its massive store of explosives, Midway was a sitting powder-keg.

Major "Red" Parks, commander of Marine Fighter Squadron 221, was checking the breech mechanism of a fighter-plane machine gun which lay on the repair bench of a sandbagged maintenance revetment. Parks had a feel for guns and planes. They were his life, next to actually flying, that is. He had never quite lost the crazy, light-headed sensation of sheer joy that had almost overwhelmed him the first time, years ago, when he took the stick of a trainer at the old Pensacola Naval Air Station. When he thought about it, which wasn't often since the war started, he was a little frightened for fear that someday he would lose that heady feeling and flying would become just another job.

He worked the breech a few times and, satisfied, he turned to the chief aviation mechanic at his side. "Okay, Chief, you can install this one . . ."

Someone shouted: "Attention!" He turned and saw an inspection party approaching, headed by Midway's commanding officer, Navy Captain Cyril T. Simard. Salutes were snapped and Simard said: "I want to talk to you, Major Parks."

"Yes, sir."

"Let's take a walk. The rest of you get on with your work," Simard ordered.

They moved out onto a little beach and skirted the looming barbed-wire barrier. Simard was plainly disturbed and he made no effort to hide it from his Marine colleague. He said: "What's the count, Red?"

"I'll be able to put up half a dozen F4F's, sir. Fifteen . . . maybe sixteen Buffaloes."

"Buffaloes! . . . Bastardly relics! How the hell does CINCPAC expect us to stop the whole damn Jap carrier air force with a handful of obsolete planes that ought to be rusting in some museum?"

Simard took out a cigar and bit off the end. He spit it out but he didn't light up. He chewed the cigar for a moment and then he asked: "You know what we're up against, Red?"

"I've heard rumors."

"Well, I can tell you now . . . a task force of four

first-line aircraft carriers, according to our intelligence boys at Pearl. And that's just a starter. They say the carriers are backed up by an invasion force of battleships and transports carrying five thousand officers and men. And in reserve is Yamamoto himself with more battleships and heavy cruisers and you-name-it."

Simard removed the cigar from his teeth and took a long look at the frayed end. Then he said in a quiet voice: "They mean to kick the shit out of us, Red."

"Is CINCPAC certain about all this, sir?"

"Yes. Don't ask me how, but they're certain."

"Are they sending Halsey's carriers to help us?"

Simard bit down hard on the cigar and said: "When Nimitz was here on his inspection tour, I asked that question. He told me that was information I didn't need to know. He was right, of course, but I sure as hell would like to feel we're not being left to entertain the whole bastardly Jap fleet by ourselves."

Red Parks picked up a seashell and winged it into the lagoon. He could see his CO was fuming, and he wanted to give him a moment to cool down. He said, at length: "When is this bliffer supposed to hit us?"

Simard spat. "That's the maddening part of it. CINCPAC says invasion is imminent. That's all. They claim to know every damned ship in the enemy invasion force, their commanders, their courses, everything . . . but they can't tell me *when* the axe is going to fall."

Nothing ever seemed to stifle Parks's easygoing optimism. Grinning, he said: "I guess we can answer the *when*, Captain. It'll be when they're good and ready to hit us with everything they've got." He picked up another seashell and sailed it at a sitting gull. The bird protested with a harsh squawk and took to the air. He went on: "We'll be ready for them."

"Jesus Christ, Major," Simard spat, "haven't you heard *anything* I've said?"

"Yes, sir. You're worried about how my fly-boys will do in our Buffalo Brewsters."

"You're damn right I am."

"Well, those Buffs are sure as hell obsolete, sir. But as long as we can get them in the air, as long as we can fire their guns, they're fighting planes." He looked Simard in the eye and grinned again. "We'll let the Japs know we're up there, sir. And we might even get lucky."

Captain Simard wished he felt half as confident as Parks sounded. And he wondered if the Marine major really believed what he was saying.

The vast cobalt-blue Pacific Ocean stretched interminably below the PBY Catalina flying boat, mile upon mile upon mile of *nothing*.

"Strawberry Five" had taken off from Midway in the predawn darkness with twenty-three other PBY's to patrol a seven-degree slice of the semicircle extending seven hundred miles to the west of the island. The slow, ponderous, parasol-winged amphibian was flying its assigned sector, the fourth pie-shaped wedge of water in the search plan which Nimitz had ordered to locate the enemy fleet.

Strawberry Five was cruising smoothly on autopilot while Lieutenant Howard Ady and his copilot, Ensign Al Kuhn, were scanning the sea with their binoculars. Kuhn kept glancing at the fuel gauge which showed less than half full. Ady didn't seem a bit concerned. He never worried about such trifles. As long as he was in the air he was totally content. He lowered his glasses and dug his knuckles into his smarting eyes.

Ady said: "For the last hour I've had the crazy feeling we're not moving . . . just hovering over the same patch of water."

"Might as well for all the good we're doing."

"I wonder if the other guys have sighted anything?"

Kuhn didn't respond. His attention was on the fuel gauge again. He said: "Time to turn for home, Howie." He jabbed a forefinger at the gauge.

Ady lowered his glasses, glanced at the gauge, grunted noncommittally and continued to search the sea. After a moment, he leaned forward and said: "Something down there, Al. Seven o'clock."

Kuhn brought his binoculars up and located the object. "Looks like a small boat."

"Let's drop down and check it out."

Ady eased the Catalina down into a slow, lazy circle. Kuhn depressed the intercom switch and spoke to the crew. "There's something below us. Keep your eyes peeled."

The crewmen-gunners responded with an assortment of "Yes, sirs" and "Aye, aye, sirs." Then one of them piped up: "It's a dinghy, Ensign Kuhn. It's empty."

Another voice added: "Off a fishing boat, looks like."

Kuhn was getting more and more edgy about the fuel. He wanted to chill Ady's interest in this sighting, and quickly. He said: "Probably swept overboard in a storm. No telling where. Happens all the time."

Ady continued to study the dinghy. Then, at length, he said: "Yeah . . ." He sighed and lowered his binoculars. "Well, we sure as hell didn't find us a Jap carrier on this run."

He took over the controls from the autopilot and pushed the amphibian into a slow turn, back to the east and Midway Island.

In the cockpit of Strawberry Nine, copilot Ensign Hardeman was chain-eating Graham crackers and dropping crumbs all over his new, tailor-made uniform. He brushed them carelessly off onto his pilot, Lieutenant Jewell "Jack" Reid.

Reid glared at him, his eyes red-rimmed with fatigue. His temper was shorter than usual this day. He said: "Keep your goddamn crumbs off me, Hardeman."

"Sorry, skipper," Hardeman said with an easy grin. Then he added: "Christ! Could I go for a long, cold beer right about now. Damn crackers make me as dry as a maiden witch's teat."

"My God, where do you dig up those cornball similes?"

"That what they are, similes?"

Reid shook his head in utter disgust and went back to searching the vast emptiness of the sea.

Hardeman stowed away the remainder of the crackers and said: "That's what I like about flying with a university-educated man . . . you learn things all the time. Similes. That has a nice, educated sound. Gotta remember it." Then he added: "By the way, if you don't turn for home in the next three minutes, we ain't gonna make it."

Reid glanced at the fuel gauge and saw that his co-pilot was right. He took the controls off autopilot and put the Catalina into a slow turn which would take Strawberry Nine back to Midway Island.

"Okay . . . okay . . . Another day, another joyride!"

Hardeman said: "Do you think they're really coming, Jack?"

"If Nimitz says they're coming, they're coming. What worries me is that we don't have enough of these fat-assed gooney birds to patrol the other side of the island."

In the CINCPAC battle plot room, seven hundred miles away at Pearl Harbor, Admiral Nimitz was sipping cold, black coffee as he worried over the plot. Lieutenant Wold and the battle room personnel watched him, and felt the tension of his apprehension.

Lieutenant Commander Blake entered with the latest dispatch from Midway. "The air-search report, Admiral."

Nimitz turned to Blake, but his unexpressed hope was shattered by Blake's summary: "No sightings, sir."

Nimitz did not take the dispatch Blake held out. He turned back to the plot and said, almost to himself: "Is there *any* defense measure we've overlooked? Anything Midway needs?"

Blake answered: "They've had top priority, Admiral. We've sent them everything we could scrape up . . . tanks, barbed wire, PT boats, antiaircraft guns . . . everything we're able to supply."

The admiral looked up at him and Blake added: "They're about as ready as they'll ever be, sir."

Nimitz nodded and took a sip of his coffee. Blake's smile was wry and deprecatory. He said: "It would be a helluva comfort if we were really *sure* that Midway was where Yamamoto was going."

The admiral grimaced. "After all this planning,

he'd better be." He set down the coffee mug and leaned with both hands on the plot table, his glance fixed on the small spot which represented Midway Island. "Damn! It's miserable to loll around here waiting for an attack on your own people . . . and hoping to hell it happens."

"More pressure from Washington, sir?"

"Suddenly not a whisper. I'd rather have them raising hell."

One of the battle plot staff leaned across the huge table and moved the model which represented the *Yorktown* a bit closer to the rendezvous position northeast of Midway.

Wold, who had been silent for longer than was usual for a young man of his assertive nature, said: "I wonder if she's really on schedule? With three of her boilers out of commission, she'll be lucky to maintain the eighteen knots that we've anticipated."

"She's still under radio silence," Blake said. "Same as *Hornet* and *Enterprise.* So we're not going to know until it's all over. But my hunch is that Admiral Fletcher will have her there right on time."

Wold said: "At Point Luck . . ."

"That's right, Lieutenant," Nimitz said. "At Point Luck."

Blake wasn't certain, but he thought the admiral's statement sounded less like an affirmation than a prayer.

Matt Garth gazed around the flight deck of the *Yorktown,* marveling at the miracles Yardmaster Gillette and his Pearl Harbor dry-dock crews had accomplished.

He turned as his son came up, a Marine guard with him. Tom snapped off a salute, and said briefly: "Reporting as ordered, Captain."

Matt returned the salute. He looked at the Marine guard. "Thank you, Corporal."

He waited until the corporal had gone. "Sorry to have to send the Marines after you, Tom. But you've ignored my messages."

Tom was still rigidly at attention. "I didn't feel we had anything to discuss, sir."

Matt said coolly: "And you can drop that midshipman's crap. You're talking to your old man."

"I'll try to remember that, sir."

"Tom, for God's sake . . . It's time we straightened things out between us. Or are you going to spend the rest of this war sulking over a mistake that maybe, just *maybe,* your own father made when he was doing his damnedest to help you?"

Tom remained at attention. His father sighed and said quietly: "All right. Have it your way. But for whatever it's worth, I'd like to set the record straight. In fact, I insist on it."

"Whatever you say, sir."

Matt ignored the remark. "Tom before I left Pearl Harbor I personally vouched for the loyalty of Haruko and her parents. I went out on a limb . . . *way* out . . . to get them cleared . . . and *released!*"

There was a look of surprise and puzzlement on Tom's face.

Matt went on: "I don't know how much weight my request will carry, but there it is."

He waited for his son to respond, and after what seemed to be an interminable moment, the boy said simply: "Thanks."

Tom turned to leave. Matt caught his arm and said: "One more thing. I didn't ask your CO to have you shipped out."

Now, the veiled hostility was there again, tight, controlled, but still visible. "But you told me you spoke to him . . ."

"Yes, I did. He asked me how I felt about you and Haruko. I didn't tell him."

There was a definite note of accusation in the boy's voice. "Why not, Dad? . . ."

Matt suddenly felt as if he was choking on his own words again, but he was determined to tell it exactly as it had happened. He knew that Tom would see through any evasions, and that would be the end of any chance he might have, however remote, of reaching his son. He said simply: "It was one of those times when anything you say isn't going to do a damn bit of good. Jessop made it pretty obvious that he's caught up in the anti-Japanese hysteria. I . . . well, I just let it pass. Maybe I gave the impression that I agreed with him . . . Apparently, I did . . . without meaning to . . ."

There was an anguished look on Tom's face. "My God . . . Why didn't you just stay out of it?"

"Look, Mister," Matt said, angry and incensed now. "I've been honest with you when it would have been a helluva lot easier all around to have been just a little . . . devious. Jessop thought he was doing us both a favor. I've done all I can, and a damn sight more than I should have. And just remember one thing. You're being paid to fly fighter planes, not sit down there in your cabin and stare at your girl's picture. So you'd better shape up, boy, or some hot-shot Jap pilot is going to flame your ass."

Choked with emotion, he turned and strode off, leaving his son there staring at him.

17

The rain was beating down on the decks of the *Yamato*. The vicious storm had rushed down on them from the north. It was totally unexpected and unnerving. Inside the bridge, huddling over the chart table, a young weather officer was briefing Captain Kuroshima.

"There is simply no way to predict how far this front extends, Captain."

Kuroshima frowned and asked: "How long will it last?"

"I have no way of telling, sir. These mid-Pacific storms are impossible to forecast."

Yamamoto was staring out of the rain-splattered window, listening to the exchange at the chart table. He said sharply: "Another twelve hours? Twenty-four? You must have some idea."

The young weather officer was chagrined. "No sir. I can't say, sir."

Kuroshima straightened from the chart table. He knew the concern which was foremost in Yamamoto's mind, and he attempted to mollify it. "But is it not entirely possible that Admiral Nagumo's carrier striking force is running well ahead of this storm front?"

"Yes, sir." Then the young officer added: "Or plowing through it, just as we are."

Kuroshima shot a look at the nervous weatherman, to which the latter could only reply: "I'm sorry, Captain."

Less than three hundred miles to the east, on its final leg toward Midway Island, Admiral Nagumo's first carrier striking force was actually caught in the same slashing storm as Yamamoto's battleship armada. The decks of the four great aircraft carriers and their escorting cruisers and destroyers were lashed with rain. The *Akagi* was in the lead, with the *Kaga,* the *Hiryu* and the *Soryu* following in line astern.

On the bridge of the *Akagi,* Admiral Nagumo shifted his glance from the chronometer to the streaming windows. Captain Aoki, skipper of Nagumo's flagship, stood beside him. Nagumo was more edgy and morose than ever, and the report that Aoki had just given him did nothing to lighten his spirits.

"In less than five hours, Hosogaya will attack in the Aleutians. The operation will start and we will be groping toward Midway in this filthy squall. Is that your report, Captain Aoki?"

"The weather officer's report, yes, sir."

Nagumo turned to his Chief of Staff, the brainy, erratic Rear Admiral Kusaka, and said: "Yamamoto should be notified."

Kusaka replied coolly: "Sir, we're not due to launch our first air strike for thirty-six hours yet. Conditions could clear long before then."

Aoki, who had been growing increasingly concerned about Nagumo's blackening mood, said: "I agree with Admiral Kusaka, sir. So far this storm has been a godsend. It has served to hide our approach from any patroling enemy vessels. I'm confident that it will break just when we want it to."

Nagumo seemed swayed by their optimism, but his

reply was grudging. "In the morning. If it hasn't cleared in the morning."

He might as well have been speaking to Kuroshima, the "God of Operations" himself, for Kusaka was also totally convinced that the key to the success of Operation MI was surprise. And that meant the strict observance of radio silence. However, he was not a man to dispute his superiors head-on. He preferred to disagree in a tangential manner whenever possible. So he said mildly: "Yes, sir. In the morning we can decide whether or not to break radio silence and ask Admiral Yamamoto for instructions."

Nagumo nodded and spoke to Aoki. "How is my air operations officer?"

"Commander Genda is about the same, sir. The doctors are doing everything they can."

Nagumo turned away to stare again at the miserable weather. He was acutely aware of his feelings of gloom and apprehension, and the effect it was having on his staff. But try as he might, he could not seem to find that confidence, that sense of well-being that had attended his victories at Pearl Harbor and at Ceylon against the British.

At length, he said: "Damned communications blackout. I keep wondering, Kusaka . . . what did Operation K discover at Pearl Harbor? Were the American carriers there?"

It seemed perfectly obvious to Kusaka, and he couldn't understand why his commander didn't see it. He said, as patiently as he was able: "Since we've heard nothing from Admiral Yamamoto . . . no warning to the contrary, that can only mean that the enemy carriers were there."

At that very moment, in the battle plot room aboard Yamamoto's flagship, a young staff officer was removing the models which represented Submarine Squadrons 3 and 5 from their stations on the screening cordon between Midway and the Hawaiian Islands.

Watanabe was in heated debate with Kuroshima.

"Admiral Nagumo was not advised that our reconnaissance flight to Pearl Harbor had to be scrubbed—

on your insistence, Captain Kuroshima. Now *this* delay . . ."

Kuroshima cut him off. "Does *not* justify breaking radio silence, Commander."

He turned to see Yamamoto hurry in. Kuroshima handed the admiral the radio dispatch and said in a matter-of-fact tone: "Just received from Tokyo, sir. Submarine Squadrons Three and Five will be late in reaching their screening stations."

Yamamoto studied the dispatch, plainly disturbed.

"Sir, it's imperative that Admiral Nagumo be warned at once," Watanabe said intensely.

Kuroshima kept his voice quietly cool, although he was considerably irritated that the young aide should have the temerity to challenge him so directly. "The commander extravagates the situation, sir. Admiral Nagumo undoubtedly picked up Tokyo's transmission when we did."

Watanabe felt the blood rising to his face. He tried to match the captain's unemotional tone. "The captain is forgetting the *Akagi*'s poor radio antenna system."

Yamamoto said: "His point is well taken, Kuroshima."

Kuroshima smiled slightly. "Granted, sir. But it now appears that our submarine screen is unnecessary. The latest intelligence places the enemy carriers entirely out of the picture . . . " He leaned across the plot and pointed, "Here. In the Solomon Island area."

Yamamoto waited for further clarification of the surprising news, but Kuroshima remained silent.

"Is that all?" the admiral demanded. "Were there no details? How many carriers?"

"Tokyo didn't say, sir. So we must assume that all, or most of the American carriers were sighted there."

There was another tight little pause which Watanabe broke. He looked Kuroshima straight in the eye and said: "Go on, please, Captain."

Kuroshima's smile hardened and died. Yamamoto looked from one to the other.

At length, almost grudgingly, Kuroshima responded: "We received another intelligence report. I did not want to bother the admiral with it until more details came through. It was sketchy. Transmitted from the I-128."

He turned to the plot and indicated the submarine model laying off Midway Island. "As you are well aware, sir, submarine reconnaissance is difficult at best. Always open to question."

Yamamoto said sharply: "Get to the point, Captain."

Watanabe could not restrain himself. He preempted Kuroshima's reply. "The Americans are beefing up Midway, sir. Particularly in air strength."

The admiral was visibly shocked. But the lightning mind of Kuroshima had already formulated a response. "Sir, if it turns out to be true that the enemy is increasing his air power at Midway, surprise on our part would be all the more vital. Admiral Nagumo's carriers *must* strike the first blow. To break radio silence . . . as I am sure Commander Watanabe is again about to urge upon you . . . might very likely deprive Nagumo of a first strike. It might bring the enemy carriers charging in from the Solomons before he has neutralized the island's defenses and sets his trap for them."

Yamamoto pondered over the plot for what seemed to Watanabe to be an eternity. The young aide had the feeling that his admiral was not entirely convinced by Kuroshima's argument, but, at length, Yamamoto simply nodded and walked out.

Kuroshima did not deign to look at the deeply troubled Watanabe. Instead, he turned his attention back to the plot, like a gambler who had just out-guessed the roulette wheel and knew exactly where he was going to place his next wager.

18

On the broad flight deck of the *Yorktown* Admiral Fletcher was inspecting his Grumman Wildcats, all armed, fueled and spotted for take-off.

Steaming in circles around the great carrier, the destroyers *Hamman, Hughes, Morris,* and *Anderson* were serving as the protective screen, with the cruisers

Astoria and *Portland* within the huge ring, close astern of the *Yorktown* itself, and the destroyers *Russel* and *Gwin* far out on the flanks.

On the horizon, some sixteen sea-miles away, the smoke of the *Enterprise* could be seen as she turned on-to a parallel course, with the carrier *Hornet* behind her, her six cruisers in convoy, the four oilers struggling to keep up with the main body, and the nine destroyers out on her flanks for protection.

The two columns had steamed straight through the intended Japanese submarine cordon before the enemy subs, late because of repair foul-ups in the homeland shipyards, had arrived at their picket stations. Now, safely on the Midway side of Yamamoto's submarine screen, they joined forces at Point Luck; Task Force 17 under Admiral Fletcher in overall command, and Task Force 16 under Admiral Ray Spruance.

Admiral Fletcher moved down the line of planes, with Air Operations Officer Commander Murr Arnold at his side. The *Yorktown*'s skipper, Captain Buckmas-ter, was with them, and Matt Garth followed, checking both the planes and the pilots.

The flyers stood by their machines at rigid attention, most of them youngsters not long out of school, ready now for combat. Ramos, Mansen, Stern, Eastland, Phillips, Garonsky, Barker, Cassel, Auden, Hugo, Collins, Masters, Renas, Ford, Novelli . . . Matt Garth knew them all by name, knew their problems, their fears, their hopes.

He was looking for their emotions now—the deter-mination, the excitement, the well-hidden apprehensions; for most of them, this would be the first test of their capabilities and of their courage.

And Tom Garth was among them, too. His eyes were fixed blankly on the far horizon as his father moved past him; they did not waver.

The officers moved slowly on; a ritual not so much looking for anything wrong as making sure the young men knew that nothing would be *allowed* to be wrong.

Suddenly a seaman-messenger raced along the flight deck from the companionway that led to the carrier's communication center. Panting, the red-faced boy pulled up short when he reached the admiral, fumbled a hasty salute, and held out a radio dispatch.

Fletcher read it carefully, then his eyes went to the distant northern horizon, as though trying to pierce beyond it where, at the edge of the frigid Bering Sea, the twelve-hundred-mile-long chain of the Aleutians swept westward from the extremity of the Alaskan Peninsula all the way to Russian Kamchatka.

The Admiral took a deep breath, and there was a grim set to his mouth as he handed the dispatch to Matt Garth. "Well, it's started. The Japanese are bombing Dutch Harbor."

It was 6:30 A.M., June 3rd, in the year of our lord 1942.

Fletcher turned to Captain Buckmaster: "We'll signal Ray Spruance, Captain."

Buckmaster nodded. He took the message from Matt, glanced at it briefly, handed it back to the messenger with a curt nod. He looked at the air operations officer. "Dismiss the crews, Commander . . ."

The group hurried back to the bridge to be met by another messenger. He, too, saluted and handed over a dispatch. Fletcher read it and announced: "Attu and Kiska Islands are being invaded. Pass it on to Spruance."

He was calm and thoughtful as they climbed to the bridge. "Dutch Harbor, Attu, Kiska . . . three separate strikes. Or are they all part of the same assault? That's a vital question, isn't it?"

Matt said, puzzled: "The only worthwhile objective of the three is Dutch Harbor. Both Kiska and Attu are well away to the west. If Yamamoto really wanted to hold Dutch Harbor, wouldn't he try and protect his right flank as well?"

"Yes, I'd say that sensible strategy would almost make that mandatory. He'd have to go for a landing on the peninsula itself, at Perrivale or Chignik. And they'd almost certainly have to be hit *before* his main target."

He rubbed a gnarled hand over his chin. "Are we estimating? Or simply guessing, Matt? Is their main target the Aleutians after all?"

Matt frowned at him. Fletcher went on: "You know,

it's entirely possible that the Japanese know that we've broken their Purple Code . . . and that the Midway part of their Operation MI is a phony."

"You mean, have we come all this way to the middle of the Pacific for nothing?"

It was a thought that was also occurring to Admiral Nimitz fifteen hundred miles away at Pearl Harbor.

He stood in front of the huge battle plot at CINCPAC and watched his staff sliding into position the known elements of the attacking Japanese forces. Hosogaya's northern force had split into three elements: the first was clearly shown as descending on Dutch Harbor; the other two were behind the first, and a long way to the west.

Nimitz's face was grim. "All right, gentlemen. Dutch Harbor could well be the diversion we've been expecting. *But* . . . does that mean that Attu and Kiska are the main targets after all?"

He turned to Commander Blake. "What's he got up there, altogether?"

Blake was scanning the plot, jotting down the figures as he spoke. "So far our reconnaissance flights have confirmed the heavy cruiser *Nachi,* that's Vice Admiral Hosogaya's flagship. Two carriers, one of which is the *Ryujo,* the other not yet identified but probably the *Junyo* . . ."

"Not the *Akagi?*"

"No sir, we're sure about that."

"Good. Go on."

"Only one light cruiser, believed to be the *Abukuma,* the flagship of Vice Admiral Kakuta, two heavy cruisers, as yet unidentified, but one of them is probably the *Takao,* and a total of nine destroyers. One minelayer, one large transport."

"No battleships?"

Blake stabbed at the plot. "Further south, four battleships and two light cruisers moving in at flank speed, together with four or possibly five supply ships. Obviously a support force."

Nimitz nodded. "So there's not a sign of the *Akagi,* which means Admiral Nagumo hasn't shown up yet.

And neither has Yamamoto in the *Yamato,* is that correct?"

"Correct, sir."

"From what I know of the Japanese Admirals, Yamamoto would hold back. He'd have to, until the operation is well under way. But Nagumo . . . I'm sure he'd want to spearhead the attack himself, and that means the *Akagi*. Am I right?"

"Without a doubt, Admiral. And the *Akagi* is *not* leading the assault. They've committed a total of less than thirty ships. It's a wider diversion than Rochefort's intelligence led us to expect, but it's still too small a force for a major strike. We were right."

"Don't be too sure of that, Blake. Yes, it's a feint all right, a diversion. But the main assault still could be on the West Coast. Or right here in Hawaii."

"Yes, that's possible. That's always been possible. But, Admiral, I'm sure we're defended against the real threat."

Nimitz said: "Let's take another look at our search plan."

Blake gave the order, and one of the staff flipped a transparent decal into position over the outline of Midway Island.

For seven hundred miles southwest of Midway, and for seven hundred miles to the north-northwest, a large segment of a circle indicated the search area of twenty-three PBY Catalina flying boats. It was a piece of pie a little wider than ninety degrees that spread out far beyond the line of eleven American submarines fanned out to the west of Midway, a staggered, double line of sentries.

Nimitz studied the search plan closely, then he said quietly: "Today, Blake. Our PBY's should tell us today whether we're right . . . Or wrong."

In the crowded cockpit of Strawberry Nine, Ensign Hardeman was again expending his nervous energies on a box of Graham crackers. Jack Reid reached across the controls, took the box out of Hardeman's hands, and tossed it into the passageway.

Hardeman grinned. "Jesus, Jack! That's the only security blanket I've got . . ."

"Goddamn crumbs everywhere . . ."

He brought his binoculars up again and scanned the brilliant blue patches of water far below the cotton clouds that floated peacefully beneath them, big and little puffs tinged with the palest gray at the edges.

And then his eyes almost popped out of his head. "Hey! One o'clock! *Look!*"

Hardeman raised his glasses and stared at the water. He heard Reid's voice, yelling now: "You see what I see? Jesus! . . ."

"Damn right I do . . ."

The clouds were thicker now, obscuring most of the sea below, opening up here and there with the vagaries of the wind. They seemed to part miraculously, momentarily, and there below—two ships were knifing along on a course exactly opposed to that of the Catalina.

The clouds closed and Reid jammed the controls over until the clumsy PBY broke through them again, and below . . . He stared and said, his voice hushed: "My God, an armada! . . ."

He counted two, three, six ships, and then the clouds came together again and the ships were gone.

Reid yelled into his intercom: "Sparks! Raise Midway, urgent! Radio: 'Main Body.' "

The radio operator's voice came back: "Is that all? Just 'Main Body?' "

Reid yelled: "Send it!"

He turned to Hardeman: "Let's go down for a closer look. And you want your crackers back, buddy, you can have them . . . "

He pushed the nose of the plane down in a steep dive.

Vice Admiral Kondo stood on the flying bridge of his flagship, the heavy cruiser *Atago,* and peered through his binoculars at the diving plane, far off but approaching his occupation and support force convoy fast. He said to the aide who stood at his side: "Silhouette chart . . ."

A staff officer answered him: "An American PBY, sir. Reconnaissance seaplane."

Kondo said calmly: "Then at last we've been seen."

The phone was buzzing, and the staff officer picked it up.

"Bridge."

He listened for a moment and replaced the receiver. "The radio room, sir. They've picked up a transmission from the enemy plane. It's alerting Midway."

Kondo took a long, deep breath.

He said at last: "Well, we have come closer than we might have expected." He picked up the phone and pressed the buzzer which sounded in the radio room.

He said clearly: "This is Admiral Kondo speaking. Break radio silence. Advise Admiral Yamamoto that we've been spotted. That is all."

He replaced the receiver and turned to his aide. He was almost grimly thoughtful. "Well, at last we shall put Operation MI to the test . . ."

Admiral Yamamoto received Kondo's radio flash in his quarters. Kuroshima had also brought him a follow-up which reported that nine B-17 bombers had been sent from Midway to attack the invasion force armada. They had dropped their bombs in crystal-clear visibility from ten thousand feet. They had scored only one near miss on Kondo's ships. No casualties, no damage whatsoever.

But Yamamoto took little satisfaction in the news. At length, he looked up from the dispatches and said: "This is not as we planned, Captain Kuroshima."

Kuroshima was elated. "No, sir. But our intelligence estimates have been confirmed. The quality of the American pilots *is* poor. Imagine! Scoring only one near-miss . . ."

Watanabe, who was at his admiral's side as usual, said: "But we've lost the advantage which you thought was so vital to the success of the operation, Captain. The element of surprise."

Kuroshima treated the young aide to a buoyant smile. "It is of no consequence now, Commander Watanabe. Our carrier strike force will be attacking in less than twelve hours. The Americans can't possibly bring their fleet on scene in time to interfere."

Despite his dislike for the egotistical "God of Operations," Watanabe found Kuroshima's jubilation infectious. He nodded and returned the smile.

Yamamoto remained uneasily silent as he reread Kondo's dispatches.

Word had arrived at the CINCPAC battle plot room, where Admiral Nimitz was keeping his vigil. There was a repressed excitement as Nimitz read the message that Blake had handed him.

"Six large ships in a column, bearing two hundred and sixty degrees, distance seven hundred miles from Midway. This seems to be it, gentlemen." He turned to Lieutenant Commander Wold. "Get Joe Rochefort for me."

"Yes, sir."

Wold hurried out, and when he came back with the intelligence man he saw that Nimitz was still puzzling over the plot as though something weren't quite right. He turned and said: "Joe, I wanted to tell you myself. You were right. It is Midway."

Joe Rochefort beamed. *"Hoo-ray!"*

He corrected himself, a little sheepishly. "What I mean is . . . Well, you know what I mean, sir."

"Indeed I do, Joe. And thank God Fletcher joined up with Spruance in time."

Blake was at the phone, and he looked at the admiral and said: "Another one from Strawberry Nine, sir. Eleven ships, course oh nine oh . . ." He broke off and frowned. "Course oh nine oh? Well! Speed nineteen knots."

Nimitz puzzled. "But what kind of ships? The first transmission said 'Main Body.' Yet there's no mention of any aircraft carriers."

Blake too was studying the plot. "That PBY, Strawberry Nine, was at the extreme leg of his seven hundred-mile range when he sent the message 'Main Body.' It could easily be that Nagumo's carriers are following the 'large' ships he reported."

Rochefort agreed. "They could be just beyond the pilot's horizon, Admiral."

Nimitz's face was grim now. "If they are, then Fletcher is waiting in the wrong place. He's too far north." He thought about it for a moment in silence, then said frowning: "He'd have to move right now, and at flank speed, to get within striking distance before sunset."

He tapped at the plot: "But if Nagumo's carriers are up here where we figured, coming in from behind this storm front? What happens then?"

Joe Rochefort said promptly: "Fletcher would be caught between two forces."

"Exactly. So . . ."

It was a vital decision and he did not hesitate. He turned to Commander Blake and there was no doubt in his voice at all.

"Top-priority signal to Admiral Fletcher: This is not, repeat *not,* the 'Main Body.' Expect the enemy carrier force to strike tomorrow from behind the storm front, to your northwest, as previously anticipated. Signed, Nimitz."

Joe Rochefort was smiling gently to himself. He was thinking: "That's what makes a man a great admiral."

On board the *Yorktown,* Fletcher and Matt Garth were at the vertical Plexiglas plot in the giant carrier's combat information center. The information it revealed was drawn in by a petty officer who stood behind the large, transparent display. It was the same information that Nimitz had and it was, being updated when the message arrived.

Fletcher read it and then repeated: ". . . to your northwest, as previously anticipated. Signed, Nimitz."

He thought about it for a moment, and nodded. "Well, that settles *that.* CINCPAC must think that the PBY sighted only Kondo's invasion force."

Garth was worrying about it. He said slowly: "But if it's Nagumo's attack force . . . with his carriers following . . . and they scout us out before we find them? . . ."

Fletcher nodded. His face was drawn and anxious. He turned to Captain Buckmaster. "Captain . . . Go to battle stations, and sound . . . General Quarters."

Buckmaster moved to give the order. The atmosphere in the *Yorktown*'s combat information center was heavy with repressed excitement—and doubt.

19

Admiral Nagumo stood at the farthest reach of the flying bridge, and peered up at the sky. It was 2:54 A.M. and there was no moon behind the heavy mantle of clouds to confirm the weather officer's prediction that the carrier striking force was, at last, steaming clear of the storm that had dogged them so long. However, the rains had stopped, the winds abated somewhat, and the sea was calming.

The admiral grasped the guard railing for support and heard the loudspeakers through the *Akagi* blare out: "Action stations all hands! Pilots report to ready room! All hands to your action stations! Pilots re-report to ready room!"

On so many other occasions the sound of the great aircraft carrier arousing itself for battle had quickened his pulse, sent his spirits soaring. At this moment he felt only a leaden apprehension. He made an effort to shake it and turned to go back inside the bridge.

Kusaka came hurrying on, smiling. "The weather is clearing, sir! We couldn't have timed it better! The weather officer anticipates broken-cloud cover between one thousand and twenty-five hundred feet. Ideal for concealing us from the enemy's scout planes. Above twenty-five hundred feet, our flyers will have unlimited visibility all the way to their target."

Kusaka was at a loss to understand why Nagumo did not seem to share his satisfaction. He followed his admiral inside the bridge, then said: "Sir, by some freak atmospheric, we've just picked up this radio transmission from Tokyo to Admiral Yamamoto."

He handed the dispatch to Nagumo, who snorted. "So. Intelligence estimates that the American fleet is still cruising the Solomon area . . . "

"Sir, this, combined with the continued silence from Admiral Yamamoto . . . Well, sir, whatever doubts we may have had . . . "

"Are you still with me, Kusaka?" Nagumo snapped back. "An estimate is just that. We have no definitive intelligence reports, only opinions and estimates. And continued silence from Yamamoto does not make those estimates *fact* . . . "

He broke off, astonished to see a man dressed in robe and slippers standing in the doorway at the far side of the bridge. It was Commander Minoru Genda, still a bit woozy, face flushed, red-eyed, hair disheveled. A very unmilitary sight. But his presence was welcome, indeed, and everyone's spirits were buoyed at seeing him—especially Nagumo's.

The admiral moved across to him and thrust out his hand, "Genda . . . !"

Genda shook his admiral's hand warmly, a very confident looking man in spite of his obvious illness. His eyes were sharp and bright and enquiring, his attitude one of impatience and eagerness, a good-looking man in his early thirties. "My apologies, Admiral. Forgive me. I've been away from my duties much too long."

The admiral grasped him by the shoulders, an old friend. He noted the perspiration streaming down his face. "It's good to see you, Genda, very good . . . But you still have a terrible temperature! Are you sure you should be out of sick bay?"

Genda took a handkerchief and wiped at the sweat on the back of his neck. There were great, dark patches of damp all over his cotton robe and he felt it shamed him, as though it were a disgrace to be ill at so crucial a time. He was, without a doubt, the best air operations officer in the entire Japanese navy, a man of courage and great determination, who had reached his high place in both the affections and the estimation of his admiral by constant, dedicated study and hard work.

He shook his head. "It's nothing, sir. I'm well enough to take charge of air operations."

"And so you shall, my friend. And you can start at once. I want you to prepare an air-search plan. Immediately."

Genda was surprised, and so was Kusaka. An air search? Already?

Genda nodded. "But for what area, Admiral?"

Nagumo led him to the chart. He said thoughtfully: "Well . . . where would I deploy my aircraft carriers if I were the American commander?"

He placed his finger on the map at the present position of his carrier striking force. It was very close to the spot marked: "Launch First Midway Strike." From there he traced an invisible line slightly to the north of due east, stopping when he had formed the apex of an almost perfect equilateral triangle, with his intended launch point and Midway Island at the base.

He jabbed at the point and said: "That is where I would lay in wait with my carriers if I knew Midway was going to be invaded. There. Northeast of the island. I want that area scouted, Genda."

Genda took a sheet of plastic and laid it over the map. He found a red wax pencil and quickly sketched in his plan, explaining it as he drew in the sharp, incisive lines.

"Very well . . . Two sections here, to the south and west of the island, to cover any possible enemy activity on our right, each of them three hundred miles long and sixty miles wide at the farthest point of range. Then, to the north and the northeast, two similar plots to cover a forty-five degree segment here. Another three hundred-mile segment further north and northeast, also sixty miles wide, and two more to the north, of which this one need only be . . . a hundred and fifty miles by forty."

Nagumo studied the sketch in silence for a while, nodded at last, and said, satisfied: "That's an area of sixty or seventy thousand square miles, I would say. Good, very good. And how soon can we begin, Genda?"

Genda said eagerly: "The scouts can be airborne in half an hour, sir. We will use seaplanes."

"Seaplanes? . . ."

"Yes, sir. I do not recommend diverting any of our bombers for scouting duty."

Nagumo seemed doubtful, but he listened as Genda went on: "We'll launch two each from the *Akagi* and the *Kaga*. And our cruiser escort will launch . . . five seaplanes. Two from the *Tone,* and three from the *Chikuma.*"

"Very good. But until our scouts have searched that area, we will hold our most experienced pilots in reserve. And half our aircraft."

Kusaka was astonished, and felt he must protest.

"Sir, I agree that an air search may be a wise precaution but . . . to hold back our best pilots from the Midway strike! . . ."

Nagumo gave him a look which warned against any further argument, but Kusaka continued, his conviction too overwhelming to permit silence on what he considered to be a horrendous mistake.

"Admiral, even if Tokyo is incorrect . . . if the American carriers *were* at Pearl Harbor, and not in the Solomons when we sailed . . . they couldn't possibly have passed through our submarine screen without being detected. And we've had no warnings of any kind from Admiral Yamamoto. His silence can only have one meaning. The American fleet is nowhere near Midway."

Nagumo replied sharply: "We've been over this ground, Commander."

Kusaka would not be silenced. "Sir, our first strike *must* be decisive. Midway's airstrip and planes must be destroyed in one massive blow. Otherwise, we invite a counterstrike against our carriers and Admiral Kondo's troop transports."

Nagumo was swayed by Kusaka's intensity as much as by his argument—swayed only enough to be floundered in indecision. He turned away as if to give the matter serious thought. But at length he said: "Commander Genda? . . ."

There was no doubt in Genda's mind. He replied

with easy conviction, "I'm inclined to agree with you, sir. Let the novice pilots fly the first strike. Led by a few veterans, such as Lieutenant Tomonaga, I am confident they can get the job done. If not, we can always launch a second strike."

Nagumo did not turn to face them. He simply nodded and said: "That is how we'll have it."

Then he left the bridge.

Kusaka wanted to shout after him: *Wrong, wrong, wrong!* . . . But he knew it was useless. Instead, he said bitterly: "Suddenly the man who led us to victory at Pearl Harbor and at Malaya and at Ceylon is choked by caution."

Genda felt a certain sympathy for the young commander. It was not easy for these brainy, superconfident types, upon which the Imperial Navy relied so heavily, to lose an argument. He said mildly: "They say, Kusaka, that old warriors live as long as their instincts don't betray them."

He indicated the air search area on the chart. "Our admiral smells danger out there."

Kusaka would not be assuaged. He said flatly: "Nonsense."

The intelligence, because of the continued radio silence, was severely limited on both sides now. There were only the reports of the scouting planes, and even these were kept to a minimum for fear of intercepts.

In the distant headquarters at Tokyo and Pearl Harbor, it was known that the battle was about to begin; but what form it would take remained a matter of guesswork. At CINCPAC HQ, Nimitz was sipping coffee while the staff, under Blake's guidance, slid the models representing the searching PBY's into their allotted places on the plot. Everyone was showing signs of the long vigil.

Nimitz said offhandedly, "Times like these, Joe, I miss the flatlands."

Joe Rochefort looked up in surprise, and the admiral went on: "That's a mighty big body of water out there, and I'm just a fella who came out of a Texas prairie town."

After a pause, he continued, "The nearest stretch of water to where I lived when I was a kid was a hundred and twenty miles away, and all it was was a lake you could wade across at the height of the rainy seasons. Hell, during the summer, we used to make clay pots out of its bottom."

The admiral snapped out of his reverie and looked hard at Rochefort. "No matter how this turns out, Joe, I want you to know one thing; you've sure as hell earned your salary *this* month."

Rochefort smiled. "Thank you, sir."

"There was a time back there, remember when all you had to go on was . . . what did you call it? A gut feeling. Just a code name, 'AF,' and who the hell could guess what it might mean?"

Joe grinned. "Like I always said, Admiral . . . Ten or fifteen percent of the time, it turns out we know what we're doing."

Nimitz nodded. "You know what Matt Garth told me? He said: 'Long as we've got guys like Joe Rochefort to tell us where the enemy is going to be, we'll be in good shape to give them a run for their money. Joe was right about Coral Sea, and he's right about Midway, too . . .' That's what he said, and I guess I wouldn't ever have told you, but . . . hell, this waiting's getting me down."

Nimitz paused and sipped at the coffee, stone-cold now, but to his liking. He went on: "But it's got to be a helluva lot worse for the boys on the *Yorktown.* Out of one battle by the skin of their teeth, more dead than alive, and they're back in another before they've had time to shake a stick at a rattler."

On board the *Yorktown,* sailing in the predawn darkness, Admiral Fletcher and Matt Garth were studying precisely the same plot.

Garth indicated the letter "K" which designated Kondo's invasion force. "We know the course he was on when he left Guam. We know his speed. We can assume that he'll hold that course, if they believe their diversion ploy in the Aleutians is going to trick us. So, by now, he's got to be . . . somewhere about here."

Fletcher nodded.

Matt went on: "Seems to me, the important thing is that they wouldn't bring their transports close enough for us to knock hell out of them if they didn't intend to invade damn soon. That means that Nagumo is close on Kondo's heels somewhere. I think CINCPAC is right, Admiral, Nagumo will hit Midway today."

Fletcher agreed. "I'm sure of it, Matt. But from where? He could pop out anywhere along the edge of this storm front. And when he does, he'll have his own scout planes out looking for danger."

Matt said blandly: "Then we'll just have to find him before he finds us."

"But if we're wrong, Matt . . . if he comes at us from our blind side? . . ."

Fletcher indicated the area: Outside Midway's PBY search pattern to the north, the tract of sea was vast, and empty—a dangerously unknown expanse.

Matt worried it over in his mind, and said at last: "Then perhaps we'd better put some eyes out there, too, Admiral. About ten SBD's could cover our northern flank, fill in the blind spots."

"All right. But I'll want to recover them fast if the Catalinas should make contact where we expect the Japs to be. So . . . no more than a hundred miles out. Get them up in the air for a quick search, and a quick return. If I need them in a hurry . . . that's *how* I'll need them; in a hurry."

"I'll see to it at once, sir."

Matt left the combat information center to give the orders to the air operations officer. Then he went to the flight deck to watch the take-offs.

In a matter of minutes, the line of Dauntless dive bombers were spotted on deck and were hurling themselves into the air. He saw some of the other pilots were watching the take-offs, too, Ramos, and Mansen . . . and his son.

From where he was standing, on an antiaircraft platform above them, he could hear their voices coming up to him on the wind.

Ramos was saying: "Poor bastards. They're gonna

miss all the fun. There's nothing north of us but empty ocean."

Ramos was a lanky, awkward sort of kid, who stumbled over everything as though his legs were not properly articulated. He liked to have the ship's barber run the clippers over his oddly-shaped head so that the top of it looked like a bristle brush.

Eddie Mansen answered him. He looked at Tom and said, grinning: "He gets all his dope straight from Tokyo Rose. Right, Chili Bean?"

Ramos grinned back at him and patted the top of his crewcut. "Wrong. I get it up here. When it bristles, there's Japs around."

"I heard all you gotta do to shoot a Zeke down is take a good look-see where the pilot is, and let him have it."

"You get close enough to see the pilot, you better push that ejector button fast, and start that l-o-n-g swim home. Hell, I saw one stand on his tail and go straight up like a rocket."

"You saw a Zeke? You been dreaming, Gerry?"

"Well, some guy told me . . . I'll find out, I guess. If it's true, you know what I'm gonna do? I'm gonna get up there first and just . . . wait for him. Surprise, surprise . . ."

They were all laughing together down there, kids horsing around with each other to hide their anxieties.

Mario Novelli joined them. Though he was no older than they were, barely into his twenties, he had seen combat and they looked up to him. Tom asked him, serious now: "You were with Thatch at Coral Sea, Novelli. How good *are* the Zeke pilots?"

Novelli was a handsome boy from the North Beach district of San Francisco. He had never been known to raise his voice or show any anger. He seemed to be totally self-contained and without a nerve in his lithe body. He considered his reply for a moment, then said: "Damn good. And they've got a hot little plane. I mean *hot*."

He studied their faces for a moment. "You guys aren't worried? . . ."

Mansen piped up: "Us? . . . Worried? . . ."

"Well, you'd better be. You'll live longer."

Ramos grinned. "That's how you lucked through at Coral Sea?"

Novelli said, with an intensity that surprised them all: "I stuck close to Thatch and prayed a lot. But this time I'm gonna shaft the bastards . . ."

Matt saw Commander John Thatch approaching, saw them snap smartly to attention and salute. He heard Thatch bark: "You pilots should be sacked out. What the hell are you doing up on the flight deck?"

Tom Garth answered him: "Just couldn't sleep, sir."

"Well, get below and *try!* We've got a heavy day ahead of us."

Matt watched as the young men turned away and moved off to their quarters. His son had not once caught his eyes, and he went back to the bridge with a heavy heart.

He was thinking: *It was just an accident, a misunderstanding, and we're both on the same ship as a result of it, heading into God knows what. Well, at least we're together . . .*

20

The hands of the big brass chronometer on the bulkhead of the *Akagi*'s bridge stood at 04:30 hours. It was eighty-two minutes before sunrise on the morning of June 4th.

Admiral Nagumo was on the flying bridge, surrounded by his staff officers and his aides, looking down on the *Akagi*'s flight deck where the long lines of aircraft were spotted for take-off. The roar was monstrous as the pilots revved up their engines. Genda, still sweating heavily, was beside Nagumo; in spite of the pain that was throbbing in his head, he was pleased.

He turned to the admiral, shouting to make himself heard: "The weather forecast is holding, sir. It couldn't be more suited to our purpose. There's broken

cloud cover up to two thousand feet to conceal our
ships from the enemy's scout planes. And above two
thousand, there's unlimited visibility straight into Midway for our pilots."

Nagumo did not respond. On the flight deck all was
ready for launching. The handlers and the pilots and
their crews awaited the signal from the flying bridge.
It did not come. All eyes were on Nagumo, but he
seemed mesmerized by the cacophony of the engines.
The staff officers exchanged puzzled glances. Kusaka
shot an impatient look at the pocket watch he kept so
carefully synchronized with the ship's chronometer.

At length, Genda said: "When you are ready, sir."

Nagumo nodded. "Commander Genda, you may
commence launching."

Genda picked up the flight deck officer's telephone
and spoke into it. "Commence launching."

This was the moment they had all been waiting for,
the commitment that culminated the months of planning and debate and replanning. Genda, Kusaka and
the staff officers and aides watched with great satisfaction as the planes roared, one by one, into the predawn
sky, clawing their ways off the deck, the Val dive-
bombers first, then the Kate torpedo-bombers—the latter now carrying contact bombs for the Midway assault—and last of all the sleek Zeke fighters.

The other three carriers of Admiral Nagumo's striking force, the *Kaga,* and *Soryu* and the *Hiryu,* having
received the order by signal light, were also launching
their aircraft to the cheers and *banzais* of every crew-
man who could get topside to see them off.

At ten thousand feet, Lieutenant Joichi Tomonaga,
the strike leader, leveled off and put his Kate into a tight
circling pattern as he watched his planes form up,
thirty-six dive-bombers, thirty-six torpedo-bombers,
and thirty-six fighters, all of them circling to find their
correct flight positions, the Kates at the lowest level,
the Vals above them, and the Zekes higher still, three
great V's slicing their way through the predawn sky.

The moment the last plane was in position, Tomonaga shoved the throttle of his Kate into maximum
power, and took his place in the lead. He waggled his

wings once in a signal, and held his arm upraised; he swung it forward in a gesture that meant: *On to Midway!*

The three V's of the planes, one hundred and eight in all, headed straight and fast for the island.

And silence had come over the *Akagi* again, the roar of its planes muted now to a distant hum, growing fainter all the time. Even Nagumo seemed more relaxed now. He had seated himself in his chair in the corner of the bridge, and a steward was serving him tea in a tiny porcelain cup.

The steward was a lank, elderly man who had served with the admiral for many years now. Nagumo looked at him. "And you, Takahashi, what do you think of this battle?"

The old man bowed. He said quietly: "The honor of the empire, sir, hinges on it. All of Japan is praying for your success."

He poured the tea, bowed, and went out. The admiral sipped in silence, and steeled himself for the trial that he found most difficult—the trial of *waiting*.

It was out of his hands now. Now it all depended on the eager young men whom he, and Genda, and Admiral Yamamoto himself, had molded from a ragged and undisciplined group of arrogant extroverts into the tightest-knit body of fighting flyers in history.

Genda was checking over the reports as they came in. He frowned over one of them. Kusaka saw the look on his face, "Trouble, Genda?"

Genda shook his head. "No, not really. All the scout planes from our cruisers are in the air . . . except one. It's late taking off."

Kusaka turned away.

A solitary scout plane delayed? It didn't seem very serious. But Admiral Nagumo had overheard.

"Late taking off? How long will it be, Genda?"

"Half an hour, sir. It's the cruiser *Tone,* she's having trouble with her catapult. So Scout Four will be half an hour behind the others."

Nagumo said, frowning: "Scout Four? From the cruiser *Tone?*" He got up and went to the plot.

"That's one of the vital segments, almost due west of Midway."

He sounded deeply disturbed, and Genda, knowing well what was on his mind, said: "Sir, in case the Americans *should* suddenly appear . . . I suggest the second flight wave be brought up on deck right away."

Kusaka was suddenly very angry. This was always the time when the squabbling would start, the moment something unforeseen happened and quick decisions had to be made. He believed firmly in the most careful planning, with no deviations at all from those plans that were the result of long and trying sessions, where every possible alternative had been studied at leisure and accepted or rejected after thoughtful debate. He hated snap decisions, and was convinced that they could lead only to disaster.

He said caustically: "The second flight wave? Armed with *torpedoes,* no doubt, to deal with enemy carriers we haven't even seen yet? Is that your plan?"

Genda said firmly: "Yes, it is. Our remaining planes and the *Kaga*'s, armed with *torpedoes,* for use against any enemy carriers that might appear. *Soryu* and *Hiryu*'s second wave can stand by with contact bombs . . . in the very unlikely event they'll be needed at Midway for a second strike."

Nagumo caught the frustrated anger on Kusaka's face. He looked at Genda. "Give the order, Genda."

Both sides, now, were probing the blue sky with their search planes, each with almost identical pie-shaped wedges spreading out to cover every possible square mile of water, the Japanese quarter-circle extending to the east, and the American to the west.

Each flew his own rigid pattern, and all eyes were staring down and around, above and below, as they searched each other out in the intolerable immensity of the mid-Pacific.

Strawberry Five was on autopilot flying toward one of the many billowing clouds that scattered the dawn sky. Howard Ady and his copilot, Al Kuhn, were searching the sea below them; it seemed that they were spending all their lives in this useless endeavor, with nothing to show for their trouble but the constant weariness of red-rimmed, smarting eyeballs.

They relaxed for a moment as the PBY ploughed through a towering white cloud, Kuhn knuckling his eyes. Then the flying boat cleared the cloud and Kuhn suddenly yelled: "Howie! Lookit down there! Christ! It's the whole damn Jap navy! . . ."

Where only a few moments ago there had been nothing but that constant, blinding blue of the sea, the golden sun low on the horizon and seeming to set it on fire, there were now four great carriers speeding northeast in line astern, their cruiser and destroyer escorts flanking them. It was an awesome sight.

Ady threw the switch on the intercom: "Radio, get with it! Raise Midway! Send . . . 'Enemy carriers' . . ."

The port belly-gunner's voice broke in, urgently: "Bandits! Three o'clock! Three o'clock, Lieutenant!"

Kuhn twisted around and looked out the window on his side of the cockpit. He answered: "We have them."

Ady was already nosing the Catalina steeply down toward a bank of cloud. He yelled: "What are they, Al?"

"Zekes! Jap fighter cover for the carriers! A swarm of them!"

"Jesus . . . I don't want to tangle with any goddamn Zekes, not in this flying apple-box. Here we go . . ."

He swung the plane around into the cloud cover, and looked at Kuhn anxiously: "You keep a good lookout, Al. *Four* carriers . . . Christ! You know what that means? They'll have a hundred, a hundred and fifty fighters up there somewhere."

On board the *Yorktown,* Fletcher was staring, puzzled, at the message he had been handed.

He said: "Enemy carriers . . . That's all?"

Matt Garth was studying the Plexiglas display, the petty officer behind it marking the report of the sighting. Fletcher hurried to him. "He didn't complete the message, Matt. Just —'Enemy carriers.'"

Matt shook his head. "That's all he sent, sir. If he

was on schedule and on course, he made his contact here . . . about two hundred and fifty miles out."

Fletcher was furious. "He damn well better get on the ball! I have to know how many! And where!"

"He'll probably be in contact again, Admiral, as soon as he gets a closer look."

"Good God, I hope so. Meanwhile send it on to Spruance."

"Aye, aye, sir."

In the cockpit of Strawberry Twelve, Lieutenant William Chase was also puzzling over the uncompleted message. Beside him, his copilot, Ensign Newman, was working out the navigational problem involved; the spoke that Strawberry Twelve was searching was immediately adjacent to, and to the south of, Strawberry Five.

Chase switched on the intercom and said: "Radio, are you damn certain it was Strawberry Five you heard?"

The radioman's voice came back at him: "Positive, skipper. It was their call letters. Besides, I recognized Rufano's fist. He's Five's operator. Strawberry Five, all right."

The lieutenant twisted around to Newman. "How far are we from that contact?"

"Well, we're about fifteen minutes behind schedule, so . . ."

He broke off. The voice on the intercom was yelling at them: "Bandits! Bandits! Sweet Mother . . . Hundreds of them!"

Chase yelled into the intercom: "Where, damn it? *Where?*"

"Four . . . no, five, five o'clock!"

Newman was staring out through the side window. In the middle distance, appearing one by one out of a dense mass of heavy cloud, he saw the V-formation of Kate torpedo bombers.

He yelled: "Torpedo bombers, Jesus . . ."

He stared and corrected himself: "No, bombers, they're Kates, but they're carrying bombs. Ten, fifteen, eighteen . . ."

He broke off, counting quickly, watching their steady

flight above the cumulus. He heard Chase's voice: "Fighters? They got to be up there someplace."

He was straining his neck, peering up and back, and suddenly he yelled: "There they are! Christ, we're right in the middle of them . . ."

Newman broke off and began to search the chart table frantically. "Where's the code book? Where's that fucking code book?!"

Chase yelled: "To hell with that! This is no time for coded messages!" He made an effort to calm himself and said clearly into the intercom: "Radio, send in the clear—'Many planes heading Midway. Bearing . . .' "

He motioned wildly at Newman for the bearing. Newman flipped on his intercom switch and said: "Bearing three hundred and twenty degrees. Distance one five oh."

The radio operator bleated: "Sweet Mother, skipper . . ."

Chase said angrily: "Send it!"

In the *Yorktown*'s combat information center, Admiral Fletcher and Matt Garth were still puzzling over the signals. The admiral was fit to be tied, his anger mounting visibly.

Garth was on the phone, his face dark with frustration. He said: "You're certain?" He waited. Then: "All right, let us know the moment anything else comes through."

He hung up the phone and turned to the admiral. "Nothing more, sir, that's all there was. 'Many planes heading Midway'—with the bearing and distance." Almost automatically, he glanced at the Plexiglas display to check that the petty officer was making the necessary annotations.

Fletcher said furiously: "And was it Strawberry Five that sighted the 'many planes?' Or one of the other PBY's? We have to know that, Matt!"

Matt sighed. "No call signals were sent, sir. Radio says the operator seemed very agitated."

Commander Murr Arnold, the *Yorktown*'s air operations officer, had joined them. He said: "It could be that they were jumped by enemy fighters, Admiral."

"My God, I hope not." Then the admiral's fury returned. "Damn it! How many carriers? What's their course? Their speed? Are they carrying torpedoes and looking for us? Or carrying bombs and headed for Midway?"

"Heading for Midway is what he said, Admiral."

Fletcher sighed and said wearily: "Send it on to Spruance. He must be thinking we're a bunch of idiots."

Strawberry Five was having trouble. The big Catalina was being bounced around in turbulence so heavy it seemed to be bending the giant wings. Ady was fighting the controls, trying to keep the PBY on course, and Kuhn was peering ahead into the thick, swirling mist.

He said: "One thing at least. Those Jap fighters'll never find us in this soup."

Ady said grimly: "No. And we won't find their carriers either, unless we break into the clear, and damn soon. Shit! . . . I should have gone straight in and risked it."

"We'd have been jumped by those Zekes in ten seconds flat. It's a long swim home, Howie."

Suddenly the clouds parted and they were in open sky again, the horizon ahead of them a brilliant red with the sunrise.

There was nothing down there, nothing but vast and limitless water. Ady said, dismayed: "We lost them . . ."

The voice was on the intercom again, setting him right; it yelled excitedly: "Lieutenant! Lieutenant Ady! There they are, behind us! I can see two carriers, and a battleship!"

Ady banked the plane sharply and yelled back: "I see them! Send it, Sparks! Send it now!"

On board the *Enterprise,* Admiral Ray Spruance was standing on the signal bridge with Captain Miles Browning, his Chief of Staff, watching the rapidly-blinking light on the horizon. A signal officer passed the first part of the message to the admiral. "Fletcher to

Spruance. Second sighting reported by Strawberry Five. Two enemy carriers and battleship bearing Midway three hundred twenty degrees, distance one hundred eighty miles, course one hundred thirty-five degrees, speed twenty-five knots."

Spruance checked the chart an aide held out for him. His face was alight with satisfaction. He said: "The storm front is right behind them. They came right out of the slot where Nimitz said they'd come . . ."

He took the second part of the message from the signal officer and read: "Proceed southwesterly. Attack enemy carriers. Will follow as soon as search planes recovered. Fletcher."

He looked at Browning.

"Signal *Hornet,* Captain Browning . . . and let's get to battle stations."

21

At Midway Island, the air-raid siren was building its mournful wail up to a shriek of alarm.

On the island's little airstrip, an odd assortment of planes was lining up to scramble—a B-17, a Navy TBD, two more B-17's, a PBY, a handful of Brewster Buffaloes, two F4F's . . .

In the underground command post, Captain Simard was watching the blips on the tiny radar screen. Simard's aide, Lieutenant Carl Simonton, was furiously cranking the handle of one of the field telephones set along the sandbagged walls.

Simard went over and took the phone from him, and said: "Andy? Has Major Parks got his fighters up yet?"

The connection was very bad. He could barely hear the crackling voice on the other end: "Yes, sir. All twenty-three. The SBD's are on the line now."

"Damn it! Get them airborne. *Now.* We've got a large number of enemy planes on our radar. They're due to hit us in less than fifteen minutes."

"You're not holding any in reserve, sir?"

"No. I want everything that can fly cleared off this island! Fifteen minutes! Then get your people to the shelters!"

Simard slammed down the receiver and turned to face the young staff officer awaiting his attention.

"Captain, our torpedo group radios that they've rendezvoused with the army bombers. They're headed for the enemy carriers."

"How many did we get up?"

"Six Avengers. The army put up four Marauder bombers rigged with torpedoes."

"Do those army pilots have any idea how to make a torpedo run?"

"They were briefed before they took off, Captain."

"What about the Marine's 221st?"

"Major Henderson's sixteen SBD's, sir. They're on the same course as our torpedo group."

"Well, that's everything we've got. Christ, I hope it's enough," Simard said grimly.

Simonton was at the bank of radio receivers that lined the other wall of the command post. He called across to Captain Simard: "Sir, we've got Major Parks's fighter frequency."

Simard hung up the field telephone and hurried across to where the third class radio operator was bent over the near-obsolete receiver. The operator caressed the tuning dial and, suddenly, there it was, loud and clear, the voices of Major "Red" Parks and his fighter pilots.

Someone was shouting: "Red Four to Rainbow Leader! Rainbow Leader! Bandits! Two o'clock!"

Someone else chimed in: "Jap fighters! Forty . . . fifty of 'em. Below us, Red! Zekes . . . Vals, Kates! . . ."

Then they heard Red Parks's voice, calm and very confident: "All right . . . all right. Calm down. I see them. Everybody set?"

"Blue Flight ready."

"Red Flight ready and willing, Major."

"Sitting ducks! . . ."

"Let's go, for Christ's sake! . . ."

Parks cut in: "I said calm down, damn it! Nice and

easy now. Let's see how many we can drop on the first pass."

There was a long moment when nothing but static came over the loudspeaker. Then the voices were heard again, rising to a pitch of frenzy as the pilots engaged the invaders.

"Blue Three, Blue Three! . . . Under you!"

"Jeez, lookit that Jap bastard climb!"

"Red Four, on your tail, look out!"

"Get that bastard off me, somebody get him off me! . . ."

"I'm hit, Rainbow Leader, I'm hit . . . Oh my God! . . ."

"Mayday, Mayday! . . ."

"Billy, four o'clock low! . . ."

"On your tail, Blue Two, three of 'em, look out! . . ."

"Bail out, Blue Three, bail out! . . ."

"I'm hit, I'm hit . . . Mayday, Mayday! . . ."

"Get him for me, somebody, get him for me. I've lost my controls! . . ."

"Rainbow Seven, Rainbow Seven, coming down on you! . . ."

"Okay, okay, I got one of them . . . My engine's on fire! . . ."

"Rainbow Leader, look out, look out, two of them, dead ahead of you! . . ."

"My God, they got Major Parks! They got Rainbow Leader! . . ."

"I'm on fire . . . I'm on fire! . . ."

And then, abruptly, there was only the static.

Captain Simard stared at the radio man as he called into his mike: "Rainbow Leader! Come in Rainbow Leader!"

There was only silence. He shook his head and looked back at Simard, who said savagely: "Keep trying!"

The operator called again: "Rainbow patrol, anyone from Rainbow patrol, come in please, come in please, report your condition. Report please. What is your condition? Anyone from Rainbow patrol, come in please."

There was no answer at all.

Only four minutes had gone by since Marine Fighter Squadron 221 had engaged the enemy.

Simard went into the dugout entrance and wearily climbed the sandbagged steps. He took his binoculars and looked at the distant sky. He saw that a lone F4F, heavily damaged, was wave-hopping its way back from the carnage out there, limping home to the strip.

The only one?

He searched the sky with his glasses. There were the incoming Japanese formations, specks in the bright distance, three layers one above the other, each in V formation.

Simonton came up out of the dugout and said: "We raised one of the cripples, Captain. His report was confusing but it's confirmed that Major Parks went down in flames . . . along with a dozen or so more. The survivors are regrouping."

"Enemy losses?"

"Two . . . maybe three bombers. Possibly one fighter . . ." Simonton stopped short. "My God! Do I see somebody up on the powerhouse?"

"It's that movie director, John Ford. He has my permission, Lieutenant."

Simard turned his attention back to the approaching enemy formations for a moment, then went down into the dugout and picked up the field telephone.

He said quietly: "Andy? They blew right through Major Parks's fighters. It looks like at least a hundred coming. Gunners standing by?"

"Standing by, Captain."

"They're our only hope now, Andy. Get your people into the shelters, right away."

He put down the phone and turned to the others. He said grimly: "All right, now we sit here and take it."

Tomonaga's assault force, only slightly damaged, was proceeding inexorably on its way. Midway was below him now, wide open to his assault. As he checked his planes quickly for their correct positions, his rear gunner's voice came to him over the intercom. "Lieutenant Tomonaga! We've been hit! We're losing gas!"

Tomonaga looked and saw a steady stream of gasoline vapor trailing out of his right-wing tank.

He answered calmly: "We have a full tank in the other wing. More than enough to get us home."

He rechecked the formations, switched on his radio transmitter and gave the order: "Attack in squadron order."

The Kates, armed with bombs which would explode on contact, would be the last to attack. Tomonaga lead them in a wide circle around the island, just out of the American's antiaircraft range, and watched his Vals wheel over into their dives. He thought for a moment how beautiful they looked with the silver reflecting the red and gold of the morning sky and the white puffs of cloud drifting among them. He saw the leading Val release its 600-pound bomb, saw it twist over and over in the air and strike, saw great geysers of red and yellow flame shoot up as it landed on an aviation fuel dump. He saw the bombs of the other Vals exploding across the hangers and the airstrip.

When the last Val had screamed down and released its bomb, he signaled his Kates, with their 1,650-pound loads, to follow him for a saturation run across the island.

It seemed that both the tiny twin islands were exploding, the sand erupting with timbers and sheets of galvanized iron and slabs of concrete being hurled through the air. The black smoke billowed up everywhere.

At last, the Kates circled and headed out to sea after the Vals, flying through the little black puffs of smoke marking the flak from the defenders' guns. He saw one of them go spiraling down into the water, and then another. He watched as the Zekes came down to sea level and raced in for their strafing runs, watched the bright flashes of flame from their cannon and machine guns, saw the bullets smashing their way into the targets. He watched the wing of one of the Zekes blow off, and the plane tumbling over and over onto the beach, saw it explode in a cloud of flaming smoke . . .

And then, just as suddenly as it had begun, it was over. The Japanese planes were all on their way back to their carriers, and the only sound on the island was the crackling of flames and the cries of the wounded and dying.

Midway was devastated. In less than twelve minutes one aircraft hangar and one seaplane hangar had been heavily damaged, three buildings burned out, one seaplane platform destroyed, two fuel storage tanks exploded, and two antiaircraft emplacements destroyed.

Five thousand feet above the carnage, a lone Japanese Kate lingered to assess damage. It was Tomonaga, and he was not satisfied.

Lieutenant Carl Simonton emerged from the dugout, with Captain Simard, and stared around at the wreckage in shock.

"My God, they creamed us . . ."

Simard shook his head. His face was grim. "Not entirely, Simonton. We're not out of business yet. Our airstrip is still operational."

Genda hurried out onto the flying bridge of the *Akagi,* fairly bursting with the good news. He handed Nagumo the dispatch and said: "Tomonaga's combat report, Admiral. He estimates more than forty enemy aircraft were shot down or destroyed on the ground."

For the first time since they had put out of Hiroshima harbor, his staff saw their Admiral beam.

He said: "Well, it seems your novice pilots got the job done, Genda. Very good. Very good, indeed."

"Thank you, sir."

Nagumo looked at Kusaka, whose expression gave no hint as to whether he was pleased or disappointed that Genda's advice had proven sound. The Admiral handed him the dispatch and said: "Kusaka, have Captain Aoki pass the news on to the officers and crew."

"Yes, sir," Kusaka said, and went inside the bridge.

Captain Aoki smiled broadly as he read the dispatch. He said to Kusaka: "More than *forty* enemy planes destroyed! . . . A great victory, Kusaka."

"Indeed it is . . . if it is not exaggerated."

Aoki gave the young rear admiral a puzzled look and Kusaka added, coolly: "Be that as it may, Tomonaga's report has put some heart into our gloomy leader. I can say it to you, Aoki . . . Nagumo has seemed old and uncertain. Not at all like himself . . ."

He broke off as a telephone clamored nearby. A watch officer snatched it up.

"Bridge."

The watch officer listened for a beat, then turned to Aoki. "Skywatch reports enemy torpedo planes, Captain! Coming in from our port quarter!"

Aoki was a cool oldtimer. He moved to a port window and located the attackers with his field glasses. They were mere specks coming in low on the horizon. He said calmly: "Sound air-raid alarm. Helmsman. Hard left!"

Twenty minutes later, in Pearl Harbor, Midway's Avenger and Marauder attack planes were being removed from the CINCPAC battle plot. Nimitz had just hurried in, and Blake handed him a radio dispatch.

"Simard's report from Midway, sir. Nagumo smashed his torpedo plane attack."

"What about his airstrip?"

"Barely usable. But he's trying to regroup for another attack before Nagumo hits him again."

Nimitz said in a quietly furious tone: "Damn! What the hell are Fletcher and Spruance doing? . . ."

The pitifully weak American torpedo attack had been easily repulsed. Three of the four Marauders which had attacked from the *Akagi*'s port side were quickly shot down by the Japanese Zekes. The fourth was driven away, trailing thick, black smoke.

Only one of the six Avengers which came skimming in from the starboard side of the great carrier survived the murderous Zeke cannon fire and the curtain of flak thrown up by the *Akagi*'s escorting cruisers and destroyers.

Now, the excitement ended, Admiral Nagumo and Genda were being served tea.

A communications officer hurried onto the flying bridge and handed Nagumo a dispatch. He read it and handed it to Genda, a definite note of recrimination in his voice.

"Tomonaga is asking for another strike."

Genda was surprised. He frowned over the message and said, at last: "Yes, sir . . . but this is a report of a great victory! Tomonaga says we lost only seven planes and we destroyed more than forty enemy aircraft, in the air and on the ground."

Kusaka had followed the communications officer out from the bridge. He could no longer conceal his impatience. He held out his hand for the dispatch and said: "Commander Genda, may I?"

Genda gave it to him in silence. Kusaka read it through and said coldly: "Certainly, a ratio of seven to forty is a very satisfying one. But one thing is very, very clear, Commander Genda. The pilots you chose, the second-line pilots, did *not* destroy the airfield. In Tomonaga's own words, it is still operational. Holding back our best pilots was, as I said it would be, a very damaging mistake."

Genda gave him a hard look, but did not reply. Kusaka turned to the admiral. "Sir, we have one hundred and eight planes, and our best pilots waiting on our flight decks. The entire force should be sent out without delay."

Nagumo said acidly: "The entire force, Kusaka? Our planes are armed with torpedoes, also on Commander Genda's advice. Hardly suitable for use against an airstrip."

Kusaka was well in control now. He said steadily: "They should be taken below and rearmed with bombs, sir. As I suggested before, we *must* make certain that no air attacks against us can be mounted from Midway."

Nagumo shot a glance at Genda, who remained silent.

Kusaka pressed his point home. "Sir, Lieutenant Tomonaga's request is also a warning. Midway is still a threat to us."

The admiral felt his anger rising. He said grimly: "And so are the American carriers, Kusaka!"

"If they're nearby, sir, yes! But our scouts have been gone for more than two hours, and they've reported *nothing.*"

"You are forgetting Scout Four," the admiral said. "It was half an hour late taking off. It won't reach its maximum search range for another hour yet. We *must* expect enemy carriers, until we are absolutely sure that they are *nowhere* near us. And that includes the whole of Scout Four's segment!"

He found that his voice was rising, the edges of his temper showing. He was thinking: two good men, Kusaka and Genda, and their points of view are diametrically opposed.

Kusaka continued to press. "With respect, sir, guarding against an improbable danger should not take priority over eliminating a known threat. Midway's air power is a very definite threat."

It was a telling point, but Nagumo seemed mired in indecision. At length, he looked at Genda and said: "Commander? . . ."

But Genda himself was not too certain now. He stared down at the flight deck where the planes of the second strike force were spotted for launching. At length, he turned back to the admiral and said: "Tomonaga's planes will be returning soon. When they are recovered, they can be quickly refueled and rearmed for a sea action. In case our scouts sight any enemy ships."

It was not the definite kind of advice that Nagumo wanted. He waited, but Genda said no more.

Kusaka's tone was insistent now: "If you would give the order, Admiral?"

Nagumo waited a long time before replying. He said at last, heavily: "Very well. Order the torpedo bombers rearmed with contact bombs. As soon as they're ready, we'll launch a second strike at Midway."

Not looking at the others, he left the bridge and went to his cabin.

Kusaka looked at Genda with just a hint of triumph in his eyes.

The *Enterprise* and the *Hornet* were knifing their way through a cobalt-blue sea at close to maximum speed, their flight decks jammed with aircraft, armed and ready for combat.

In the combat information center of the *Enterprise,* Admiral Spruance was studying the plot on which Nagumo's carrier force had been fixed. Browning was at his side.

"We've got fifty-seven planes on the line, Admiral. Ten fighters, thirty-three dive-bombers, fourteen torpedo-bombers. The *Hornet* will launch about the same number."

Spruance nodded. "What's our distance to the enemy carriers?"

A plot officer responded: "One hundred and thirty-five miles, sir."

The admiral spoke quietly to Browning. "Suppose we launched immediately? . . . Would our pilots have enough fuel to make the attack and return?"

"Yes, sir. *If* this weather holds. *If* their navigation is perfect. And *if* they don't lose any time over the target."

"In other words, some of them would have to ditch on the way home?"

Browning nodded.

The admiral turned back to the plot again as his staff officers exchanged surreptitious glances. They had the highest admiration for Ray Spruance, all of them. But for the most part, they had spent their entire careers on aircraft carriers, whereas the admiral had earned his considerable reputation on cruisers: the best cruiser skipper in the navy, they called him.

And now they were wondering how and when he would commit his planes.

The admiral said at last: "If we launch now . . . we might just catch Nagumo recovering his Midway striking force . . . On the other hand, if we wait to get in any closer, we'll give him the time he needs to rearm and refuel his planes . . ."

Browning said urgently: "Sir, that PBY reported only *two* carriers. Intelligence says he has four in his strike force. If those other two suddenly pop up near-by . . ."

Spruance broke in: "We'd be sitting ducks, yes. But there are two certain targets one hundred and thirty-five miles away . . . who don't expect us."

After a beat, he added: "Alert Admiral Fletcher, Captain Browning. And let's get *Enterprise* and *Hornet* turned into the wind."

When Fletcher, on board the *Yorktown,* received word of Spruance's intentions, he was visibly startled by its audacity. But Matt Garth noticed that as he studied the message, there was a kind of grim satisfaction on his face.

He said mildly: "Ray Spruance . . . He's quite a remarkable man . . . for a cruiser skipper."

22

On the flight decks of the carriers *Akagi, Kaga, Soryu,* and *Hiryu,* the armorers were swarming over the Val dive-bombers and the Kate torpedo-planes. In accordance with Admiral Nagumo's orders, the armor-piercing bombs were being removed from the Vals and replaced with contact-exploding bombs; the Kates were being stripped of their torpedoes and also armed with contact bombs.

They were sweating over their work, driven hard by the armorers-in-chief, and the little mechanized trucks that carried the armaments were speeding along the great flight decks, carrying their loads—some of them —to the elevators that went down into the bowels of the ship for storage.

But only some of them; there was simply not enough time to get the loads of high explosives properly stored, and a great many were simply stacked on the deck itself awaiting disposal.

Aboard the *Akagi,* Nagumo seemed more relaxed as he watched the activity from the flying bridge. Having made the decision, a great load had slipped from his shoulders.

Kusaka was on the phone. He listened for a moment, nodded his satisfaction, then turned to the admiral, saying, "The air controller reports that Tomonaga and the Midway strike force will be overhead in exactly one hour, Admiral. Just the time we need to finish rearming our planes and get them launched for a second strike. And this time . . . I promise you, sir, there will be *nothing* left of their airstrip."

There was a note of pugnacity in his voice, and Nagumo said dryly: "Your confidence is very reassuring, Kusaka."

"I hope you share it, Admiral."

Nagumo shook his head slowly. "Not entirely, I'm afraid. Convictions, certainties, a blind faith that what we are doing is right . . . These things were never a part of my philosophy, Kusaka. The fortunes of war are far too tenuous. They can be swayed one way or the other by the slightest of chances. It would indeed be comforting if we could persuade ourselves that we are highly-skilled, intelligent men and, as such, incapable of making mistakes. But we are also human, and miscalculation comes very easily to all of us. And if we do not realize this, then confidence becomes . . . arrogance." •

Kusaka refused to be chastened.

"Our scout planes have still not reported any enemy carriers within a radius that might endanger us. And now . . . they've come to the end of their segments and are starting the homeward leg. And they have made no sightings at all."

The hint of "I told you so" in his voice, sent Genda to the chart. He stared at it in silence for a moment, finding it hard to restrain his anger. At last he said, touching the search plan overlay with his forefinger: "There is still one large area to the northwest of Midway about which we can have no assurance whatsoever. The scout plane from the cruiser *Chikuma* developed engine trouble and turned back, without completing coverage of its segment . . ."

Kusaka interrupted him with a deprecatory wave of his hand. "The *Chikuma*'s plane is covering the second segment to the far north of the island. We already decided, Commander, that this area was of secondary importance."

"We did indeed, sir. But the *Chikuma*'s scout is not the only one having difficulty. I am much more concerned with the scout plane from the cruiser *Tone,* Scout Number Four. It took off half an hour late, you remember. It has only completed half its leg on the outward journey." He drummed the tip of his finger on Scout Four's search area and went on: "This is the most crucial area of all. If there are any American ships nearby, this is where I'd expect them to be waiting for us."

Kusaka chuckled. His tone was irritatingly condescending. "The commander is still feeling the depressing effects of his illness."

Genda was stung, and it was an effort for him to keep his reply to the young rear admiral properly respectful. "Perhaps. But until Scout Four reports no sightings . . . as the others have done . . . I cannot share the admiral's confidence."

Genda's fears were justified.

Scout Four was having considerable trouble with the engine of his two-seater amphibious reconnaissance plane. It was stuttering badly and choking on itself. The pilot was a half hour behind his tight schedule and was pushing his craft in a desperate attempt to make up the delay.

He was stiff and weary from the tension, his eyes strained from constant staring at the dazzling blue of the empty ocean below.

Empty until . . .

A vision flashed by below him, so quickly gone that he thought for a moment he had imagined it. A patch of cloud was below and around him now, enveloping him in its heavy mist, and he swore and pushed the nose of the seaplane down, hard, and swung it around in a tight turn.

And then he was below the cloud again. He stared at the sea, switched on his intercom, and said to his radioman, his voice full of repressed excitement: "Radio . . . message to the *Akagi:* 'Ten enemy ships sighted.

Bearing oh one oh degrees, distance two hundred and forty miles from Midway. Course one-five-oh degrees, speed twenty knots.' "

He heard the staccato message going out, and he swung the plane round again for another look. The ships were very clear now, far, far, below him, and he said into the intercom: "Make sure that message is acknowledged. We are going down for a closer look."

He eased the throttle forward and began his dive.

Admiral Nagumo was stunned.

He stared at the message that had been urgently taken to him, read it through again, and said: "Which scout radioed that contact?"

The communications officer had heard the squabbling going on between Genda and Kusaka, and he had views of his own on where the danger lay. But he said, stolidly enough, not even glancing at Genda: "It came from Scout Four, sir. The one that was late taking off."

The admiral hurried to the chart. He tapped at its surface and said: "Then he should be . . . about where? . . ."

The plot officer quickly located the position.

"Exactly here, Admiral."

Nagumo turned to Genda. "How far along is the rearming of our planes, Genda?"

"Almost halfway, sir."

Nagumo said tightly: "Order it halted."

Genda hesitated. "But, sir . . ."

The admiral ignored him. He turned to the communications officer and said: "Radio Scout Four, Lieutenant. 'Ascertain ship types and maintain constant contact.' "

"Yes, sir."

He said to Genda, very quietly: "We may have made a mistake after all. I want no more rearming done until we *know* exactly what types those ships are."

Kusaka, fuming, was silent.

Admiral Fletcher was studying the radar screen in the *Yorktown*'s combat information center. Matt Garth and the air operations officer of Task Force 17, Commander Murr Arnold, were at his side, watching the tiny blips at the extreme end of the northern quadrant.

Arnold looked at the radar operator and raised his eyebrows.

The operator said quietly: "Friendlies, sir. Our scout planes returning. They've completed the search."

Arnold checked his watch. "We should have them all back aboard in less than fifteen minutes."

Fletcher nodded. "All right. See to it, Murr."

Arnold hurried out, as Fletcher moved with Matt Garth to the big Plexiglas plot, saying: "So, let's see what Ray Spruance is up to now . . ."

The legends representing the attack groups from the *Hornet* and *Enterprise* were well on their way now toward the line that had been indicated for the Japanese force. Matt noted Fletcher frowning at it, obviously dissatisfied about something. Unsure of what was troubling the admiral, he said: "Admiral Spruance's attack groups from the *Hornet* and the *Enterprise* should make contact with the enemy carriers in about one hour, sir."

"On that same course? Two-four-oh degrees?"

Matt nodded. "That's right, sir. Spruance is counting on Nagumo being pinned down until he recovers his Midway attack group. Two-four-oh degrees ought to get our people to the homecoming at just about the right time. Imagine, the sight that's going to be! Four enemy carriers with their flight decks jammed with unfueled, unarmed planes."

The admiral did not share Matt's optimism. He studied the plot, then said: "Spruance is cutting it awfully thin, Matt. If we miss on this first crack, you realize what it means?"

"Yes, sir. It means that Nagumo will have us cold."

The admiral was worried. He lit up a cigar, exhaled a cloud of smoke and said: "Let's just hope Ray's strike leaders are on the nose with their navigation. He hasn't left them any margin for error. Not the slightest."

They were flying at low altitude in good formation, fifteen of the Devastator torpedo-bombers from the carrier *Hornet*. Their leader was Lieutenant Commander John Waldron. His gunner/radioman, Horace Dobbs was squinting into the sky above and behind them. He spoke into the intercom.

"I don't see our fighters anywhere, skipper. They shoulda caught up to us by now. And where the hell's Diving Eight, I don't see them either."

Waldron said nonchantly: "Diving Eight's where they belong, Dobbs. With Fighting Eight. They took off together."

"Yeah, well ain't they supposed to be tagging along with us?"

Waldron did not respond. His attention was on his compass as he carefully corrected the heading on which he was leading his torpedo group. He glanced back over his shoulder and saw that the fourteen other TBD's had aligned themselves with his course. On his right wing he noticed the pilot, Ensign George Gay, bending forward in his cockpit. He wondered what the hell the kid was up to now.

What Gay was up to was tapping his compass and muttering to himself. At length, he switched on his radio transmitter and spoke into the microphone:

"Red Fox Leader from Kit Three. Skipper, either my compass is haywire, or we're not headed on two four oh."

Waldron replied dryly: "Don't worry about your compass, Mr. Gay. It's probably just as good as mine."

"Sir?"

"Just follow your leader, Mr. Gay. Stick on my tail and you won't get into any trouble."

"But skipper, our orders . . ."

Waldron interrupted him: "There's nothing out on two four oh except empty ocean, Mr. Gay. I *know* where the Japs will be. And that's where we're heading. I figure they musta *moved* since we launched. And if they did, which way will they go? I'll tell you. They'll be heading east. *Away* from Midway. Over and *out*, Mr. Gay."

Waldron's *"out"* left no room for argument, and Gay switched off his transmitter. His gunner/radioman,

Third Class Petty Officer Huntington's voice came over the intercom. "What the hell good's our orders if the skipper is gonna lead us off on his own? I don't like it, Mr. Gay."

"Take it easy, Huntington. If anybody can track down the Japs, it's Commander Waldron. He's part Sioux Indian."

The second radio flash from Scout Four had advised Admiral Nagumo that the ships sighted consisted of five enemy cruisers, five destroyers. No carriers. Nagumo had been vastly relieved and had ordered the rearming of his planes to continue. The moment they were ready and spotted they were to be launched for a second strike on Midway.

But before the rearming could get underway, sixteen SBD's had appeared overhead. They were from Midway, Major Lofton "Joe" Henderson's Marine dive-bombing Squadron 24. The Japanese had been astounded when, instead of screaming down on their carriers from high altitude, the Americans came in at low level, like torpedo planes, although they carried armor-piercing bombs. They could not know that Henderson was leading pilots who were barely out of flying school and who had had no dive-bombing training. His only chance to score a hit, Henderson had felt, was a glide-bombing attack. He had concentrated on Admiral Yamaguchi's carrier, the *Hiryu*. The *Hiryu* came through the suicide attack absolutely unscathed.

Now, a short while later, a third flash was radioed from Scout Four. Nagumo studied it in dead silence. He read: "Two additional enemy ships . . . apparently cruisers . . . sighted two hundred and fifty miles from Midway . . . speed twenty knots. Carrier with group. Believe to be the *Yorktown*."

Kusaka shook his head, baffled. "The *Yorktown*? That's impossible! The *Yorktown* was virtually blown out of the water at Coral Sea! It *cannot* be the *Yorktown!*"

Nagumo said coldly: "At Coral Sea, was she seen sinking to the bottom, Admiral?"

"No, sir, she was not. But our estimation was that

she was almost certainly not able to reach Pearl Harbor for repairs, and that even if she did, she would require *months* of work to get her seaworthy again!"

"So our information, as always, is purely negative."

"Sir, they cannot possibly have repaired her and moved her this far west in so short a time."

Nagumo said angrily: "We have to assume they have done exactly that, Admiral Kusaka!"

Kusaka threw up his hands. "Well, if it *is* the *Yorktown,* we must destroy her at once. We have no alternative . . ."

Now Nagumo was furious.

He said, shouting: "I see! Now, suddenly the threat from Midway's bombers seems less to you than it did when you urged me to switch our planes from torpedoes to bombs."

Kusaka said tightly: "Midway will have to wait, sir. I doubt if they have much to throw at us after their first failures."

Genda corrected the young Admiral, bluntly. "Failures? . . . Not quite, sir. We've had to send up most of our second-wave fighters to beat them off."

"Then recover them, Genda," Kusaka said heatedly. "Get them refueled and rearmed quickly."

He turned to Nagumo and said in a more controlled voice: "Sir, we should rearm our bombers immediately, and attack the enemy carrier."

Nagumo was furious.

"Back to torpedoes again, Kusaka, is that it? More wasted time! I thank you!"

There was the distant sound, overhead, of a hundred planes, and Genda quickly raised his binoculars. He turned back to the admiral and said urgently: "Lieutenant Tomonaga's strike is returning, sir. Do I have your permission? . . ."

The admiral nodded, and Genda picked up the phone. He still watched the bombers as he spoke into it: "Communications, put me onto Lieutenant Tomonaga's frequency . . ."

He waited a while, and they listened to the heavy static coming over the speaker. He said at last: "Tomonaga? This is Commander Genda. Do you read me?"

The voice was faint, distorted by the heavy static: "I read you, Commander."

"Report."

Tomonaga said: "Request permission to land, sir. Many of my pilots report near-empty fuel tanks. Many have antiaircraft hits. Urgent we land immediately, Commander."

Genda turned back to the admiral. The communications officer was handing him another message, and he waited for the admiral to read it.

Nagumo looked up at him and gestured with the message form: "Admiral Yamaguchi advises that we launch an attack on the American carrier immediately. That we send out our bombers at once with whatever they are armed with."

Genda said urgently: "And while we are launching, sir, Tomonaga's pilots will be crashing into the sea."

Nagumo fingered the message from Yamaguchi, then stared up at Tomonaga's circling planes. He hesitated, then said, at last: "Very well. We will wait until we've recovered all our airborne bombers, Tomonaga's flight. While the flight deck is in use for the recovery, we will send the other planes below and rearm them with torpedoes and armor-piercing bombs. Then . . . we'll launch one massive attack on the American carrier."

Genda nodded. He picked up the phone again and began giving the necessary orders.

And now the *Yorktown* herself was entering the battle. On her flying bridge, Murr Arnold and Captain Buckmaster were watching the last of the scout planes touch down, the landing signal officer bringing them down perfectly. Admiral Fletcher and Matt Garth came out from the chart room, and the admiral asked:

"That's the last of the scouts?"

Arnold nodded. "The last one, Admiral."

"Good."

He turned to the skipper. "Captain Buckmaster . . . launch everything we've got. Immediately."

"Aye, aye, sir."

The captain nodded to his air operations officer, and Murr Arnold picked up the phone and gave the order.

Moments later, a stentorian voice came at them over the P.A. system. It was the sound they had all been waiting for: "Pilots! Man your planes."

They watched as the flight deck was suddenly teaming with activity. Ramos, Mansen, Novelli, Tom Garth, Commander Thatch, all were racing to their planes.

As Tom Garth climbed up onto the wing of his Grumman Wildcat, he felt, strangely, that he was being watched. He looked up and saw his father's eyes on him. He held the look, but his face was frigid and unforgiving. Then, without a sign or a gesture, he climbed into the cockpit.

The order came over the P.A.: "Stand by to start engines! Stand clear of propellers!"

There was a moment of silence, and then the final order: "Start engines!"

The sound of the planes roaring to life was appalling. The exhausts were spluttering, coughing black smoke and then hissing blue flame. The signal officer swung his arms and signaled the first of the F4F's into the air.

It was Tom Garth's plane, and his father watched as it shot off the end of the deck and wheeled up high, climbing at its maximum two thousand-plus feet per minute. He saw the other F4F's follow, and then the SBD's, one after the other in rapid, ordered succession.

He turned away, his emotions mixed. He was worried for his son's safety, and also worried about his failure to reach him.

He glanced at the admiral, and saw that he was smiling gently.

Fletcher said, quietly: "He'll do all right, Matt."

Matt Garth nodded. "Thank you, sir. I'm sure he will."

23

However empty the ocean had once appeared, its replica on the *Yorktown* plot now indicated that it was teeming with activity.

The latest additions, now, were the carriers' attack groups, on their designated course of two-four-oh, heading for Nagumo's fleet. There were three of them —Bombing Three, Torpedo Three, and Fighting Three, and Arnold was reading out their status report for Admiral Fletcher and Garth.

Arnold's voice was calm with a self-imposed restraint he found hard to maintain. "Torpedo Three at fifteen hundred feet, sir. Bombers and fighters are going in at nineteen thousand. Fifteen minutes to target, course constant."

The admiral looked at Matt Garth. "Who's coordinating the attack?"

"Max Leslie, sir. He's leading Bombing Three."

"How many?"

"Sixteen SBD's, Admiral. Armed with thousand-pounders."

Fletcher moved to the window and stared down to the huge flight deck. It was almost empty now, and he could see the newly-welded plates that Gillette's ship-fitters at Pearl Harbor had positioned to repair the gaping hole in her flight deck.

He said, brooding: "It was an eight hundred-pound bomb we took at Coral Sea. If they'd hit us again, we'd have been out of action forever, but they didn't. They broke off the attack, and I'll spend the rest of my life wondering why."

"They lost a lot of planes, Admiral."

"They still had plenty of bombers left, on board the *Zuikaku*, but . . . they thought we were dead. They didn't believe a carrier could take eight hundred pounds of high explosive amidship and still survive."

Matt nodded. "It was a miracle that she did."

Fletcher went on, brooding: "You ever go hunting, Matt?"

He was surprised. "A little, sir."

"It's like when you're after big game. The golden rule is . . . *make sure your quarry is dead before you turn your back*. That's what the Japs should have done, and they didn't. So now . . . Now we'll see what Leslie can do to them with his thousand-pounders."

Commander May Leslie was flying precisely at nineteen thousand feet, and he was checking his compass and his watch. He counted the seconds, flipped on his radio, and said clearly: "Helen Leader to Helen Group. Time to arm our bombs. I say again. Arm bombs."

He reached down to the manual-arming control. Close by it, there was a newly-installed electric arming-switch, one of the complicated devices which had given the armorer so much trouble back in the assembly and repair factory at Pearl Harbor.

For three days they had worked on the circuitry, and had almost decided to tear them out as Matt Garth had ordered; but, at last, the arming-switches had begun to function correctly.

Leslie flicked it on, and the plane bounced crazily up into the air. He swore soundlessly, and looked through the Plexiglas window and confirmed what he already knew was true; his bomb was falling uselessly into the sea.

He threw the radio switch and yelled: "Helen Leader to Helen Group! Keep your hands off those damned electric switches. We've still got a snafu! Use manual control!"

But he was too late. The voices came back at him over the radio circuit, confused, excited, and angry:

"Mine dropped too, Commander! . . ."

"Jesus, there goes mine too! . . ."

"What the hell can we do now, sir? Drop spitballs on the Japs? . . ."

"All right, pipe down! The rest of you use manual control. Helen Leader out."

Leslie was barely able to restrain himself from kicking a hole in the side of his ship. His rear-seat man, Aviation Gunner, Third Class, George Wilson didn't help matters when after a long moment, he got on the intercom: "Commander Leslie? . . ."

"What is it, Wilson?"

"Aren't you going back to the ship for another bomb?"

Leslie was too furious to reply. At length, he heard Wilson supply his own answer. "Yeah . . . I guess they'd keep us aboard, wouldn't they? The show would be over . . ."

Yorktown's Bombing Three continued on its way, sixteen SBD's holding their precise formation.

Only a few minutes' flying time away, across the distant horizon, the last of Tomonaga's Midway strike force was landing on the *Akagi's* flight deck. The moment it touched down, Genda hurried to the bridge. He saluted Nagumo and said: "All aircraft now on board, sir."

The admiral turned to him. "And Lieutenant Tomonaga?"

"The *Hiryu* reports that he was the last to be recovered, sir. With less than a teacupful of fuel in his tanks."

"Very well."

He turned back to the plot and studied it for a while, and said to Captain Aoki: "Now, I want as much sea space as possible between us and Midway. We'll close the range on that enemy carrier. Reverse course, and steer northeast at battle speed."

"Yes, sir."

Nagumo went out on the flying bridge where he could get a better view of the activity on the flight deck. The Kates and Vals were being lowered in the elevators for refueling and rearming. There was exhaustion on the sweating faces of the handlers as they swarmed over the planes, and the contact bombs, hastily removed, were stacked wherever they could find room on the deck.

Kusaka and Genda were at the admiral's side, and

he said to them: "We're very vulnerable now. The sooner we get out and away from the island, the better I'll like it."

It was precisely as Commander Waldron had predicted. Torpedo Eight was flying on its changed course at fifteen hundred feet, strung out in a long scouting line abreast. Waldron was watching the ocean. He flipped on his radio. "Red Fox Leader to Kits. Okay, fellas, keep your eyes skinned now. This is where the Japs ought to be. Somewhere close by . . ."

A voice cut in, excited, shouting: "Commander Waldron! . . ."

"I see it."

There was a dark column of black smoke on the horizon, and he went on: "If that smoke is what I think it is . . . V formation, move into position behind me. We're going in."

Close on Waldron's right wing, moving up fast now, Ensign Gay and his gunner were staring out at the smoke, too. Ensign Gay was grinning. He said into the intercom: "What did I tell you, Huntington?!"

Huntington's reply was caustic and apprehensive. "Yeah. If you're going hunting Japs, to hell with orders or fighter protection . . . just follow a gung-ho Indian."

Waldron pushed his plane to its maximum. The air speed indicator showed two hundred and fifteen when he looked back and checked the position of the others, noting with approval that their formation was tight and precise.

He flipped on the intercom: "Dobbs? See if you can raise Bombing Eight and Fighting Eight."

He heard the radioman's voice coming back at him: "Okay, skipper, but we lost 'em when we changed course."

"They can't be too far away. I want to coordinate our attack."

Dobbs switched on his radio transmitter and began calling, his voice tinged with anxiety.

"Red Fox Eight Leader to Badger Eight Leader. Red

Fox Leader to Badger Eight Leader and Bobcat Eight Leader. Do you read me? Do you read me? Come in Badger Eight . . . Bobcat Eight . . ."

There was a long silence, and the smoke on the horizon was rapidly getting nearer. Dobbs called again, more urgently now: "Badger Eight . . . Bobcat Eight! Come in please! Come in! Do you read me? . . ."

There was another long and frustrating silence. He said at last over the intercom: "No use, Commander. I can't raise anyone. They're out of range."

The smoke had taken on a clearer form now, and the outline of the Japanese carrier was taking shape. Then another was coming into sight, and another . . .

Four of them!

Waldron could scarcely control his excitement. He said, forcing a calm into his voice: "Okay. We can't wait all day."

He snapped on his radio transmitter. "Red Fox Leader to Kits. We're going in. Flight Two and Four hit the carriers on the left. Flight One and Three ram it into the other two bastards."

Ensign Gay said: "Oh, Jesus. We're going in without fighter cover! . . ."

On board the *Akagi,* the air-raid siren was already sounding. Genda picked up the phone and said urgently: "Where, Skywatch? *Where?*"

He listened, his face grim, and put down the phone and said: "Off the port quarter, Admiral. Enemy torpedo bombers."

Nagumo was very calm now. He looked at the flight deck and back to Genda and said: "The rearming?"

"Finished, sir. The *Kaga, Soryu,* and *Hiryu* have signaled that they are also finished and ready to launch against the American carrier. But first we'll have to deal with this torpedo attack."

"Then launch your fighters, Genda. Signal the others to do the same. Let's get this over with as quickly as possible."

"Yes, sir."

Genda picked up the phone, and almost at once the

signal lights were flashing, the launch officer racing to his position, and the first of the Zekes was hurtling into the air.

The American torpedo planes were closing fast, skimming in at wave-top level. Waldron was on the radio. "I say again. Flight Two and Four attack the carriers on your left. One and Three take on the other two. Hold in tight. Stay in section as long as you can. Good luck to all of us!"

On the bridge of the *Hiryu*, Admiral Yamaguchi was watching the oncoming TBD's through his field glasses. Captain Tomeo Kaku was close beside him, a look of astonishment on his face.

He said, disbelieving: "They're coming in without fighter protection? It can't be!"

Yamaguchi was searching the sky high above. "It seems to be, Captain, nonetheless."

"But it's . . . suicide. Mindless suicide."

"Perhaps. But it's an effective technique."

"Sir?"

"We can't launch our attack against their carrier while we're busy dodging their torpedoes. And they're using up our fighters."

Captain Kaku shook his head. He said again: "It's suicide!"

Now, Torpedo Eight was mounting its attack. The lumbering TBD's were wheeling off for their individual strikes, and Ensign Gay, on a collision course with the beam of one of the giant Japanese carriers, heard the frantic voice of his gunner: "Zekes above us! . . . Jesus, a hundred of them! . . ."

He heard the bullets ripping into his fuselage, splattering into the cockpit, and he heard Huntington shriek once: "My God! . . ."

Gay swung around in his seat and saw that Huntington was slumped over his gun, dead. He turned back and flew straight into the inferno of antiaircraft fire that was coming at him from the *Kaga*, zigzagging now in evasive action, while the black puffs of exploding shells splattered the skies around him.

Now he was at zero feet, skimming the tops of the waves, and he worked at the release mechanism of his torpedo frantically. It would not release. He kicked at it in frustration, and felt the plane suddenly rise as his torpedo finally fell away into the water. As he tried to retrim his ship, he saw that the cockpit was a shambles. There was a bloodied mess on the side of his seat, and he realized with a shock that Huntington's dead body had been blown apart by a burst of Zeke cannon fire.

There was another Zeke on his tail, and one diving at him from dead ahead. Infuriated, he pulled back on his stick and tried to ram it. He barely missed clipping its wing. Another swathe of bullets sliced into the cockpit, flak from the *Kaga*'s AA batteries. Gay threw the stick forward again, and skimmed over the carrier's deck so close that he could see the faces of the men on board turned upward to stare at him, bringing him for the first time a personal aspect to this battle. It had seemed, for so long, a question of one machine against another, and now . . . now the angry faces were there, wide-eyed and open-mouthed as he zoomed over their heads.

Gay's plane took two more Zeke cannon shells, staggered, and pancaked into the sea. He fought open the cockpit canopy and rolled himself out, hitting the water hard and gripping the cushion that was unexpectedly in his arms. Wiping the oil and the blood from his eyes, he looked up to see the planes of his flight crashing into the sea one by one, the skies above them crowded with Japanese fighters diving on them, climbing fast to dive again, shooting them down with an ease that was appalling.

Waldron was the last to go.

His flight had managed to get close enough to the *Akagi* to drop three torpedoes but all of them missed their mark by a wide margin as the flagship executed a hard turn to port. Then two Zekes were diving on him from his right, a third coming up on the left. Machine-gun slugs were raking his plane, and a quick glance over his shoulder showed that Dobbs was dead.

His cockpit was on fire now, and he struggled desperately with the canopy. He could not free it. Then it came up at last and he tried to push his way out. Burning fuel was everywhere, and he himself was on fire as the plane hit the water and exploded in a great ball of flame.

In the water, Ensign Gay clutched his air cushion and struggled to stay afloat. The explosion of Waldron's plane signaled the end of Torpedo Eight's attack. Not one of his flight had survived.

There was only the sound in the air now of the Zekes receding, and he was all alone.

Admiral Fletcher, Matt Garth, Murr Arnold, and the entire staff of the *Yorktown* combat information center had listened to the loudspeakers which had piped in Waldron's radio frequency. It was garbled by static and fading badly. They could catch an excited word or two, a shouted warning by one pilot to another, but that was all. Now only the crackle of static and hiss of white noise issued from the combat circuit.

Fletcher looked at Garth. "What the hell happened?"

Matt said, grimly: "One of our torpedo groups attacked, sir."

"But which one? What happened?"

On board the *Akagi,* Admiral Nagumo lowered his binoculars. There was no triumph in his voice. He said heavily: "A whole squadron. Fifteen very brave crews . . ."

Kusaka replied: "Foolish, sir. They hurled themselves into our fire like so many moths at a candle."

The admiral turned to Genda. "Do we have the casualty report yet, Commander?"

"We should have it momentarily, Admiral."

Nagumo looked at the dispatch which Genda had just been handed. Genda explained it. "A routine signal, sir. One of our screening vessels . . . the destroyer *Arashi* . . . reports an unsuccessful torpedo attack on her by an enemy submarine. She's left her station to make a depth-charge attack."

The admiral nodded, and as they waited for the casualty report Genda watched him covertly and wondered about the emotion that was barely showing on the stolid face.

A moment later, the communications officer hurried in, and Genda took the message and read it with quiet satisfaction.

"Admiral . . . one of our fighters suffered a minor hit, and has already been safely recovered. All the other planes are landing now. No casualties."

The admiral said: "Shipboard damage, Commander?"

Genda said: "None, sir. None at all."

24

Lieutenant Commander Stanhope "Stan" Ring was scanning the sea 14,000 feet below. He had absolutely clear visibility. He had led the ten F4F's and the thirty-five SBD's of Fighting Eight and Bombing Eight off the *Hornet* and now it was 9:47 A.M. and they were supposedly at the point where they should be making contact with the Japanese carrier strike force. The sea was absolutely empty. Ring was puzzled and angry. He flipped on his radio transmitter and said to Lee Berg, one of his veteran pilots to whom he had entrusted the navigation: "Eagle Leader to Navigator A-One, check your figures again. I don't see a goddamn Jap ship anywhere."

Berg's voice came back: "I've checked and double-checked, Commander. We flew two-four-oh degrees for exactly a hundred and sixty miles. That's what our orders said."

"Well, where the hell are they? We've been criss-crossing this area for damn near half an hour."

Another pilot's voice chimed in. "We'd better do something quick, Stan. We're using up a lot of fuel."

Berg said: "The Japs must have moved, Commander."

The pilot responded, acidly: "Good thinking, Navigator. But which way?"

There was some rather grim laughter over the circuit and someone else suggested: "Yeah. Work that one out on your Ouija board, Lee!"

Ring cut in. "Knock off the chatter. Lee?"

"Yes, sir."

"They probably went toward Midway. They'd want to get in closer for their next attack. We'll head southeast. Give me a beeline course for the island."

The navigator quickly worked it out and Commander Ring led the *Hornet*'s forty-five planes on a course exactly opposite to that which the Japanese carriers had taken . . . an error in judgment that was to put them out of the battle, once and for all.

At 10:01 A.M., Lieutenant Commander Eugene E. Lindsey, leading the fourteen TBD's of the *Enterprise*'s Torpedo Six had the Japanese carriers in sight on his horizon. He was on the radio, calling urgently for the fighters and dive-bombers with whom he was supposed to coordinate his attack.

"Robin Six Leader to Raven and Eagle Six! Come in! Raven Six, Eagle Six. Do you read me? I've made contact! Four enemy carriers! Come in!"

He flipped off the transmitter and raised the gain on his receiver, but he heard only the empty wash of static.

He hit the transmitter key again and said to his pilots: "Robin Leader to Flock. It's no use, guys. We'll have to go it alone."

One of the pilots responded angrily: "Shit! Whoever dreamed up these midocean rendezvous ought to have his goddamn head examined! They're too tricky . . ."

Another voice cut in. "Jap fighters dead ahead! Angeles Five!"

Lindsey said: "I see them. Keep bunched up. Follow me!"

Fighting Three, out of the carrier *Yorktown*, was flying at fifteen thousand feet, in V formation, through scattered white clouds that obscured, and then disclosed, the brilliant, blue-green sea below.

Commander Thatch was in the lead. His first-wing

man was Tom Garth, nervous and tensed-up, thinking of his father, of the hard look in his eyes when he'd taken off.

Hard? Or had there been a loneliness there, a sadness, even?

He was thinking too of Haruko, and wondering what she was doing at this moment, wondering whether she was still in the Honolulu internment facility or if she had been shipped back to the mainland with her parents.

A motion caught his eye. He glanced at the F4F on his left, and saw Mansen gesturing at him and grinning broadly; he looked the other way and saw Ramos, on his right, rubbing the top of his crew-cut head with rapid, excited motions.

He looked back at Mansen, who grimaced and tapped his forehead as though to say: "He's nuts, don't pay him any attention . . ."

What was it Ramos had said: "When it bristles, there's Japs around . . ."

And then, suddenly, a voice boomed out of the combat circuit: "Bertha Three Leader to Mabel Three Leader. Jim! On the horizon! Three . . . Jesus! *Four* Jap carriers!"

He was startled, yanked sharply out of his daydreaming. It was the voice of Lieutenant Commander Jim Massey, leading his twelve TBD's with their twenty-one-inch torpedoes, down there far below him somewhere. He heard him yell to his radioman: "Send it, send it!"

He looked below and saw them now, an awesome sight. The four great carriers, with their escorting cruisers and destroyers, were streaming at flank speed on a northeasterly course. They looked enormous. He saw that on his right Ramos was gesturing at him again, grinning from ear to ear and kissing the tips of his fingers, then planting them squarely on the top of his head.

He heard Massey yelling at Jim Thatch, "Are you ready up there, Jim?" And Thatch's answering voice: "Let's go, Lem. We're running low on fuel up here."

Massey's voice again, talking to his flyers now: "Bertha Three Leader to Small Fry. We'll concentrate on the closest flattop. Push in close and get hits. Let's go!" He heard Thatch's voice: "Mabel Three Leader. Stand by, fellas, they're going in. Keep your eyes skinned. Keep your altitude."

There was a terrible tautness in the pit of Tom's stomach. He looked at Ramos again and saw the wide grin was still there; it did not comfort him at all. He found he was trembling, and looked across at Mansen and saw the tight, grim look on his face. He wondered if Novelli and the others felt as scared as he did, if Ramos's grin was a subterfuge, meant to convince himself and the world at large that he was not in the least apprehensive.

He heard a voice coming over the radio, and wondered whose it was: "Hey, Lem, have they seen us yet?" And another unidentified voice answering: "I don't know. I guess not. Not yet; we're coming in out of the sun . . . We'll soon find out."

He saw, below him at 1,500 feet, the V formation of Massey's torpedo planes, and thought: "My God, they're the ones that will get all the crap thrown at them . . ."

And then, to his astonishment, he caught a brief glimpse, no more, of another formation streaking in from the opposite direction, and he knew it was Torpedo Six, the TBD's from the *Enterprise,* joining in the battle that was about to begin. Before the clouds swallowed them up again, he counted fourteen of them; and there was a sudden elation in him, as though the battle were practically over, and won.

There was relative peace on board the *Akagi.*

Admiral Nagumo was sipping his tea as he watched the quick movements of the aides at the plot, and Kusaka said, a note of expectation in his voice: "Ten more minutes, Admiral. And we'll be within striking range of the enemy carrier."

"Very good. Perhaps now we can finish what we began at Coral Sea, if that really is the *Yorktown.*"

Kusaka, beaming, was about to answer when the sudden wail of the air-raid siren sounded. He moved to the phone. But Genda was there first, snatching it up and saying urgently: "Again? Where are they, Sky-watch?"

He listened for a moment, frowning darkly, hung up the phone and said to Nagumo, very quietly: "Two separate groups, Admiral. Torpedo planes."

Nagumo was shocked. *"Two* groups? Both torpedo planes?"

"Yes, sir. Coming in at low level from opposite directions."

"Our fighter cover?"

"They're scrambling now, sir."

Nagumo picked up his glasses and hurried out onto the flying bridge. They both followed him, and soon they were able to pick the enemy planes up, mere specks in the distance but closing fast. They watched them in silence for a moment, and Genda said at last: "I count twelve coming in from starboard, fourteen from port, Admiral."

"Twenty-six planes, and all torpedo-bombers?"

"Yes, sir."

It was hard for Nagumo to contain his anger. He said harshly: "Then they can't all be coming from one carrier."

Kusaka said, blustering: "They *must* be coming from Midway, sir, it's the most obvious explanation . . ."

Genda interrupted him, caustically: "Or a *second* carrier." He turned to the admiral and said; "Sir, we have still heard nothing from Scout Four since it sighted the one enemy carrier. I think the *Soryu* should send out one of its fast scout planes for another look. We *must* be certain of what we're up against!"

Nagumo said quickly: "See to it immediately."

Torpedo Three was down to attack-level now, skimming over the surface of the water. Commander Massey was holding his course steadily and watching the sky above him. He saw what he was expecting, the Japanese fighter cover coming in to their ships' defense. He yelled into his mike: "They're lining up to jump us, Jim! About a dozen Zekes!"

Thatch's voice was strong and confident: "We're

right above 'em, Lem! Mabel Three to Hustlers. Let's break 'em up."

The F4F's began to peel off, diving steeply down for the Japanese fighters. Tom Garth was the third in the formation, and the clutching at his stomach was almost intolerable now. He saw the Zekes far below and gunned his throttle. Suddenly one was in his sight. He fired a burst, and was startled to see that it simply wasn't there any more.

He wondered, for a moment, what had become of it, and then a voice came at him: "Tom, behind! Behind you!"

It was Ramos. He swung round in his seat and saw the Zeke on his tail, closing. He went into a tight dive and pulled up sharply, and saw the enemy fighter sweep past him, climbing higher still for another pass.

He made a tight right turn, and it was on his tail again. He swung left so hard he thought his wings would fall off, and it shot past him again. But when he looked round, there it was once more, close behind him.

He was beginning to panic now, twisting, diving, turning, climbing. Twice he almost, but not quite, got it in his sights, and he fired his guns furiously; once, he thought he had clipped its wing.

And there it was again. Only now Ramos was barreling in on it from the port side. Tom saw the burst of Ramos's machine-gun fire rip into the Zeke. It disintegrated in a massive cloud of smoke and exploding debris that seemed to fill the air all around him, but he had not time to feel any elation over Ramos's victory. Dead ahead of him, one of his flights' F4F's went down, twisting over and over, on fire. Then another F4F lost its wing and he saw the pilot bail out and hang there in the sky like a doll on the end of a string.

Then suddenly there were two Zekes on his tail, closing in on him fast. He jammed the controls over and went into a tight roll. One of the Zekes swept past him, its cannons blazing.

The burst shattered his instrument panel, and he felt a hot, sharp pain in his left leg. His engine was on fire. He struggled to keep his craft in a shallow dive as he hit the extinguisher button. Smoke was pouring into the cockpit now, and the CO_2 gas was smothering him with its fumes.

The sea was rushing up at him now, and he closed his eyes and fought to bring the nose of the crippled plane up. He was barely conscious, and he was thinking: "Haruko, Haruko . . . will I ever see you again?"

The Zekes were tearing into the slower, less maneuverable F4F's, scattering them, cutting them open, sending them down into the sea in flames, and all the time the antiaircraft guns of the four carriers and their escorts were blazing, taking their toll as the gunners kept up a rapid, accurate fire.

And then it was over. The sky around the carriers was suddenly empty, and there were shattered wrecks of smoking planes in the water, burning and hissing out clouds of steam as they slipped beneath the water.

Over the *Akagi*'s PA system came the order: "Cease firing! Cease firing! All guns cease firing!"

Admiral Nagumo and Kusaka were on the flying bridge throughout the raid, and Genda was at the telephone, talking with the fighter director.

There was triumph in Kusaka's voice: "Admiral, we've crushed every one of their attacks. And not a single torpedo has even come close."

Nagumo did not share his pleasure. He said quietly: "They sacrifice themselves like samurai, these Americans. It is not a pleasant spectacle, Kusaka, to see so many brave men die. So uselessly."

"As long as they are the enemy, Admiral . . ."

Genda had hung up the phone, and there was a worried look on his face. Nagumo noticed it, and felt the anxiety, too; it seemed to him that this man, this old friend of his, was always right. He said: "What is it, Genda?"

"The fighter director, sir. He reports that the last attack pulled our entire cover down to sea-level. They're off now, wave-hopping after the survivors."

Nagumo said, startled: "Then we have no fighter umbrella over us?"

"No, sir. We're trying to recall them now, sir, trying to get them back to their patrol altitudes."

"How many fighters are standing by to cover our attack against the American carrier?"

"Barely enough to do the job, Admiral. I don't advise diverting any of them. We'll have our umbrella back in short order."

"Warn the fighter director that it's imperative."

"Yes, sir."

As he turned away, Nagumo said: "And the fast scout plane from the *Soryu*, Genda?"

"It's searching now, sir. We should know very shortly, one way or the other."

The *Soryu*'s scout was coming to the end of its segment, far from its carrier. The pilot was flying high above the clouds, at his maximum of close to thirty thousand feet.

He was staring down at the water now, watching the line of ships that had just come into his sight. He caught his breath and said urgently: "Radio! Three carriers, three American carriers! Get through to the admiral's flagship, and be quick about it. I repeat, three American carriers, *Yorktown*-class!"

He heard the radioman's answer: "Yes, sir!" and he waited to hear the message transmitted.

But there was only silence. The radioman was flipping the power switch repeatedly and tapping at the glass over the dead carrier-wave meter. He tapped it again and again; the needle would not swing up. He checked the power plugs into the transmitter and found them all in order. The pilot said impatiently: "Send it, man, what are you waiting for?"

"The transmitter isn't working, sir. We're not sending out any signal."

"Well, fix it!"

"I'll try, sir."

"Try? . . . Damn it, do you realize what's at stake?"

"Yes, sir. I'll try."

But the operator was not able to make the necessary repairs. The tide of the battle was beginning to turn. On the tranquil sea far below the Japanese scout plane, the three American aircraft carriers steamed on, detected but unreported.

They were the *Enterprise,* the *Hornet* . . . and the *Yorktown.*

25

Now it was the time of the dive-bombers.

Out of the carrier *Enterprise,* the thirty-one Douglas SBD's of Bombing Six were flying steadily through cloud which looked like huge white boulders strewn across a vast quarry.

In the lead plane, Lieutenant Commander Wade C. McClusky was trying to focus his binoculars on a tiny speck in the ocean fourteen thousand feet below. His engine had been smoking for the last half hour, making it necessary for him to advance his throttle to maintain cruising speed. One of his section leaders, Lieutenant Hans Donig, was eyeing the ugly wisp of black trailing from McClusky's ship. He heard the engine cough and saw the wisp become thicker and more ominous.

His radioman-gunner, Bob Greer, was also watching McClusky's plane, and he spoke over the intercom. "There he goes again, Mr. Donig . . . coughing up more oil. He must be running awfully hot and using a lot more gas than the rest of us."

Donig did not reply. Greer said: "If we don't find the Japs pretty damn pronto, we'll all be out of gas."

Donig said: "Take it easy, Greer. Commander McClusky knows what he's doing."

"He's taking us back and forth across the same water for the last thirty minutes, that's what he's doing. And I don't get it."

Donig replied with forced patience: "We were ordered to fly two four oh for a hundred and sixty miles. That's where we are."

"Yeah. Nowhere."

When McClusky's engine protested again with a cough and a belch of smoke, Donig flipped on his radio transmitter. "Raven Leader from Black Bird One. Commander McClusky . . . better take a look at your fuel gauge. If we don't turn back damn soon . . ."

McClusky's voice cut him off: "I know, I know. But take a look down there. Two o'clock. What's that look like to you?"

Donig squinted through his binoculars. At fourteen thousand feet, the object McClusky had sighted was a mere speck. Donig said, not at all certain: "A Jap destroyer? . . ."

"That's what I figure it is. And it's going somewhere in a hell of a hurry. I wonder where?"

"Why don't we drop down and blow it to hell and gone, Commander?"

"A single destroyer? You gotta be out of your mind, Donig. No, we'll keep our altitude and follow it. Let's see where it leads us." He raised his voice a trifle: "Raven Leader to Flock. Maintain formation. Out."

Bombing Six droned on, unaware that the enemy destroyer they were tailing was the *Arashi,* which had broken off its depth-charge attack on the American submarine and was returning to its screening station with Nagumo's carrier striking force.

The clouds were thicker now and McClusky began to fret about losing contact. There was a thick layer of stratocumulus, standing out in sharp relief against the cobalt of the water below which showed through from time to time in a sharply-defined, striated pattern. And then they changed to patches of small, white globular masses, a kind of tufted circus, and there was much more of the sea visible now, and on it . . .

McClusky sat bolt upright in his seat. He heard the excited chatter of his pilots coming at him, fast and furious:

"Raven Leader! . . . There they are!"

"Dead ahead, Raven Leader! Sweet Jesus, lookit them! . . ."

"Commander, down there, whoo-ee! . . ."

"Raven Leader, Raven Leader, the whole bloody Jap navy! . . ."

He yelled: "This is Raven Leader! Pipe down! Everybody pipe down! Stay off the air till I report contact!"

More calmly now, watching the three carriers in close formation, a fourth one standing off far on the northern horizon, he called; "Raven Leader to Mother Goose. Raven Leader to Mother Goose. I have them in sight. Four, repeat four, enemy carriers. I say again. I have sighted four enemy carriers."

He looked back, checked over the positions of his bombers, and knew that now he was going to find out just how good his pilots were. And how good the Japanese antiaircraft gunners were, as well.

It was almost exactly twenty minutes after Torpedo Three, Fighter Three and Torpedo Six had been blown out of the skies: 10:21 in the morning.

And at almost exactly the same moment, Bombing Three, out of *Yorktown,* led by Max Leslie, was coming up from the opposite quarter and sighting Nagumo's carriers as well.

Leslie was staring down at them, too. He took a long, deep breath and spoke to his radioman. "Billy? Rustle up the fighters and the torpedo-bombers. We're supposed to coordinate our attack. And by the size of that force, that's what we damn well better do . . ."

He heard Billy Wilson's voice, calling urgently: "Helen Leader to Bertha Leader. Helen Leader to Mabel Leader. Come in please." There was a long pause, and then again: "Come in Mabel, come in Bertha. Where are you? Come in, come in, we've made contact! Come in Mabel Leader, come in, Bertha Leader."

He could not know that he was talking to men who had died. He tried for a while longer and then he said over the intercom: "It's no use, Commander Leslie. Torpedo Three and Fighter Three don't answer."

Leslie swore. "Keep trying, Billy. They can't be too far off, for Christ's sake."

"I don't know, Commander. Maybe they balled up on their navigation."

"Keep trying, damn it!"

"Yes, sir."

On the other side of the carriers, Bombing Six was closer. McClusky was studying them through his glasses, watching as they began to turn slowly. He said into his radio: "Raven Leader to Flock. Looks like they're turning into the wind. You guys know what that means, they're getting ready to launch."

He heard his number-five man answer him: "Where's their fighter patrol, Commander? I don't see any Jap fighters."

McClusky said, searching the skies around him: "Anyone see any fighters up there?"

A voice answered back : "Looks to me like they don't have any up, Commander."

Someone else chimed in: "That doesn't make any sense, fella. The Japs aren't gonna leave their carriers unprotected! Jesus, four of 'em!"

McClusky couldn't believe it either. "Look sharp. They've got to be up here somewhere."

The answers came back at him:

"Nary a sign of them, Commander . . ."

"Negative . . ."

"No, sir, not a fighter in sight, anywhere."

He was jubilant. "We won't wait for them . . . not while we've got four sitting ducks down there. Follow me!"

He peeled off into his dive. One by one, thirty SBD's streaked down after him.

And closing now on the opposite quarter, Commander Leslie was still trying to raise his fighter escort. Billy Wilson said, frustrated: "Sir, it's no use. Commander Massey and Commander Thatch don't answer."

Leslie was angry. He said: "Okay, Billy, hang on. We're going in."

"Sir! We don't have a bomb!"

"I know that. But we can keep some of their gunners busy while the others drop theirs."

He switched on the radio: "This is Helen Leader. We're going in. We'll concentrate on that big bastard up front. You guys who lost your bombs, strafe their antiaircraft. Let's try for hits, everyone. Down we go!"

He nosed his plane over at a seventy-degree angle and began his dive. Sixteen SBD's followed him, their engines screaming.

The *Akagi*, the admiral's flagship, was in the lead, turning now head-on into the wind.

Nagumo was worrying over the plot. He turned to his Chief of Staff and said: "The last two attacks were made by more than fifty torpedo planes. Fifty! There's more than one enemy carrier nearby. There must be!"

Kusaka didn't seem to be in the least concerned. The slight smile on his face moved Nagumo to anger. He banged the palm of his hand down hard on the plot table and repeated: "Fifty, Kusaka!"

The rear admiral nodded, the smile still fixed. "Yes, indeed. And they were almost all destroyed. More importantly, they scored not a single hit! Not one! It was a notable victory, Admiral, one of which we can all be very proud. Of which the empire can be proud!"

Nagumo said angrily: "I am well aware of the excellence of our fighter pilots and of our gunners!"

He turned to his air operations officer. "Genda, why hasn't the *Soryu*'s scout plane reported?"

Kusaka answered quickly and calmly: "If he had seen anything to report, sir . . . he would have reported it."

Genda was not so optimistic. He said: "Something must have gone wrong, Admiral. It should have contacted the American ships more than ten minutes ago."

"Have you been trying to raise him?"

"Yes, sir. We have not succeeded."

Nagumo gripped the edge of the plot table and brooded over the area where the enemy carrier was sighted by the *Tone*'s Scout Four. "First Scout Four is late. It's reports are confusing . . . contradictory . . . and now silence from the *Soryu*'s scout . . ."

Genda said with quiet urgency: "Admiral, I suggest that this is no time to speculate. All our bombers are rearmed and ready."

Nagumo straightened. His voice was once more firm and, Genda thought, as decisive as it had been at Pearl Harbor. "Then signal all carriers: Launch immediately."

Genda moved to the phone and gave the order.

The torpedo-carrying Kates were waiting for the Zekes to take off; they were bunched up tightly at the rear of the long flight deck, and the flagmen were getting ready to launch the fighters into the air.

The noise of their fast-revving engines was ear-splitting, and then, over them, came another sound, the piercing, ominous note of the air-raid warning, sending its shrieking wail out across the decks and over the water.

Genda bolted for the flying bridge, aware that Nagumo and Kusaka were close behind him. One of the junior officers was pointing skyward and yelling something he could not hear over the thunder of the planes. He saw him swing his arm around and point in the opposite direction, too, and there was a moment of terrifying panic as he looked at the decks and saw the bomb- and torpedo-laden planes bunched like sheep in a holding corral. And off on the sides of the flight deck were the stacks of contact bombs which there had been no time to store in the magazine belowdecks.

The antiaircraft guns were firing already, and he looked over to his left and saw that on their flank, the *Soryu* and the *Kaga* were firing, too; the *Hiryu* was out of his sight.

The guns were pounding, the gunners reloading furiously, but their effort was too little and it was too late. The enemy dive-bombers were plummeting out of the sun, and nothing could stop them now.

The first bomb crashed harmlessly into the sea, close on the starboard bow, a great column of water shooting up as it exploded, and then, as the second, third, and fourth enemy planes dived in, three thousand-pounders landed in a dead straight line on the decked fighters.

Genda was blown across the deck with the force of the explosion. When he staggered to his feet he saw that almost half the bridge had been shattered. He gripped the railing and saw, on his flank, that the *Soryu* was taking a line of bombs along her flight deck, too, four of them sending up great columns of fire and smoke as her planes exploded. He saw that beyond the *Soryu,* the *Kaga* was in flames; he could not know it, but the first direct hit had been a bomb dead-center

on the group of waiting torpedo planes, and the second
and third had straddled her midship elevator.

Genda turned his attention to his own ship, and
looked around wildly for his admiral. Just then another
thousand-pounder landed almost exactly on the big
yellow circle that marked the middle of the flight deck.

The ship reeled under the enormous force of its
blast. The planes on the hangar deck below were burning furiously now. The superstructure and the antiaircraft batteries were being raked with a savage fusi-
lade of machine-gun fire, and he saw the gunners in the
foremost turret lying dead across their bulwarks, their
guns silent.

Amidst the holocaust, the stacks of contact bombs on
the flight deck were exploding, hurling shrapnel in
every direction. The Vals and Kates at the far end of
the flight deck were ripped apart, their gas tanks erupting and pouring flaming fuel down into the holds.

Men were fighting their way out of the companion-
ways, some of them on fire, some of them helping
their wounded comrades, and the great geyser of
steam that had erupted from below told him that the
boilers had been ruptured.

He fought his way through the flames and the smoke,
and found the half-disintegrated bridge. There were
men lying dead there, killed by flying splinters, and he
thought, for one terrible moment, that Nagumo was
one of them.

The admiral was lying on the deck with his eyes staring, but he was still moving, his face taut with agony.
Kusaka was trying to help him to his feet. Genda
helped lift him and Nagumo shook his head as though
to force the pain to the back of his mind. They found
an undamaged corner of the bridge and propped him
up against the bulkhead.

There were flames closing in all around them now.
Admiral Nagumo struggled to make himself heard over
the fearful din: "Damage . . . damage report, Commander?"

Genda shook his head. He was inhaling great gulps of
smoke, and he saw that the helm was spinning wildly,

the helmsman, his body bloodied, fighting it hopelessly, trying to bring it hard right.

Another bomb exploded just outside the bridge. He saw the helmsman's head blown open and the officer of the deck leaping into his place, taking over the wheel. He heard him shout: "Captain . . . the helm is dead!"

Captain Aoki was staggering to his feet, his uniform ripped almost entirely off his body. He shouted unsteadily: "Switch to secondary steering! Notify the engineering officer!"

The OD gestured helplessly: "All communications are dead, Captain!"

"And the radio?"

"Destroyed, sir."

Kusaka turned to Admiral Nagumo. He could scarcely make himself heard above the terrible sounds of the dying ship. "Admiral, you must transfer your flag! The cruiser *Nagara* is close by. I'll signal for a boat."

It did not seem that Nagumo heard him. There were tears in Captain Aoki's eyes, and he added his own urgency: "Admiral, please! Shift your flag to the *Nagara,* sir. Leave the *Akagi* to me!"

Now, with infinite weariness, Nagumo raised his head, looked at Genda and said: "The *Kaga?*"

"Very heavily damaged, sir."

"And the *Soryu?*"

"The *Soryu* too."

"The *Hiryu?*"

"We have no news, sir. We have no communications with anyone now. Please, you *must* shift your flag . . ."

Admiral Nagumo looked blankly over the wreck of his flagship and slowly nodded his head.

The planes of Bombing Three and Bombing Six turned away from the carnage and headed back for their carriers. A few of the pilots turned to look back and saw that the brilliant blue of the sky was being darkened now by great clouds of oily black smoke, marking the dying place of the giant Japanese aircraft carriers.

Nine hours later, exactly, the *Kaga,* a floating grave-yard, was to topple over and sink. Within nineteen hours, the *Akagi* would slide to the bottom. And four and a half hours later, the *Soryu* would follow Nagumo's flagship to a deep, deep grave.

26

The carrier *Hiryu,* thirty-seven miles from the burning hulks of the *Akagi,* the *Kaga,* and her sister ship the *Horyu,* was not under attack.

On the bridge, there was a stunned dismay, as Rear Admiral Yamaguchi, Captain Kaku, and the officers of the staff watched through their binoculars the distant columns of smoke that represented all that was left of the three great carriers.

With the invasion force and the supporting cruisers, with the destroyers and supply ships from Guam, with the mine-sweepers from Saipan and the twin columns of the main convoys from Hiroshima, with the ships of the diversionary force out of Ominato—two hundred assorted vessels had been scheduled to take part in this operation.

And the nucleus of all this power lay in the four great carriers. Now three of them, in the space of a few minutes, had been reduced to burning wrecks.

Below, on the flight deck, the pilots and flight crews were dazed; they could not believe that the mighty, invincible carriers of the Imperial fleet could be so quickly reduced to burning hulks. Lieutenant Nichio Kobayashi and Petty Officer Pilot Nakoda were among them, trembling with rage and in the depths of despair.

A messenger ran up to Kobayashi and saluted him. "The Admiral, sir . . . Would you report to him at once."

Kobayashi hurried to the bridge. He found Admiral Yamaguchi there, speaking angrily into the phone. "Radio flash to Admiral Yamamoto on board the flagship *Yamato.* Message begins: 'The *Akagi,* the *Soryu,* and the *Kaga* are on fire. I am attacking!' "

Yamaguchi put down the phone. His face was

drawn; he seemed to have aged, and had lost his jaunty, self-confident bearing. He said, his mouth set and determined: "Ah, Kobayashi. Come, I have a job for you."

He pointed to the plot, indicating the open sea to the northeast of them. "Here, in this general area. This is where the American carriers *must* be. I can't tell you exactly where, but you must find them, Lieutenant. The final outcome of this battle depends on it. And the honor of the *Hiryu,* too. We're the only carrier left in the fight now."

Kobayashi looked dubious. He was a skilled leader and keen fighting pilot, but the area the admiral had indicated seemed enormous. Yamaguchi saw the look on his face and went on: "Their last position was radioed by Scout Four. But it's several hours old."

The pilot was puzzled. "But the fast scout plane from the *Soryu,* sir? Hasn't it reported yet?"

Yamaguchi said gravely: "It hasn't been heard from since it was launched."

"Then how shall I find them, sir?"

"You must lead your group toward their last reported position, northeast of us. And trust to luck that somehow you'll make contact."

Luck? Was all the careful planning for nothing, then? Kobayashi stared out across the water to the smoke that marked the three funeral pyres; then he turned back and saw the grim determination in his admiral's eyes. He saluted and said: "I'll find them, sir. If they're out there anywhere . . . I'll find them."

He was airborne eight minutes later, flying his Val at the head of his V formation, seventeen others behind him and six Zekes flying cover high above them.

He was worried as he stared down at the empty sea ahead, flying at a steady two hundred and ten miles an hour, checking his compass, his watch . . . He flipped on the intercom: "Radioman?"

The radioman's voice was depressed, as though there were dishonor in finding nothing. He said: "Nothing, sir. All enemy ships and aircraft frequencies are silent."

And then, suddenly, there was a note of elation in his voice. "But we have planes below us, sir! Five, twelve . . . seventeen bombers, sir! Enemy SBD's . . ."

"I see them!"

Kobayashi dropped one wing slightly for a better look. It was Bombing Three returning from its successful attack. They were flying carelessly now, in loose formation, their work done, relaxing at their controls.

He heard his radioman again, reporting calmly: "Our fighters are forming up for an attack, sir!"

Kobayashi said quickly: "Signal them to lay back! We will not attack! Use your light and stay off the air!"

"We're not attacking, sir?"

Kobayashi said patiently: "I say again, use your light, maintain radio silence, signal the group to stay back. We have a better target than a handful of bombers. The enemy planes are heading for their carriers, and that's what we are looking for. We'll simply follow them."

He looked across to his wingman. It was Petty Officer Nakoda. The look on his face, tight and grim, seemed to say: "Now . . . it's *our* turn." He pushed forward on the throttle, eased the plane up, and climbed close to the maximum height of thirty-one thousand feet.

Safe from discovery, they watched the American SBD's far below, and kept on their tail.

Commander Leslie was taking it easy. He could hardly believe what had happened back there, and it was difficult not to turn back and make sure that *three* carriers really were burning, crippled to the point of complete destruction. One alone would have been a tremendous victory, but *three* . . . And the *Yorktown* was ahead of them, waiting to recover them, waiting for the excited belowdecks talk that always went on after a kill.

Billy Wilson came in on the intercom. "When do you estimate we'll be touching down, skipper?"

Max Leslie yawned. "About an hour. If our gas holds out and our navigation is right on the nose."

It was less. In forty-five minutes, there was the

Yorktown below them, turning into the wind, with the senior officers out on the flight deck watching their approach with their binoculars.

Matt Garth said, staring out at the tiny specks in the sky: "I count all of Commander Leslie's bombers, sir."

Fletcher nodded. "Good. But where the hell are the rest of Thatch's fighters?"

Arnold moved quickly to the other side of the flying bridge, using his glasses on the open sky. He said: "Off the port quarter, sir. But not all of them," he added grimly.

Matt Garth felt the muscles in his stomach tighten. Then Arnold announced: "I'll bring the fighters down first. They'll be lowest on fuel."

Matt's heart pounded as he watched the F4F's landing, pulled up short and viciously by the arresting cables. One by one they barreled their way in, some of them unsteadily, some of them expertly, some of them barely making it. One by one, the pilots threw back their canopies and climbed out of their planes, almost tumbling down from their cockpits.

The first was Mansen, clutching at a wounded shoulder; then Ramos, reeling with blood streaming down his forehead; then Novelli, his face and body blackened by smoke.

Of Tom Garth, there was no sign at all.

Matt watched them staggering below, desperately anxious to *ask*, but not knowing how to phrase the question.

Another question was on Admiral Fletcher's mind. He looked at his air operations officer and said anxiously: "Did they get any hits, Murr? What's your guess?"

"I haven't the foggiest idea, sir. Damned static! Three carriers with a ringside radio connection . . . and none of us could understand a thing our pilots reported . . . That's Thatch!"

Fletcher, too, recognized Thatch's bulky figure heaving out of his cockpit. He turned to one of his staff officers. "Bring Lieutenant Commander Thatch up here. On the double."

The young ensign snapped a salute and hurried off.

Just then the phone rang and the commander reached for it quickly. He said: "Arnold here." There was a beat, and then "Thank you."

Arnold turned to Matt. "That was Ramos, your boy's wingman. He says Tom's coming in now."

Matt felt a wave of relief. "He's okay?"

"His plane's shot up badly, but Tom's keeping it in the air. Ramos says—the way he's flying, he's got to be able to land it. Your son is a pretty good pilot, Matt."

Now he was coming in, low on the water and still smoking badly. They could hear his engine coughing ominously; one wing was dipping dangerously. The landing signal officer, Fly One, was waving his paddles furiously, and shouting: "Up! Up! Get that goddamn left wing straightened out! Good . . . *Good!* Hold it there . . No! Get it back up! . . ."

Fly One swore suddenly and signaled a wave-off. But the plane came in anyway, much too fast and off-center. It was too high. It skimmed over the first arrester-cable, and the second, touched down, bounced crazily, and swung to one side in a violent, rocking motion . . .

Matt saw the crewmen and the handlers diving for cover and he watched in horror as he saw the crippled plane bounce once more, then hook itself, at an angle, on the last of the cables.

It was not enough to stop it.

The F4F smashed into the bridge island, sheering off its entire front. He saw the engine break off and go spinning across the deck and over the side, and the plane was on fire, one wing torn off.

Already, the fire fighters were swarming over the fuselage extinguishing the flames, and dimly, through the heavy smoke, he saw the rescue crews fighting their way up to the shattered cockpit. He saw the canopy hurled out of the way, and then they were dragging his son out.

There were tears welling in his eyes, and he could not stop the sudden trembling that seized him.

The admiral's hand was on his shoulder. "Get on down there, Matt."

As Matt rushed from the flying bridge a voice came over the intercom, loud and clear: "Bridge from Combat Information!"

Arnold turned. "Go ahead, C.I.C."

"Radar has a third group of aircraft. Definitely bandits. Zero-two-zero relative. Thirty miles. Approaching, *and* climbing, sir."

Arnold looked at the Admiral, startled. "Climbing? Then they're enemy dive bombers."

Fletcher said calmly: "Order Battle Stations. Launch every available fighter. Signal Bombing Three to stay clear, we're under attack!"

Matt hurried to the side, where hospital corpsmen were handling the stretchers, getting them into the elevator. One of them saw him coming, detached himself, and said: "He's alive, Captain. That's about all."

Frozen, he watched the stretcher-bearers taking his son below.

Now, indeed, it was Kobayashi's turn.

He looked down on his quarry from fourteen thousand feet—the *Yorktown*—their old enemy from the Coral Sea, with its escort of two cruisers and six destroyers. His face was set as he began his dive, signaling to the Vals behind him to follow. He could see the Wildcats scrambling up to meet him head-on, and he prepared himself for the battle of his life. He looked back and saw, with satisfaction, that his fighter escort was diving down for the dogfights, seeking to break up the American fighters almost as soon as they were airborne.

He squinted at the massive barrage of antiaircraft fire coming at him, clamped his teeth, and hurtled straight into it, the great carrier in his sights now.

The guns were blazing, the shells exploding viciously around him, but he took his time until he was absolutely sure. Then he reached for the release mechanism and flipped it. He saw his bomb plummet down, watched it turning over and over in the air, and swung the plane hard up and over. The bomb hit dead-center into the flight deck, a perfect strike.

He was conscious of two other planes from his

group close behind him, and as he pulled out of his roll he saw two more bombs bracket the carrier, then a third slamming into the deck. He heard himself shouting a *banzai* . . .

He saw a Wildcat coming at him, its six five-inch machine-guns blazing in unison, and he felt his cockpit being ripped apart. He forced his plane down till it almost touched the water, then up again in a savage, searing climb, rolling as he climbed and getting his opponent in his gun sights. He gave the enemy Wildcat a series of short, sharp bursts, and watched it explode. Then a burst of flak from one of the carrier's escorts caught his tail and blew it off. As he flipped over, out of control, he saw that he was high above the *Yorktown* herself, and upside down.

He saw a bomb from one of his Vals go straight down the smokestack of the stricken carrier and then his plane nosed up, stalled, hung there for a moment, then plunged, in flames, into the sea.

On the *Yorktown*'s bridge, smoke from below was choking everyone, obscuring the flight deck completely. Captain Buckmaster was on the phone getting a damage report from his engineering officer in the bowels of the great ship. His expression was apprehensive and the din of exploding planes and shouting men from the flight deck made it difficult for him to hear. He listened for a moment, then shouted: "All right, Delaney, do your best! If you can maintain enough steam to keep the auxiliaries running, we can start repairs! Keep me informed!"

He hung up and turned to Admiral Fletcher. "We took a bomb down our stack, sir. All our boilers are out. We're dead in the water."

"How long to get them started again? At least some of them?"

"Delaney will let me know, sir, as soon as he's made a thorough check."

Matt Garth was hurrying up from below, and he said grimly: "Radio's down, Admiral, and in all this smoke we can't use visual signals. We're a dead ship, I'm afraid."

Fletcher looked down at the smoke-obscured flight

deck for a moment, pondering the situation. Then he turned to Buckmaster and said, heavily: "I still have a fleet to command, Elliot. I'll have to transfer to the *Astoria*."

Buckmaster spoke to the watch officer. "Order the admiral's launch lowered." He turned back to Fletcher and said: "Better hurry, sir."

Fletcher nodded and looked at Matt. "Should you come with me, or stay here? What do you think, Matt?"

"We have more planes than pilots, Admiral. If we have to fly them off . . . if we can get the flight deck cleared . . . I'd like to be on hand to take one of them."

The admiral held Matt's eyes for a moment. "All right . . . if that's the way you see it. How's your boy?"

Matt shook his head, the anxiety gnawing at him. He said: "Too early to tell, sir."

Fletcher nodded and headed out.

In the cloudless sky above the crippled *Yorktown*, circling at twenty-five thousand feet, Petty officer Pilot Nakoda was making his report to his carrier.

He said into his radio: "This is Zephyr calling Whirlwind, Zephyr to Whirlwind. Enemy carrier is ablaze. I repeat, enemy carrier is ablaze. We are returning to base."

One hundred miles to the southwest, on the bridge of the *Hiryu*, Admiral Yamaguchi, Captain Kaku, and Lieutenant Tomonaga, were gathered under the loudspeaker over which Nakoda's message was coming. They could hear, from below, the excited shouting of the enlisted men, the *banzais* from those who had heard the transmission. But Kaku said, frowning: "That wasn't Lieutenant Kobayashi's voice, surely?"

Tomonaga said, shaking his head: "No, sir, that was Petty Officer Nakoda."

Yamaguchi was deeply disturbed. "Then none of the senior officers survived . . ."

He broke off, and turned, as a staff officer hurried in. He saluted the admiral and said: "The fast scout from the *Soryu*, sir. It's approaching now. He signals that his radio is out."

"Finally. Now we'll finally know what we're up against."

Yamaguchi hurried with Tomonaga down to the flight deck, and watched the scout plane land. When the exhausted pilot had clambered out of his plane, he said to him: "Your report?"

The scout pilot could hardly control his excitement. He saluted, and the words tumbled out: "Three enemy carriers, sir. I sighted three American carriers! I was unable to report them because of radio trouble . . . I'm sorry, Admiral . . ."

Yamaguchi put a hand on the shamefaced pilot's shoulder and said simply: "Well done."

Then he turned to Tomonaga. "Well, Lieutenant . . . it looks like you have more work to do."

Tomonaga said with savage satisfaction: "We know one of the three is burning, sir."

"Yes. So we'll concentrate on the other two. We'll launch all our available planes immediately. You'll lead them, Tomonaga."

"Yes, sir."

A few moments later, the *Hiryu*'s loudspeakers were blasting out the order: "Pilots, man your planes! Launch crews, man your stations! Pilots, man your planes . . ."

Tomonaga returned to the flight deck, suited in his flying gear, and hurried across to the same Kate in which he had led against Midway that morning. The thought flashed across his mind that the strike seemed to have happened a century ago . . .

Suddenly he was aware that the engine had not been started, that the prop was idle. He turned to the handlers and mechanics gathered around his plane and saw the shamedfaced looks on their faces.

He said sharply: "Let's go. Get this ship ready for take-off."

The head mechanic raised his hand as if to stop him. "Your right-wing tank, Lieutenant. It's punctured. We haven't had time to repair it."

Tomonaga was pulling on his helmet "Is the left tank filled?"

"Yes, sir. But you won't have enough fuel to return . . ."

Tomonaga gruntcd. "Start the engine, damn you."

In a few minutes, sixteen planes were roaring off the flight deck of the *Hiryu,* Zekes and Kates, racing off to the northeast once again.

Watching them, Yamaguchi said heavily: "A few hours ago, we filled the sky with our planes. Now, we win or lose with six fighters and ten torpedo planes."

They were all that were left of the once mighty Japanese air armada.

27

The organized chaos on board the *Yorktown* was reminiscent of the struggle in the yards back at Pearl Harbor during those hectic seventy-two hours when she had been patched up for combat duty.

The damage control parties were at work with the extinguishers, the welders cutting out the ripped-open plates and replacing them; and the "black gang" in the engine room was working desperately to give her some power once more.

Captain Buckmaster was clambering over the boiler-room grills, running with oil and water, shouting to make himself heard over the din of the jackhammers and the hissing of the welders' arcs.

"Mr. Delaney! How's it coming along?"

Delaney wiped at the greasy sweat on his face and neck. "Only one boiler lit, sir, the other five are still out."

"Will that give us any speed at all?"

"No, sir. But give me an hour . . . I'll have a couple of the others on line again. By then . . . I'll give you at least fifteen knots."

"Good, very good. And Delaney . . . Pass the word to your black gang. We've got the topside fires almost under control now. Tell them . . . tell them we're hurt, but we're still in the fight."

"Aye, aye, sir."

Buckmaster went topside again and found Matt Garth. Taking his arm, he said: "Matt, we're short-handed all round, and the Japs'll be at us again for sure. Before that happens, I want to get the wounded transferred to one of our cruisers. Will you see to that for me?"

"Aye, aye, sir." Matt paused, and then, very quietly: "And thank you, Captain."

Buckmaster nodded. "Say hello to Tom for me, Matt."

There was a feeling in him that he could not quite articulate, even to himself, a feeling that when things were wrong, or simply painful, then *everyone* seemed to be standing by to offer help, or sympathy.

He found his way over the bomb-packed flight deck, strewn with wrecked planes and equipment, with men toiling like demons to get the debris cleared and every-thing working again. One of the gun turrets had been completely destroyed, and on another the armorers were setting up new mountings for the 40-mm guns, testing their traverse, getting them in shape.

The main elevator was a mass of twisted wreckage. He clambered down along the iron ladder to the main aircraft hangar, and found that there were great sheets of jagged metal hanging down from its shattered over-head girders. He climbed another ladder to the work-shops where the armorers and machinists were busy at their lathes, on down through the auxiliary lighting plant, now out of action, and down to the auxiliary en-gine-room service deck.

Immediately below him, on the seventh deck down, were the massive turbines and the boilers of the engine room. The heat was intolerable. He touched the bulk-head. It was burning hot from the recently-extinguished fires, and steam from ruptured pipes was still seeping up from the deck plates.

He squeezed through a twisted, heavy steel hatch and went down a long corridor to the fan rooms where the ventilating system was located, on through the en-gineering storeroom, through one of the small crew messes, where a dozen exhausted men were stretched out on the floor taking a quick break.

He found his way into the sick bay at last, and said to the hospital corpsman there: "Lieutenant Tom Garth, he's one of the pilots."

The corpsman saluted. "Intensive Care, Commander. Straight through that door."

"Thank you . . ."

His heart was pounding. Intensive care . . . Well, at least Tom was still alive.

He went on and found the white-painted steel room, a vault far below in the bowels of the great ship, where the critically wounded bunked, with the doctors and corpsmen working feverishly in the cramped quarters.

He walked down a row of double-tiered bunks and found his son, an I.V. in his arm, his eyes closed. He stood looking down at him for a moment, and then a doctor was close beside him, saying: "It's Captain Garth, isn't it? I'm Oringel, one of the ship's surgeons."

Matt turned to see a young officer who couldn't have been more than year or two out of internship. "How is he, Doctor?"

"Well, he's been cut up pretty badly . . . some third-degree burns . . . serious concussion. But he's tough. He'll be all right."

"We're transferring the wounded, did you know that?"

"Yes, they sent us word. They're being sent over to the cruiser . . . the cruiser *Portland,* I believe."

"That's right. Her launches will be coming alongside shortly. How many are being transferred?"

"The chief surgeon has tagged eighty-two all told."

Matt looked around at the wounded in the rows of bunks and said grimly: "They hit us pretty hard, didn't they?"

The young doctor was surprisingly matter-of-fact. "At Coral Sea they hit us a helluva lot harder, Captain."

He leaned over and felt Tom's pulse. Matt stood by, distressed, waiting. The young surgeon said, at last: "He'll be out of the war a while . . . with luck, until it's over. Wouldn't mind that myself, sitting out the war in Honolulu or some other recuperation center . . . He's coming around . . ."

There was a cry from one of the bunks at the far

end of the isle, and the doctor was moving quickly to attend a young seaman who had just awakened to discover that his right arm was missing.

Matt looked down at his son. Tom's eyes opened slowly and there was a twisted smile on his face as he focused on his father, and then, speaking painfully, said: "I made a mess of it, didn't I, Dad?"

Matt shook his head. "No. Long as you're going to be okay, it's no mess."

"In more ways than one . . . What about you, Dad? You going to be all right?"

"Sure. How do you feel? Or is that a damn fool question under the circumstances?"

"I feel lousy. But better than I did a couple of hours ago. Is the battle over?"

"Not yet. And I'm glad you're out of it."

"I'm sorry you're still in it."

Matt smiled, touched, and then he said: "I've thought a lot about you and Haruko . . . and me."

"You'll never change . . ."

"Probably not, but you and Haruko should do what's right for you. And to hell with anything else."

There was a long silence as Tom looked up into his father's face, his expression strangely peaceful. At length, he asked: "Is it always like this?"

"How do you mean, Tom?"

"A guy has to get his brains scrambled to realize that . . . that he's not as far from his dad as he thought he was?"

Tom lifted a hand, and Matt took it gratefully.

Two corpsmen were moving in with a stretcher, and one of them said cheerfully: "Sorry, Captain, got to get these guys out of our hair. They don't give us nothing but trouble . . ."

His son's grip was firm and warm. He held the hand for a moment, and said: "See you back at Pearl, son."

Tom nodded. "In no time at all. Do me a favor?"

"You bet."

"I left all my stuff in the footlocker. There's a picture of me and Haruko. Bring it ashore when you come back?"

"Sure thing, Tom."

They grinned at each other as the corpsmen shifted him over to the stretcher and moved out with him.

Matt headed back to the *Yorktown*'s bridge, moving quickly up the ladders and over the tangled mess of cables and power lines. He suddenly felt a tremendous sense of elation.

He found Captain Buckmaster and Murr Arnold watching the refueling of the few remaining F4F's below on the flight deck, reported that the evacuation of the wounded was underway, then went to his cabin and quickly changed into his flying gear.

Admiral Nimitz hurried into the CINCPAC battle plot room at Pearl Harbor. He found Rochefort and Blake grinning like a couple of school kids. He addressed Blake: "Did you confirm it?"

"Yes, sir. Admiral Fletcher's reply just came in." He read the message. "Fletcher to Nimitz. Confirm previous report. Three enemy carriers afire."

Nimitz slapped his palms together gently and said in a whispered tone, his gaze on the huge plot table where the models representing the Japanese carriers were shown to be out of action: "Hallelujah! . . ."

Rochefort wasn't about to let it go at that. He looked the admiral straight in the eye, and said: "Three of their first-line carriers, Admiral. *Three*. I'd say that calls for a stronger comment . . . like, 'Hot diggity damn!' Or . . . 'Stone the crows!' "

Nimitz couldn't help but be moved by Rochefort's infectious enthusiasm. "I'll take it under advisement, Commander. Meanwhile, there's a fourth enemy carrier to deal with."

Blake hated to squelch the moment. There had been so few times since Pearl Harbor that any of them had had anything to feel good about. But he had no choice. He said: "There's more from Admiral Fletcher, sir."

"More?"

"Yes, sir. The *Yorktown*'s been hit."

"Badly?"

"Apparently. But she's underway again, Admiral. Operational."

Nimitz was deeply concerned. "That's very well . . . but the enemy has located *Yorktown* . . ."

He moved to the large wall-map which included Yamamoto's Aleutian operations. He studied it for a long moment, then said: "Yamamoto sent two carriers to attack our Aleutian bases. When were they last seen?"

"Not since they hit Dutch Harbor, sir. Twenty-four hours ago."

There was a moment of silence which Rochefort broke. "Are you thinking what I'm thinking, Admiral? . . ."

Nimitz continued to ponder the map. "Yes . . . It's entirely possible that Yamamoto has set a *double-jawed* trap for us."

Blake frowned. "I don't understand, sir."

Nimitz moved back to the battle plot and said: "Suppose those two carriers that hit Dutch Harbor recovered their planes and then immediately turned south. At flank speed they could be within striking distance of our carriers by dawn tomorrow."

Rochefort added: "A pincers movement."

"Exactly, Commander. With the *Yorktown* already damaged, they'd have superior forces and superior position."

Rochefort hesitated, then he suggested: "We've already won a great victory, Admiral. Maybe we ought to forget that fourth Jap carrier?"

"Break off and run for home, eh?"

"Before they can hurt us again, yes, sir."

Nimitz brooded over the plot for a long time before he replied. "That would probably be the smart move, Commander. The staff in Washington would undoubtedly commend me for being sagacious." He took a deep breath and exhaled slowly. "Trouble is, I don't feel sagacious. Radio Fletcher that I *want* that fourth enemy carrier."

The *Yorktown* was underway now, and Matt hurried back to the flying bridge to wait for further orders. The engineer's phone rang and Matt answered it. He heard

Delaney's voice projecting over the boiler-room din. He listened for a moment and then said to Buckmaster: "It's Delaney, sir. He's got his boilers on the line again."

Buckmaster was elated. "What have we got now . . . seventeen knots?"

The officer of the deck piped up: "Eighteen, sir."

Matt spoke into the phone. "Can you maintain this speed, Delaney?"

He listened for a moment and then repeated for Buckmaster's benefit: "Eighteen knots. No sweat."

Buckmaster and Fletcher exchanged grins, and Matt answered the question that Delaney posed. He said into the phone: "You're damned right, we're ready to hit back. But we don't know where that fourth Jap carrier is . . ."

A voice cut in over the combat information speaker: "Bridge from Combat Information."

Buckmaster swung around. "Go ahead, Combat."

"Sir, we have a report from Scouting Five. Lieutenant Adams has just located the fourth enemy flattop."

"Good, very good!"

Matt spoke into the phone again. "Did you hear that, Delaney?"

"I heard it, Matt."

"Well just keep us going full-bore. Every extra knot you can give us . . . counts now."

Delaney's voice came back from the depths: "Aye, aye, Captain."

Buckmaster turned to one of his aides. "Signal to Admiral Fletcher aboard the *Astoria:* 'Fourth enemy carrier located. Stand by for bearing and position. Buckmaster.' "

The aide moved off, and almost immediately the voice came over the intercom again, more urgent now: "Sir! Radar has bandits! Distance thirty-five miles and closing. This time, they're coming in low. Torpedo attack!"

Buckmaster looked at Arnold. "What have we got that's airworthy?"

"Eleven planes, sir. Eight F4F's and three SBD's."

"Then launch them all immediately." He turned to the OD. "And order Battle Stations, Lieutenant."

Matt waited until Murr Arnold gave the launching orders, and he said to Buckmaster: "With your permission, sir? . . ."

"Sure thing, Matt. You'll be leading the flight?"

Arnold said: "Yes, sir, he will."

"Then you'd better get air-borne. And hurry home soon, uh, Matt."

"Yes, sir." Matt grinned.

The Battle Stations alarm was still booming as Matt ran across the flight deck, slipped on his Mae West, and climbed into the cockpit of his SBD, the one spotted first in line for launching. His radio/gunner was already in the rear seat. He closed the canopy, adjusted his goggles, and waited for Fly One to signal him off.

He felt the tremendous surge of power as the Dauntless hurtled into the sky. He pushed the stick forward and watched the air-speed needle move quickly up to two hundred as he climbed at better than fifteen hundred feet per minute. The planes of his flight were moving into position behind him. He raised his arm and signaled: Follow me.

Five minutes, Combat Information's radar had said, and four of them had slipped by already. The distances were great here, but the speed of the planes diminished them. It seemed like seconds only when Matt spotted, fifteen thousand feet below, the ten Japanese Kates with their eighteen-inch torpedoes, heading straight for the *Yorktown*.

Matt switched on his radio transmitter, his voice calm, almost casual. "Yankee Leader to Blue Coats. Okay, SBD's let's get some more altitude. Wildcats . . . go get 'em."

He watched his group split up into two forces, the F4F's diving down and skimming over the wave-tops as they headed for the incoming enemy torpedo planes. He looked up and there were six Zekes high above him, diving straight for his trio. The other two SBD's had seen them also and they swung around in unison with him so as to give their gunners the best possible firing angle. His rear-seat man opened up first, then the others were shooting, too. But the Zekes did not return their fire. They dived, at an enormous speed, straight past the SBD's and into the American F4F's, who were already hammering the low-flying Kates with murderous fire.

Reluctantly, he set a course for Admiral Spruance's *Hornet,* recognizing that this was no fight for a slow-flying SBD which was burdened with a 1,000-pound bomb under her belly. He watched the air-sea battle rage far below and saw that two of the Kates had already dropped their torpedoes, and that the *Yorktown* was making a hard turn to the right to avoid them. He saw the Zekes slamming into the Wildcats and scattering them, engaging them in plane-to-plane combat, twisting and looping and diving across the sky, like autumn leaves blown by the wind. A Kate torpedo-bomber blew up and tumbled into the sea, missing the turning carrier by only a few hundred feet, but another Kate, forcing its way through a wall of antiaircraft fire, headed straight for the *Yorktown*'s bridge.

It was Lieutenant Tomonaga. All around him, the carrier gunners' flak was bursting in vicious black clouds, but he ignored it completely and held the great ship in his sights. He saw the two torpedoes already in the water holding their course as the ship turned out of their path, and swore as they both sliced harmlessly past its port beam.

He reached down and pulled the release handle, and felt his plane bounce up as his torpedo dropped away from the plane's belly. He knew it was going to strike, and he nosed the plane up hard and skimmed over the carrier's deck, the machine-gun bullets slamming into him and wrecking his cockpit as he climbed and executed a tight roll.

There was blood on his face now and his gunner was dead. He looked down and saw his torpedo strike home amidships. Another was streaking its way in, and he watched it hit and explode, a great column of debris shooting up high from the *Yorktown*'s deck.

He swung his Kate round and dived straight for its superstructure, watching the flak coming at him, grit-

ting his teeth and holding his crippled plane dead
straight onto its target.

A split-second before he would have crashed into the
carrier, a shell caught him head-on. His last memory
was the *Yorktown* smoking furiously and heeling slowly over.

Lieutenant Hashimoto's Kate had been badly chewed
up by antiaircraft fire, but he had seen his torpedo
strike the enemy carrier dead amidships and had managed to limp away at wave-top level. Now, he was level-
ing off at ten thousand feet and heading back for the
Hiryu. His radioman/gunner was mortally wounded,
dying . . . and there was nothing Hashimoto could do
for him.

He flipped on his radio transmitter. He said, not trying to hide the excitement in his voice: "Whirlwind,
this is Zephyr Two. We have scored two torpedo hits on
this carrier. I repeat, two torpedo hits on this carrier.
We are returning to base."

On board the *Hiryu,* Admiral Yamaguchi and Captain Kaku were on the bridge where the pilot's combat
circuit had been piped in. Kaku was beside himself
with excitement. "Scratch enemy carrier number two!
It's now one against one, Admiral! Please accept my
congratulations, sir."

28

The scene on board the *Yorktown* was disastrous.

The two torpedoes she had taken had struck within
moments of each other, and both of them were almost
squarely amidships.

Ninety percent of the damage done in the first attack
had still been unrepaired, and when the second had
come, in spite of Buckmaster's satisfaction with the incredible work that had been done to get her underway
again, she had been only half a fighting ship.

Her boilers had been patched, her once-formidable
efficiency only minimally restored. She had taken more

punishment than any ship could hope to survive, and she had still fought on.

But now, there was no hope left for her at all.

The corpsmen were removing the dead and the wounded from the multiple decks, and damage control parties were trying desperately to put out the fires. A dozen men were dragging parts of Tomonaga's plane from the area around the bridge, and Buckmaster, shaken but unhurt, was on the emergency phone to the engine rooms.

He said: "Delaney? What's the situation below?"

"Bad, sir. All boilers are out. No hope of relighting them."

Buckmaster cursed. "We can't counterflood without power, and we're in danger of rolling over! Get your people topside, Delaney! On the double!"

He pressed the communications button and heard the phone picked up on the first ring. "Communications? This is Captain Buckmaster. Pass the word. Abandon ship. I say again. Abandon ship. And get the signal out to Admiral Fletcher on the *Astoria* and to Admiral Spruance on the *Enterprise*."

He hung up and moved to the bridge window and looked over all that was left of his great carrier; it was a burning, listing, utterly devastated hulk.

Spruance was in the combat information center when the signal was brought to him. He read it and looked at Miles Browning grimly. "Buckmaster has given the order to abandon ship."

"We sent her all the fighter support we could, sir."

"Apparently not enough . . ."

A communications officer hurried in with a dispatch. Browning read it and said: "Sir, Admiral Fletcher has replied to your signal: 'Do you have any instructions for me?' He says: 'Negative. Will conform to your movements.' "

Spruance nodded thoughtfully and went topside to the flying bridge where he looked down on the flight deck. The SBD dive-bombers were there, spotted for launching. He said: "How many planes can we send out?"

Browning replied: "Twenty-four dive-bombers, sir.

But they'll have to try it without fighter protection."

"The *Hornet?*"

"The *Hornet* is scraping the bottom of the barrel. She's only got sixteen bombers left. Plus, we'll have the three SBD's Matt Garth is bringing over from the *Yorktown.*"

"Only three?"

"All that's left, sir."

Spruance sighed. "Very well. Signal *Hornet* we'll attack immediately."

The order was given and Spruance said, ruminating: "Do you realize, Miles, that with all this . . . enormous effort, from the top clear down to the bottom, what it all boils down to is a fight between two men?"

"You and Nagumo?"

"No, I wasn't thinking of those of us who have to *take* the orders, I was thinking of the men who *give* them. Admiral Yamamoto is probably the world's top-rated naval genius. We've got Admiral Nimitz, and the both of them . . . They stay back, and hold their distance, and watch the battle they planned fought out with models in their respective headquarters, at sea, or on land, wherever it may be . . . And what's happened? It looks like the greatest naval genius has been outsmarted by a guy from a little Texas town. It's food for thought, isn't it?"

Browning smiled ruefully. "Yes, it is. Only . . . the battle's not over yet."

"No. But the next few hours will tell us, one way or another."

Their voices were drowned out by the sudden roar of the planes' engines, leaping to life as they prepared for launching.

They watched the twenty-four bombers rocketing off the flight deck. Soon they would rendezvous with the sixteen from their sister ship, the *Hornet*. And a few minutes later, Matt Garth would be flying in to join them with his three surviving dive-bombers from the sinking *Yorktown.*

The Japanese survivors, those that were left from the second attack on the *Yorktown*—five Kate torpedo-bombers and three Zeke fighters—had stumbled their way onto the *Hiryu*'s flight deck, and the dog-tired pilots were climbing out of their cockpits, being helped by an equally exhausted crew.

The senior pilot left now was Lieutenant Hashimoto and he was reporting to Admiral Yamaguchi on the flight deck. His thigh had been grazed by machine-gun bullets, and a corpsman was attending to it. "Sir, this couldn't have been the same carrier that Lieutenant Kobayashi dive-bombed. It was undamaged and under full steam. We put two torpedoes into it."

Yamaguchi was not satisfied. He said: "Kobayashi said he left his victim afire. Did you see any smoke?"

"No, sir. It must have sunk. We didn't see any sign of a third carrier, either."

Yamaguchi gripped the young lieutenant's shoulder. "Well done. Now get something to eat. Get some rest. You'll be going out again soon."

Hashimoto bowed his head in gratitude for the Admiral's compliment. "Yes, sir." Then he snapped a salute and limped away with the aid of the other pilots.

The *Hiryu*'s skipper, Captain Kaku, watched them struggle off the flight deck, and he said to Yamaguchi: "They're exhausted. So is the ship's crew. Do you realize, sir, that since first light we've been attacked by nearly a hundred planes . . . dodged more than two dozen torpedoes and seventy bombs? Our pilots have been in the air most of the day . . ."

The admiral cut him short, a note of irritation, of impatience in his voice. "So have the American flyers, Kaku. Their ship's crewmen are exhausted, too."

"But, sir, we don't even know where that third enemy carrier is . . ."

Yamaguchi was already turning to one of his staff officers. He said: "My compliments to the air operations officer. He is to launch the fast scout plane immediately. The moment it locates the remaining American carrier, we will strike with every plane available . . ."

He broke off. The voice of a look-out was coming at them from the post in the superstructure: "Dive-bombers! Enemy dive-bombers! Starboard quarter, enemy dive-bombers!"

They were high in the sky to the south, coming in out of the sun, the first wave of the American bombers from the *Enterprise,* peeling off one after the other in rapid succession, their engines screaming as they hurtled straight down for their target.

On their quarter, a little above them, Matt Garth's three SBD's were already in their dive, and looking down, he saw the bombs of the lead group raining onto the *Hiryu*'s decks. He counted four hits and three near misses, and then the flight deck was in his own sights, and he was barreling his way through the walls of antiaircraft fire being thrown up by the *Hiryu*'s escorting cruisers and destroyers.

He held his course.

The flak was coming at him head-on. A chunk of shrapnel tore through his canopy and shattered his instrument panel. The deck was coming up at him with tremendous speed. He hit the bomb release and threw himself back on the stick, fighting the plane as though it were alive and defying his efforts to keep it from sudden suicide.

He looked back and saw his bomb land dead-center on the flight deck, saw a gun-turret disintegrate with the blast of it, saw great masses of debris hurling themselves high into the air. He knew that the *Hiryu* was dead.

His compass was gone, and his air-speed indicator, and his fuel gauges, and his altimeter. One wing was pocked with great holes where it had taken shrapnel, and one of his trailing edge flaps had been shot away. There was smoke in his cockpit, and blood and oil everywhere, and the force of the air from the shattered canopy was trying to tear him out of his seat.

But the Dauntless, living up to its name now, was answering his touch, keeping a course of sorts at wave-top level, badly damaged and staggering on.

Soon, the burning bulk was far behind him, and he was heading, he hoped, for the *Enterprise*. He looked at his watch and found that it was broken, the case driven almost into his wrist. The hands stood at a few minutes before five o'clock. He had been in the air for more than three hours, and he knew that his fuel tanks were almost empty.

He flew on steadily, willing the aircraft to hold its course, dropping down to the waves from time to time and lurching back into the sky, erratically and dangerously.

He was wounded, but he wasn't certain just how badly . . . except that his entire left side was numb. And there was blood . . . a great deal of it. He gritted his teeth and made up his mind that he would not pass out, not till he had brought his crippled plane home. He thought of his son, of the boy's desperate attempt to get down all in one piece . . .

It was dusk when he finally came within sight of the *Enterprise*.

On the flying bridge, Browning was reading out the messages as they came in, and he said: "Time for congratulations, Admiral. A clean sweep. Four first-line enemy carriers knocked out. *Four* of them!"

Spruance nodded. He was at the guard rail watching the damaged planes coming in, limping down onto the deck, the pilots being dragged from their cockpits by the crewmen. He marveled at the punishment those planes could take and still live; at the capacity for punishment of their pilots, too . . .

The phone was ringing, and Browning picked it up, "Bridge . . ."

He turned to the admiral. "That was the landing signal officer, sir. Matt Garth's coming in. His plane's shot up. They don't know whether he'll make it."

They stood together at the rail and saw Fly One getting his paddles ready, saw the distant plane, on course, heading toward them; it was very low.

Fly One, muttering a silent prayer as he watched the approaching SBD, began to use his paddles urgently, and suddenly he was shouting: "Come on, Matt! Get your nose up! Up, man, up . . . get your goddamn nose up! Better . . . better . . . *good!* Hold it now . . . *Hold it!* . . ."

Matt Garth saw, dimly, the flight deck rushing up at him. It seemed enormous, and still too small to receive him. He struggled with the controls, and they would not respond, and he knew that his plane was a dead thing in the sky, a mass of shattered metal with him aboard, hurtling uncontrolled into his carrier at more than a hundred miles an hour. The horizon was suddenly tilting crazily all around him.

He began to say a prayer, and then he hit.

The plane cartwheeled over and over, and smashed its way through everything that stood in its path, and cartwheeled again, smashed nose-on into the superstructure and disintegrated.

A wing went over the side, and the engine smashed into an antiaircraft battery, and the fuselage was a tumbling ball of fire, turning over and over as though it would never cease its terrifying motion.

It was a funeral pyre.

The battleship *Yamato,* flagship of the Commander in Chief and of the mighty Imperial Japanese Navy, was far from the scene of combat.

Admiral Yamamoto, his head tilted back, his feet wide-spaced, his hands clenched tightly, and his face pale and drawn, was staring at the battle plot.

The models of the *Akagi,* and the *Kaga,* and the *Soryu* were marked "Sunk" or "Sinking," and the *Hiryu* had beside it an annotation that read: "On fire." Their own First Fleet was still marked as being in its ordered position, far to the northeast of the islands, waiting for the carrier victory that would be their signal to move in and mop up any American vessels that might have survived.

Kuroshima was with his Commander in Chief, and he was the only one in the big battle plot room who was not in the depths of despondency. His fighting fury was not in the least cooled when Watanabe entered with the dispatch they were all waiting for.

Watanabe's voice was leaden with despair as he said to Yamamoto: "Sir, Admiral Kakuda has just radioed that his carriers, the *Ryujo* and the *Junyo,* can't join us for another forty-eight hours."

Kuroshima said quickly, intensely: "It doesn't matter, Admiral. The issue will be decided tonight when our battleships start shelling Midway. The American fleet will rush to the rescue . . . straight into Admiral Kondo's picket line of heavy cruisers and battleships."

Watanabe said quietly: "The issue *is* settled, gentlemen." He continued, addressing the admiral. "Sir, there is another dispatch. From Admiral Kondo. He has revised his earlier estimates. The bombardment group cannot get within range of Midway before four A.M. The picket group will be at least three more hours reaching their stations."

Kuroshima jerked the dispatch from Watanabe's hand. He read it for himself, then exclaimed: "Admiral, this settles nothing. Nothing at all. A little dawn light will make for better accuracy at Midway . . ."

Kuroshima broke off, suddenly aware that everyone was staring at him as if he had lost his mind. It only fed his desperate determination. "Sir, in view of Admiral Kondo's failure, it is imperative that you personally lead your battleships into a daylight attack on Midway! One crushing bombardment which will reduce the island to rubble!"

Admiral Ugaki was flabbergasted. He said sharply: "Captain! Only a fool would permit a single defeat to goad him into suicide!"

Kuroshima would not accept it. "Defeat! . . ."

Ugaki turned to Yamamoto. "The war is not lost, sir. The Imperial Navy still has eight aircraft carriers . . . and the most powerful support forces in the world." He paused, as if the words were stuck in his throat. "Admiral, we must withdraw. We have no sensible alternative."

There was a long, oppressive silence. Everyone waited for Yamamoto's reply. At length, it was Kuroshima who said, his voice strangled: "But . . . if we withdraw . . . how will we apologize to His Majesty? . . ."

Yamamoto's eyes were glazed, a veil over them as though to hide the deep disgrace that was on him. His officers waited, feeling his pain, even stronger than their own.

And then, Admiral Yamamoto said: "Leave that to me. I am the only one who must apologize to His Majesty."

No one answered him. There was only the sound of the sea outside, the steady cadence of the waves washing at the hull of the ship.

29

L'envoi

The sea around the beautiful islands of Hawaii were calm and quiet, and a brilliant cobalt blue. The seagulls were winging lazily over them, and their raucous cries were joyous for the beauty the sea provided.

The mountains, climbing up to Diamond Head, and Punchbowl, and the Salt Lake craters, had never been more verdant, and the scenic drives and parks had never been more beautiful.

There was an air of lassitude here now, as though the dangers were not quite so imminent, or perhaps had been turned back forever.

Close by the navy dockyards, the *Enterprise* was being nosed in by a team of hooting tugboats, straining to ease its huge bulk into place. The wharf was lined with navy yard workers, sailors, officers, and a scattering of civilians, taking time off from their occupations to watch the great carrier come in from battle.

There were no bands, and there were no flags waving. The occasion was thankful, indeed, but it was also solemn; the casualty lists were not yet out, but all the island knew that they would be heavy. They knew that battles were seldom won without loss of life on both sides, and that this confrontation had been a mighty one, a struggle to the death between two giant Leviathans of enormous power.

They knew, too, that the tide of battle had finally turned, that for the first time in their rapid sweep to victory across the Pacific, the Japanese had been halted.

It was as though a great tidal wave had at last been stemmed. The list of Japanese victories had seemed incredible. In the unbelievably short span of seven months, one triumph after another had been brought to His Imperial Majesty, an indisputable indication that his forces were, as he had been told, invincible.

But now, a strange and convoluted mixture of chance and courage had brought him his first defeat; not only a defeat, but a disaster of overwhelming proportions.

The *Enterprise* loomed high against the bright sky and the men who lined her rails could not quite believe that here, at last, they would find some sort of respite. There was no excitement on board, no jubilation; there was only a terrible weariness.

Admiral Nimitz stood by his car on the wharf, with Joe Rochefort, watching the slow movements of the great carrier as she was brought in, waiting for the first of the gangplanks to be lowered.

He waited, feeling the loneliness and the bitterness, and he moved aside a trifle as a navy corpsman eased a wheelchair past them. The heavily bandaged face was familiar, and he glanced quickly at the lovely young Japanese girl who was walking beside it, and put out a hand and stopped them. "Lieutenant?"

The young man in the wheelchair raised his arm in a salute. "Sir?"

"Aren't you ... Lieutenant Garth?"

"Yes, sir."

"Tom Garth, isn't it?"

"That's right, Admiral."

Nimitz nodded. "I'm sorry about your father, Lieutenant. He was a brave man. No, more than that. He was a good man. One of the best."

"Thank you, sir."

The admiral's eyes, searching, were on the girl, and there was a little silence, and he said at last, very formally: "I'd be glad if you'd introduce me, Lieutenant."

"Yes, sir. This is . . . Haruko Sakura, my fiancée." His head was high, his tone firm and strong.

The admiral put out his hand. "I'm honored to meet you, Miss Sakura." He noticed that she avoided his eyes, and he smiled and said: "I'm sure you two are going to be very happy. I wish you . . . all the best."

She raised her eyes to his now, and held them for a moment, and her hand was resting lightly on Tom's. There was a sad and distant look in her eyes, as though the pain of the trials she had been through was still with her, but there was a radiant happiness there, too, finding its way through the sadness. She smiled, very briefly, and still a little hesitantly. "Thank you, Admiral."

He watched them move away, and looked at Joe Rochefort and said: "I wonder, Joe. I wonder what's ahead for them?"

Rochefort grunted. "A lot of idiots around, sir. But they'll make it. If he's got any of his father's blood in his veins . . . they'll make it."

He thought about his old friend Matt Garth for a while, and said at last: "I wonder if Matt knew how big a battle we won? The greatest naval battle since Jutland."

Nimitz sighed. "Jutland? Yes, maybe. And there are a lot of similarities there, too. At Jutland, it was the first time the two greatest fleets in the world met head-on, the only time. And it left the Allies undisputed masters of the seas. So perhaps . . . maybe this is even more decisive than Jutland, Joe. From here on in, *we've* got the ball. But I know what Matt Garth would have said."

Joe Rochefort looked at him, and Nimitz went on: "He'd have said: 'It doesn't figure, Admiral. Yamamoto had everything going for him. Power. Experience. Confidence. Were we better than the Japanese? Or just luckier? . . .' "

Afterword:
Notes on Aircraft used
in the Battle of Midway

Naval aircraft had never fought a pitched sea-to-land-to-sea battle on the scale that shaped up at Midway. Just what were the forces that the combatants brought to this epic clash? Here is the lineup:

The American's Brewster F2 Buffalo was first designed in 1936, when the U.S. Navy, realizing that the day of the biplane was coming to an end, first switched to monoplane fighters.

The Buffalo was indeed obsolete, as Captain Cyril Simard had said. It was a single-engined plane, and it carried four 5-inch machine guns and two 100-pound bombs. It had a range of 1,680 miles, a top speed of 323 mph, and a climb rate of 2,290 feet per minute. It was 26 feet 4 inches long, and weighed 4,732 pounds empty. It was no match at all for the Japanese planes, and in the early stages of the war it had taken—and was still to take—the most appalling losses.

Far tougher, though not much faster or more maneuverable, was the F4F, the Grumman Wildcat, considered by most pilots to be the best of the American fighter planes.

The Wildcat was armed with six 5-inch machine guns instead of the Buffalo's four, was marginally heavier, and longer, and its rate of climb was slightly slower than that of the Buffalo. It did, however, have one great advantage; it was so sturdily built that it could take a considerable amount of damage and still survive. The pilots learned to refuse to engage in dog-fights; they would dive on their targets and continue the dive as a means of rapid escape.

The TBD, the Douglas Devastator, also an old plane, was first designed in 1937. Since it was the only torpedo-bomber the navy possessed at the outbreak of the war, it lingered on into the Battle of Midway in spite of its very serious shortcomings.

It was slow; its top speed was a mere 206 mph. Its rate of climb was only 720 feet per minute. Carrying a torpedo, its range was a paltry 435 miles. Its armament consisted of one 5-inch and the one 3-inch machine gun, plus one 21-inch torpedo or a large, armor-piercing bomb. It was cumbersome, unwieldy . . . and a death-trap.

The Douglas SPD, the Dauntless, was considered to be a remarkably successful plane, though no match for the vastly superior Japanese aircraft.

Its top speed was 252 mph, its rate of climb was 1,700 feet per minute, and its range 1,115 miles carrying a thousand-pound bomb. A distinguishing feature of this dive-bomber was the bomb-carrier—a crutch below the fuselage that could swing out past the propeller before releasing its load, thus avoiding the somewhat alarming hazard of having the bomb caught up in the propeller blades. It also utilized split trailing-edge flaps which could be lowered in the dive to slow the plane down and to steady it for more accurate aim. Its weight was 6,533 pounds empty, its length was 33 feet, and its wing span 41 feet 6 inches.

The Consolidated PB (Patrol/Bomber) Catalina was well regarded as being a most successful flying-boat design, though it could not compare with the huge, and much faster, Japanese Kawanishi.

It served throughout the war in many varied roles —patrol, bombing, supply, communications, transport, and evacuation. Twin-engined, its maximum speed was a slow 179 mph; its range, 2,545 miles. The Catalina carried three 3-inch and two 5-inch machine guns, plus up to 4,000 pounds of bombs, four 650-pound depth charges, or two torpedoes.

The B-17, a land-based bomber, was a solid plane

that was constantly being modified to keep abreast of the times. It was extremely well built, and because of its considerable armor plating, had the great advantage of being very hard to shoot down unless attacked from dead ahead. It had four 1,200-horsepower engines, its top speed was 299 mph, and it took 25.7 minutes to climb to 20,000 feet. Its formidable armament of twelve 5-inch machine guns, plus up to 20,800 pounds of assorted bombs, caused it to become known as the "Flying Fortress." Its range was 1,300 miles with 6,000 pounds of bombs. It was 74 feet 9 inches long, with a wing span of 103 feet 9 inches. It weighed, empty, 34,000 pounds.

Finally, there was the famous and much-loved B-25, the North American Mitchell, which proved to be one of the war's outstanding aircraft. Though designed as a medium bomber, it was also capable of carrying a greatly increased armament to improve its attack capability. It flew at a maximum speed of 284 mph, with a range of 1,500 miles (carrying 3,200 pounds of bombs) and took 16.5 minutes to climb to 15,000 feet. It normally carried six 15-inch machine guns. It was a little under 43 feet long, with a span of 67 feet 7 inches.

The Japanese had brought into the war some of the most advanced and sophisticated aircraft the world had ever seen.

The Imperial force's most popular plane, without a doubt, was the Mitsubishi Zero.

It had come as a complete surprise to the Americans. To their dismay, the Zero proved to be a superlative fighter, fast, agile, well-armed, and with an excellent range. Its top speed was 351 mph; its rate of climb, 4,500 feet per minute; and its range, a thousand miles. Armed with twin 20-mm cannon and two 7.7 machine guns, it also carried up to 264 pounds of bombs. The Zero suffered from two drawbacks: The protection for both pilot and fuel was minimal, and its relatively light construction meant that it could not absorb very much damage.

Thirty-two different versions of the Zero were produced, and they soon became known to the Americans, generically, as "Zekes." They were all good.

The second most important plane in the Japanese aerial arsenal was the Aichi B3A1, which the Allies had code-named "Val."

It was considerably slower than the Zero, with a maximum speed of 242 miles per hour, an armament of two 7.7 machine guns, and a bomb load of 684 pounds, though at Pearl Harbor it had carried only 550 pounds. With a wing span of 47 feet 7 1/4 inches and a length of 33 feet 5 1/4 inches, it was a highly maneuverable, versatile fighter-bomber with a range of 1,130 miles.

The Nakajima bomber, first introduced in 1940, was the standard torpedo plane of the Imperial Navy. It could carry either bombs or torpedoes, and had a maximum speed of 235 miles per hour with a range of 1,238 miles. Its wing span was 50 feet 11 inches, its length 33 feet 10 inches.

Then there was the incredible Kawanishi flying boat, which the Americans liked to call "Emily."

Undoubtedly, this was one of the finest flying boats ever built. It handled remarkably well on the water, was very heavily armored for the protection of the crew, and carried an offensive arsenal of five 20-mm cannon and four 7.7 machine guns. Its four Mitsubishi radial engines could push it along at a speed of 290 mph, for a remarkable range of over 4,000 miles.

But perhaps the most awe-inspiring plane in the Imperial Navy was the Yokosuka MXY, called "Okha," meaning "Cherry Blossom," by the Japanese, and dubbed "Baka," or "Fool," by the Americans.

It was, in simple terms, a flying charge of explosives, with an unbelievably short range of only 55 miles, which it could cover at a speed of 535 mph, shooting forward under the rocket power of its model 20 motor, with 1,765 pounds of static thrust. Its length was a modest 19 feet 10 1/2 inches, its wing span was 16 feet 5 inches, and it was carried to its ultimate target underneath the belly of a specially-adapted Mitsubishi G4M2 bomber.

It was a fearsome weapon. It was the only plane in

the world specifically designed for suicide missions, and became famous as the "Kamikaze" plane. During the conflict in the Pacific, 755 of these aircraft were built; and almost all of them were flown into combat by war's end, establishing a legend in their own time.

ABOUT THE AUTHOR

DONALD S. SANFORD was born in North Bend, Oregon, on St. Patrick's Day, 1918. While working as a tour guide for CBS in Hollywood, he studied playwrighting and drama at Los Angeles City College and began writing for local radio programs. The day after Pearl Harbor he enlisted in the Navy and became a technician specializing in the maintenance of antisubmarine warfare equipment. He served aboard the DD707, a modern first-line destroyer, and was discharged with the rank of chief sonarman at the war's end. After a three-year stint as a recording engineer for the United Nations, he joined Dumont Television in New York and began writing for *The Plainclothesman* and *Martin Kane, Private Eye,* two of the first cops-and-robbers shows on TV. The life of a freelance writer suited his temperament and he eventually returned to Hollywood, where he wrote over two hundred prime-time teleplays and several World War II movies. His hobbies are long-distance solo backpacking trips in the High Sierras, fishing and playing the flute.

We Deliver!
And So Do These Bestsellers.

RELAX!
SIT DOWN
and Catch Up On Your Reading!

Bantam Book Catalog

It lists over a thousand money-saving best-sellers originally priced from $3.75 to $15.00 —bestsellers that are yours now for as little as 50¢ to $2.95!

The catalog gives you a great opportunity to build your own private library at huge savings!

So don't delay any longer—send us your name and address and 25¢ (to help defray postage and handling costs).